D0405559

Discarded from
Garfield County Public
Library System

Garfield County Libraries
C[redacted]ibrary
320 [redacted] 81623
(970) 963-2889 • Fax (970) 963-8573
www.GCPLD.org

Lost and Found in ASPEN

LORI GURTMAN

A POST HILL PRESS BOOK

Lost and Found in Aspen
© 2017 by Lori Gurtman
All Rights Reserved

ISBN: 978-1-68261-617-8
ISBN (eBook): 978-1-68261-618-5

Cover design by Quincy Avilio
Artwork featured on cover by Nicole Nagel-Gogolak
Cover photography by Jennifer Cohen
Interior Design and Composition by Greg Johnson/Textbook Perfect

This book is a work of fiction. People, places, events, and situations are the product of the author's imagination. Any resemblance to actual persons, living or dead, or historical events, is purely coincidental.

No part of this book may be reproduced, stored in a retrieval system, or transmitted by any means without the written permission of the author and publisher.

Post Hill Press
New York · Nashville
posthillpress.com

Published in the United States of America

For Michael:
My warrior, my love, my inspiration.

1

1996

IT SHOULD HAVE BEEN the most exciting day of my life, but I was miserable. I had a throbbing pain in my head and couldn't decide if it stemmed from hunger or this aggravating flight. A bratty boy sitting behind me was kicking my seat over and over, until I thought I was going to explode. When I couldn't take it anymore, I squeezed my face between the seats and gave him an evil stare down. It didn't help. The next kick was so powerful that I lurched forward.

"Could you please stop kicking my seat?" I asked through clenched teeth.

His mother glanced up from her magazine. "Oh, I'm terribly sorry. I forgot to give him his Ritalin this morning."

She patted her son's head and said, "Boo-Boo Bear, you need to keep still," and then she buried her head back in the article she was reading. Before I turned back around, the little devil stuck his tongue out at me.

I didn't need this today, especially when I had so much to look forward to. I'd recently graduated from Ohio State University with a bachelor's degree in Fine Arts, and narrowly escaped having to return to Mulletville, the Podunk suburban town where I was raised. I was one step away from working the cash register at my dad's car wash and spending my days at the mall, sipping Slurpees from 7-Eleven. Landing a summer internship teaching art at Anderson Ranch Arts Center in Snowmass had been a dream come true, and if all went well, the internship could possibly turn into a full-time position. I had also lucked out when I found an affordable place to live in Aspen through some guy named Richard, who worked at the Ranch. I had no idea how the arrangement would work out, but since I didn't have any other housing options, all I could do was pray that he wasn't a serial killer.

My day continued to get worse when the woman in the seat next to me fell asleep with her head resting on my shoulder, snoring in my ear. I gently pushed her off and almost gagged when I noticed a patch of drool on my shirt. Great! She had stained me with her halitosis.

I took a few deep breaths to try to calm myself down. Then, I reached into my backpack and pulled out my sketch pad and discovered a Tupperware container my mother had packed for me. A pink heart-shaped note was taped to the box. *Good luck in Aspen. Mulletville won't be the same without you. Love, Mom and Dad* was written in purple puffy paint and sprinkled with multicolored glitter. When I took off the lid, a strong fart odor drifted into my nose. *Really, Mom? Deviled eggs, on an airplane?*

"Mommy," the boy behind me yelled out, "the lady in front of us is tooting in her seat!"

I shoved the lid back on the container, sealed it tightly, and threw it back into my bag. Sinking low in my seat, the hunger in my stomach dissipated. *Boom, boom, boom*. The kicking started up again. For the rest of the flight, I tried to block out my fantasy of ripping Boo-Boo Bear's legs off.

Finally, the plane bounced restlessly toward the runway, and the ebullient stewardess announced, "Welcome to Aspen." After gathering my backpack, I followed the line of passengers toward the exit door.

With my first step onto the tarmac, I took in a deep breath of the fresh air. My irritation drifted away with the light wind that blew through my hair. I drank in the stunning beauty around me. Majestic, snow-capped mountains lined the horizon, lush shades of green carpeted the landscape, and fleecy clouds drifted across the bright blue sky. The invigorating breeze and spectacular views resurrected every cell in my body.

* * *

Half an hour later, I had retrieved my luggage from baggage claim and climbed into a cab. I gave the driver the address to my new home, rolled down the windows, and gazed out at the magnificent mountains along the highway.

The cab pulled up to a dilapidated, seventies-style townhouse. After paying the driver, I hauled my bags up the red brick steps that led to the front door. I rang the bell and stared at the chipped paint on the house as I waited for someone to answer.

A young woman with layered, shoulder-length brown hair opened the door. "You must be Hope," she said.

"Yeah, you must be Tracy." Her cleavage was spilling out of her tight V-necked T-shirt. I forced myself not to stare at her breasts, although I was dying to know if they were real.

"Richard is at work. Come in. I'll show you around." She grabbed one of my bags, and I followed her inside. "The timing couldn't have been better when you called Richard about the room for rent. Our last roommate was a total disaster."

"What happened to her?"

"She was a major cokehead. When things got really bad, we called her dad, and he sent her to some fancy drug rehab in Malibu for, like, the fifth time."

"That's awful."

"Yeah, I know. I mean, she was fun to party with at first, but she just got out of control."

We made our way down a flight of stairs covered in matted shag carpet. "The bedrooms are this way," Tracy said.

I ignored the musty odor that filled the hallway, peeking into her room and Richard's along the way. "And this is your room," she said.

It was the smallest room, with a lopsided, full-sized bed, a rickety wicker night table, and a shabby old dresser.

"It's not the most luxurious accommodations, but at least there's plenty of room on the bed for you and your lovers." She winked at me.

I couldn't resist smiling when I threw my bag down on the floor. I wasn't used to bringing random men into my bed. Then again, a summer fling didn't sound like such a bad idea.

My stomach let out another loud roar. It was late afternoon, and I still hadn't eaten anything all day.

"You hungry?" Tracy asked.

"Yeah, starving."

"Me too," she said. "Want to go into town and grab a bite to eat?"

"That would be awesome. I just need to use the bathroom first."

Inside the bathroom, I quickly splashed some water on my face and applied a fresh coat of lip gloss. I could've used a shower, especially after that horrific plane ride, but I didn't want to waste any time. I was anxious to check out Aspen and get to know Tracy. So far, she seemed cool, and although the house was dated, it was perfect. It sounded like their last roommate was a nightmare, but it had certainly worked out in my favor. I was stoked to be there. When I was finished in the bathroom I went outside, where Tracy was waiting for me, smoking a cigarette.

* * *

It only took us a few minutes to walk to Big Betsy's, a popular restaurant in town, where Tracy worked as a bartender. A lively buzz of chatter and the loud lyrics of Tim McGraw's "I Like It, I Love It" greeted us when we opened the door with a Wild West facade. We took a seat at the bar, and after Tracy introduced me to the bartender, we ordered Coronas and cheeseburgers with a side of onion rings.

"So, how'd you end up in Aspen?" I asked.

"I moved here from Atlanta about two years ago. My family had a second home in Aspen when I was younger, so we used to come out every school vacation and most of the summer." She guzzled the last of her beer. "And then, when I was sixteen, my parents went through a nasty divorce and sold the house."

The bartender brought over our food. I poured a heap of ketchup on the side of my plate, and dipped an onion ring into it. "I'm sorry. That sucks." I flashed her a sympathetic look before taking a bite.

"Yeah, it's fine. My dad is a prick anyway," she said with a casual tone, while nibbling on her burger like a bird pecking on a seed. "I was determined to make it back here after college. What about you? What brought you to Aspen?"

I filled her in on my simple upbringing in Ohio and my dream of getting out. While chatting, I somehow managed to devour every morsel on my plate. Of course, I felt like a fat ass, especially because she barely touched her food.

After we finished eating and paid our bill, we spent the rest of the afternoon meandering through the quaint town, which was situated at the base of Aspen Mountain. The Victorian architecture and cobblestone side streets were reminiscent of the silver mining days. We strolled in and out of mountain sports stores; T-shirt shops; cowboy stores lined with hats, furs, and funky bedazzled clothes; and eclectic jewelry stores. I admired the artwork through the large windows that peered into the many galleries sprinkled around town, imagining myself becoming a famous artist one day and exhibiting my work there.

There were a few chain stores, like Ralph Lauren, Eddie Bauer, and Banana Republic, and even though many of these shops saturated the sterile malls near where I grew up, there was something more appealing and inviting about them inside historic brick buildings. The entire town was alive with energy—children could be heard giggling, people were sitting on park benches soaking in the sun, dogs played fetch with their owners on a grassy field, and patrons were sipping cocktails on restaurant patios. The town of Aspen had a vortex, and it drew me right in.

The temperature started to drop as the sun waned over the mountaintops, adding a touch of magenta to the horizon. Throwing on the sweatshirt that had been wrapped around my waist, I hugged my body for extra warmth.

"You cold?" Tracy asked.

"A little," I said, covering my mouth as I yawned.

"Want to go over to the Double Diamond? The Dave Matthews Band is playing tonight."

"Sure, but I can only stay out for a couple of hours. I start my job at the Ranch tomorrow morning. And, to be honest, I'm kind of tired. It's been a long day."

"No worries. I'll have you home before midnight, Cinderella."

Tracy linked her arm with mine as we walked across town, swapping stories about our families, our friends, and our high school sweethearts. Tracy raised her eyebrows in disbelief when I told her I'd only had sex with one guy. "Shit, Hope. That's so sad. Were you in a serious relationship?"

"Actually, we were together for about six months during my sophomore year of college, but it was far from serious. We were always fucked up when we hung out, drinking way too many beers and pulling bong hits between smoking packs of Parliaments." Looking back on that relationship, I realized that I hadn't been comfortable with him or myself.

Tracy promised to help me expand my sexual conquests while I was in Aspen. Not that I was asking, but I appreciated her concern for my inexperienced libido.

As soon as we walked down the steps into the cavernous music venue, we made a beeline to the bar and ordered drinks. Tracy signaled to the bartender, another friend of hers, and ordered two shots of Jägermeister. When he set our drinks down, she turned to me and said, "Let's liven this party up."

I watched her slug her shot back without flinching, and then I took a deep breath and followed suit. Gagging slightly, I shuddered as the fiery black licorice flavor hit the back of my mouth. The taste was still lingering when the bartender poured us two more shots. I hesitated a moment before taking the second one, and decided that after this I would milk a beer for the rest of the night, not wanting to be hungover for my first day at work.

We pushed past crowds of people standing in front of the stage. Tracy greeted dozens of good-looking guys, yelling out their names over the blaring beat of the music, trying to introduce me to all of them. With the combination of alcohol and ambient lighting, I had no chance of remembering anyone.

I let my body move back and forth to the rhythm of the music. Tracy stood beside me, her arms waving wildly above her head as she ground into a shaggy-haired guy behind her on the dance floor. Being around Tracy made me want to let go and embrace the same sexual freedom that seemed to be oozing off her. It certainly wouldn't be too difficult to meet someone. After all, the entire town was like one big meat market.

The music and energy had revitalized me, and it wasn't until the band finished their last song that I remembered I had to wake up early the next morning to start work.

Tracy's dirty dancing partner had an annoyed look on his face when the bright florescent ceiling lights came on and she kissed him on the lips and said goodbye. The poor guy probably assumed he was going to get some serious action tonight.

"Okay, let's get you home before you turn into a pumpkin," Tracy said, grabbing my hand.

Giggling all the way back to the house, we sang our favorite songs, loudly and off-key. It felt as if I had known Tracy for years, rather than a few hours. Stumbling up the steps, we lowered our voices when we opened the front door so we wouldn't wake up Richard. I whispered goodnight to Tracy and thanked her for a fun night, and then I crawled into bed, crashing the minute my head hit the pillow.

* * *

The smell of coffee brewing in the kitchen woke me up bright and early. I pulled on my oversized Ohio State sweatshirt and worn-out gray sweatpants and went upstairs to the kitchen.

"Good morning," Richard said, peeking his head over *The Aspen Times*. "We finally meet in person."

When he stood up to shake my hand, I thought if he cut off his ponytail, lost the thick-rimmed black bifocals, and tanned his pasty face, I would have considered him more attractive. He certainly didn't look threatening in any way.

"Coffee?" he asked.

"Yes, please," I said, almost too eagerly.

Richard filled a mug with steaming hot coffee and handed it to me. I thanked him and added a huge helping of half-and-half and two packets of Equal.

"Sorry I wasn't here to meet you yesterday." He took a sip of his coffee. "I was busy working at the Ranch all day. When do you start work?"

"This morning."

"I'm headed over there too. Want to grab the bus with me?"

"That would be great."

When I finished my coffee, I took a quick shower and dressed in a long cotton skirt, a black T-shirt, and my Birkenstocks. I pulled my wet hair back into a ponytail and added some bronze lipstick in an attempt to brighten my appearance. It didn't help much, but I didn't have the energy to change.

Richard showed me a shortcut to the bus stop that sat behind a condo unit. Twigs crunched under our feet as we walked along the narrow dirt path. The sun shimmered between the tall aspen trees that were perched in clusters on either side of us. Inhaling the clean mountain air made me feel like I had awoken from a long hibernation.

"So, what town are you from in Ohio? I have some family in Shaker Heights," Richard said.

"I'm from a small town two hours outside of Columbus called Mulletville."

"Mulletville? That's a strange name for a town," he said.

"I know. It's a total redneck community."

"Do a lot of guys have mullets?" he asked with a sarcastic tone.

"Actually, I only knew one guy with a mullet. His name was Ron. He worked at Video Land and was the biggest stoner in town, but last I heard he graduated from Princeton University, runs a multimillion-dollar hedge fund, and has a crew cut."

"I guess you never know where life will take you."

"What about you? Have you always lived in Aspen?"

"Born and raised. Twenty-eight years and never left." I couldn't tell if that was a good thing or a bad thing.

When we got off the bus in Snowmass and made our way toward Anderson Ranch Arts Center, tiny goosebumps shot up along my arm as soon as I spotted the rustic buildings. In the late nineteenth century, the property had been an old sheep ranch; years later, the log cabins and barns were renovated and converted into art studios for sculpting, ceramics, painting, woodworking, and photography. The intimate art community had attracted novice and advanced art students from all over the world for workshops and artist-in-residence programs.

Standing in the midst of the four-acre ranch was like hitting the lottery. For the first time in my life, I knew I belonged somewhere—in a place where I could pursue my art and live in the most magnificent mountainous landscape I had ever seen. It sure beat the strip malls of Mulletville.

Richard gave me a tour of the campus and then brought me over to the main office building to introduce me to Helen, my new boss, before heading over to his classroom. Her boy-short black hair framed her face, accentuating her bulbous nose. She greeted me with a smile and offered to take me to the cafeteria for a cup of coffee on the way to the Siegel Children's Building, where I would be teaching art classes to kids between the ages of eight to ten.

We walked toward the classroom, sipping coffee from to-go cups and discussing my new job. She apologized for the mess when we opened the door. Large cardboard boxes of supplies were piled on the distressed paint-stained art tables in the center of the sun-filled room. As soon as Helen left, I dove in immediately, ripping open the boxes and sorting the crayons, scissors, paints, and other supplies into separate containers. I felt like a kid in a candy store, salivating over the multitude of acrylic paints, brushes, and stacks of various-sized canvas paper. As if I had no control over my body, I started to play with my new toys. Pulling out a large canvas, I hung it on an easel, painted my name in the center, and added a background design of colorful mountain wildflowers. I got so carried away that I lost track of time. Eventually, I hung my masterpiece up and decided that this was going to be one of my students' assignments, but first I would take the kids outside to pick an assortment of flowers for inspiration.

When I finally finished organizing, I looked around one last time before leaving, and imagined the room filling up the following day with high-pitched voices and young faces, eager to immerse themselves in the world of art and creativity.

* * *

The days and weeks moved by quickly. Teaching filled up my weekdays, and after my last class, I would situate myself somewhere on the Ranch to paint, relishing the solitude and serene surroundings that enveloped me. I could feel an inspirational presence in nature rhythmically move my paintbrush across blank canvases, creating fields of aspen trees, vast expanses of evergreen trees draped on the mountains, and patches of wildflowers.

Richard and Tracy had become my closest friends. There was always a good time to be had when I was with Tracy. She was the ultimate concierge, taking me to the hottest bars, dance clubs, and restaurants. Since she knew every bartender and server, we were given free drinks all over town. Richard was a workaholic and not much of a partier, so he rarely joined us. I enjoyed spending time with him, discussing art and Aspen while we commuted to the Ranch each morning. We also took our lunch breaks together.

I'd only been in Aspen for a few weeks, but I was already in love with it. The thought of going back to Mulletville in the fall made me uneasy. My internship was only for three months. If things didn't work out, I would have to go back to Mulletville at the end of summer. But Aspen was where I belonged; I was sure of it.

I tried to block out my concern, but it didn't help when I received weekly phone calls from my parents. Good ol' Audrey and Jim called me every Sunday afternoon.

"Hi, Mom, how's everything in Mulletville?" I asked, ready to tune out her response.

"Oh, hello, dear, it's so wonderful to hear your voice." Her nasal Midwestern tone seemed more pronounced over the phone. "Guess what? I found the most special stick-on jewels to add to my jewelry boxes. Daddy thinks they're just wonderful and that I should consider selling them. Isn't that a hoot?"

My mom's been making crafty projects for as long as I can remember. Handpainted jewelry boxes were her specialty. She would spend hours covering them with floral designs in puffy paint. At least she finally moved on to another type of embellishment.

"How's everything with you?" she asked with genuine concern.

"Everything is great."

"When will you be able to come home for a visit? Mulletville misses you."

Fuck Mulletville, I thought to myself.

"Not for a while," I said. I couldn't let her know that I wasn't sure if I'd be able to stay in Aspen after the summer ended. "Can I call you later? I'm heading out to meet some friends."

"Wait, your dad wants to say hello. I love you, angel!"

I heard her yelling at my dad to put down his pop and grab the phone.

"Hello, pumpkin." A small burp echoed through the line. "How's Aspen?"

"All good. How's the car wash?"

"No complaints. Business is great."

I generally had more tolerance for my father than I did for my mother. He always encouraged me to follow my dreams, unlike my mother, who never dreamed bigger than her deviled eggs.

"Bethany is coming over for dinner tonight with Edward. Her belly is getting bigger every day."

My older sister, Bethany, and I were polar opposites. She dropped out of community college to marry her high school sweetheart, Edward. He worked for my dad at the car wash. Similar to my parents, Bethany never had any desire to leave Mulletville, or go anywhere, for that matter. Sometimes I wondered if maybe I had grown up in the wrong family.

"Send my love to Bethany and Edward."

"Will do. Love you," my dad said cheerfully before hanging up the phone. I breathed a sigh of relief that he hadn't asked me about my plans after the summer.

Without warning, images of working at my dad's car wash flashed before me. There I was, standing behind the cash register, taking orders: *"Would you like the ultimate wash today? It's our best value. How about the tire shine? Or the wheel brightener?"* Picturing myself spending the rest of my life in Mulletville was sucking all the air out of the living room. If I didn't find another job when my internship expired, I would be forced to move back to *Hickville*, which was the last thing I wanted.

* * *

"What's with the sour face?" Tracy asked as she stacked drinking glasses into a pyramid on top of the bar. The sound of her upbeat voice and her sun-kissed face put me at ease.

I filled Tracy in on my frustrating job situation and my fear of having to move home if I didn't get a permanent position at the Ranch.

"Here," she said, pouring two shots of bourbon and sliding one in my direction. "This will help." We both slugged our drinks back. "Why don't you ask your boss if you can stay on permanently?"

"I don't know. I feel kind of uncomfortable. I mean, I'm sure if she wanted me to stay she would've asked by now."

She raised her eyebrows and reached for the bottle of bourbon. "C'mon, Hope, don't be such a pussy. Just ask her. If she says no, at least you can start looking for another job now. And worst-case scenario, I'm sure I could get you a job at the restaurant." She poured two more shots for both of us.

Tracy was right. I had to ask Helen first, and if that didn't work out, I would have to start job hunting.

"Thanks for the pep talk. I don't know what I'd do without you." We clinked our glasses together and then threw back our second round of shots.

"Well, whatever happens, you're not going back to Ohio," she said.

The alcohol sped through my bloodstream at lightning speed, obliterating my reservations about my unsettled future.

After class the following day, I went to Helen's office, my pulse quickening with every step. The door was open when I arrived. I was about to enter when I overheard another intern asking Helen about a full-time position.

"I'm so sorry, but we've already offered the job to someone else," she told the woman.

My heart sank. *Shit, shit, shit. Now what was I going to do?* As soon as the other intern left Helen's office, I started to sneak away, but I was too late. I was only five steps down the hall when I heard Helen call my name. I froze in my tracks before turning to face her. "Hi, Helen."

She waved her arm at me. "Come in. You're just the person I wanted to see."

I stepped into her office and sat in the seat facing Helen's desk.

She gave me a small smile. "I'd like to offer you a full-time position at the Ranch, if you're interested."

"Really?" I asked in shock. "I mean, yes, of course. Thank you so much."

"No, thank *you.* I'm thrilled that we get to keep you here." Her ringing phone interrupted us. "Excuse me, Hope. I have to take this." Before picking up the phone, she said, "Why don't you meet me in my office tomorrow morning so we can discuss the details of the job?"

I thanked her again before walking out, and then I ran over to Richard's classroom to share the exciting news. When I peeked through the window, he was busy teaching, and I didn't want to disturb him. Before heading back to Aspen, I called Tracy to see if she could meet me at Red Onion for a celebratory drink, but I couldn't get in touch with her. *Screw it,* I said to myself. *I'll just have to party solo.*

2

ONLY TWO MEN WERE SEATED at the long bar that ran along one side of the Red Onion, a popular restaurant and saloon dating to the Colorado silver boom period. Historical photographs depicting life in the late nineteenth century were hanging all over the red brick walls. The empty dining tables made me feel as if I had entered a ghost town. I considered going somewhere livelier, but when I noticed the tall, dark-haired bartender, I decided to have at least one drink.

As soon as I grabbed a seat at the end of the bar, the hot bartender called out to me, "I'll be right there." Something about him struck me as familiar, but I couldn't put my finger on what it was. It might have been his striking good looks, or the fact that he looked like a younger, sexier version of Ted Danson. I flipped my hair back and waited for him to come over. After serving the other patrons their beers, he made his way toward me.

"What can I get you to drink tonight?"

Staring into his deep blue eyes put me into a stupor.

"Are you okay?" he asked.

I felt my face heat up. "Oh, I'm sorry. Yes, I'm fine; it's been a long day. What do you have on tap?"

He listed the beers on tap, but I couldn't focus on what he was saying. "I'll take a Miller Light," I said, praying that it was one of the beers he had mentioned.

"Can I get you anything to eat?"

"No, thanks. I'm fine with the beer for now."

He placed a white frosty mug in front of me. "You here on vacation?" he asked.

"No, I live here." I took a sip of the beer. "Actually, I came in tonight to celebrate that I'm officially staying in Aspen. My boss offered me a full-time position at my job."

"Congratulations." He leaned over the bar. "So, what do you do?"

After I briefed him on my job at Anderson Ranch, I was about to ask him where he was from, when the guy at the end of the bar slurred in a loud voice, "Hey, Christopher, how are the buffalo wings tonight?"

"They're wicked good!" he yelled back.

Did he just say the word wicked? *Where the hell was this guy from? Who says wicked?* As he walked to the other side of the bar, I had a perfect visual of his taut ass and solid frame. I sucked down more of my beer in an effort to ease my nerves when he came back my way.

"Sorry about that. Those guys have been sitting here since noon. What's your name?"

"Hope."

"I'm Christopher. Nice to meet you, Hope." He reached out his hand and gave my sweaty palm a firm shake. Noticing that my mug was empty, he took it and poured me another drink from the tap. I thanked him. "Where are you from?" I asked.

"Boston." He pushed his long-sleeved shirt up toward his elbows. "I just graduated from business school, and I'm taking some time off before heading into the real world."

While we were chatting, a group of young, rowdy guys walked in and sat at the bar. Christopher moved seamlessly back and forth, taking orders and serving drinks. I couldn't take my eyes off him when he walked away. After helping his customers, he always came back over to me.

Glancing at my watch, I realized I had been sitting at the bar for over two hours, talking with Christopher while he worked. The guys at the end of the bar eventually stumbled out, and then, about twenty minutes later, the drunk boys left. I didn't want to leave, but I assumed he probably wanted to close early and go home.

"Can I get the check?" I asked.

"Don't worry about it. It's on me tonight."

"Thank you," I told him, psyched he was picking up my tab, but also feeling a little uncomfortable about it. I reached into my pocket and put a ten-dollar tip on the table.

He picked up the money. "How about instead of tipping me, you and I grab a slice from New York Pizza?"

"Only if you let me pay," I insisted.

"You got it. Give me fifteen minutes to close down."

I finished my beer while I waited for him. He appeared taller when he stepped out from behind the bar; either that, or my five-foot-two, one-hundred-fifteen-pound body appeared shorter and plumper standing next to him. Walking outside into the cool night air, we made our way to New York Pizza. The sweet aroma of basil and oregano filled the tiny restaurant. Other than a couple of young college-aged kids sitting at a booth finishing up a pie, we were the only ones there. A gentleman with a head of thick, gray hair stood behind the counter, and a few trays of pizza pies lined the glass warming tray.

"Evening," the cherubic employee said. "What can I get you guys?"

Christopher turned to look at me.

"I'll have a slice of pepperoni and a soda pop," I said, pointing to the Coke machine.

"Same for me, with a large Sprite," Christopher added.

I pulled my money out of my pocket and reached over to pay.

Christopher grabbed my hand. "Sorry, I'm buying."

"No way. You didn't let me tip you at the bar, and you said I could treat you to a slice."

"I know, but I'm old-fashioned. I got it."

"Thank you, but next time, you need to let me get you dinner." It was an impulsive thing for me to say. How did I even know there would be a next time?

"You're on."

We grabbed our food and drinks and took a seat at a booth in the far corner of the restaurant. Before taking my first bite, I sprinkled a heavy coat of parmesan cheese all over my slice. I was about to ask him if he wanted any cheese, but I was caught off guard when I noticed he was looking at me. He blushed slightly when our eyes met.

"Do you always refer to soda as *pop*? I've never heard anyone use that term," he said.

"In Ohio, that's what everyone calls it. What about you? I heard you use the word *wicked*. That word is definitely worse than *pop*."

"*Wicked* is a Massachusetts term, and it's not nearly as hick-sounding as *soda pop*."

"Are you calling me a hick?" I asked between bites of my pizza, the hot cheese nearly burning the roof of my mouth.

"Totally," he replied in a playful way. "You have a little sauce above your lip." Before I had a chance to pick up my napkin, his hand reached across the table, wiping it off with his thumb. An electric current pierced through my body when his skin made contact with mine.

"Sorry," he said, finishing off his last bite of crust. "I was thinking about hiking American Lake Trail on Sunday. Any interest in joining me?"

"Sure, I'd love to."

By the time we left the restaurant, most of the town was shut down for the night. The only light came from the phosphorescent moon looming in the dark sky, surrounded by a few intermittent stars. Wandering slowly in the direction of my house, our arms lightly brushed against each other as we continued to talk the entire way.

"This is it," I said when we reached the front stoop of my townhouse. I wanted to invite him in, but I felt awkward. Tracy was definitely going to mock me for not seizing this opportunity. Our eyes connected for a moment, and despite the cool air, a heat rose between us. "Do you live far from here?"

"I live over by Smuggler Mountain."

Since he never said anything, I had assumed he lived in my neighborhood. "I feel bad you walked so far out of your way."

"I don't mind. Anyway, I didn't want you to walk home by yourself." He pushed his hands into the pockets of his jeans. "So, should I pick you up around 9 a.m. on Sunday?"

"Yeah, that would be great. Thank you for tonight. I had fun."

He pulled his head toward mine and gave me a peck on the lips that sent a tingling sensation through my body. "Me, too," he said.

An awkward silence filled the space between us. I wanted more, and so did he. Instead of reaching toward him, I reluctantly turned around and walked up the steps. Before opening the door, I looked back and waved. Christopher was still there, watching me. I floated inside, praying Tracy was awake so I could tell her about my night.

* * *

Sunday morning was a brisk, overcast day. I jumped out of bed and threw on a pair of L.L. Bean heavyweight running tights, hiking boots, and a long underwear top underneath my Ohio State sweatshirt. I shoved an extra jacket, hat, gloves, and a water bottle into my backpack. When I was ready, I sat outside on the steps and waited for Christopher to pick me up.

A jittery feeling hit my belly when I caught sight of his face behind the wheel of a black Jeep Cherokee. Christopher opened his window and called out, "Morning."

Before he had a chance to get out of his car to greet me, I walked around to the passenger side and took a seat. He looked even more handsome in the daylight.

"Morning," I said, trying not to gawk at him.

"You psyched for the hike?" he asked.

"So psyched. I hiked Cathedral Lake in August, and it was incredible."

"Both hikes are similar, so if you liked Cathedral then you'll love American Lake Trail." He turned up the volume on the radio when Blues Traveler's "Run-Around" came on. I tried not to stare at his profile while he sang along with John Popper.

Soon enough, we pulled into the parking lot of the trailhead and got out of the car. There was a raw chill in the air, but I knew once we started moving we would warm up quickly. We hiked along a stretch of moderately strenuous switchbacks. After trekking through the trail, we eventually ended up on a wooded path surrounded by evergreen trees. An inviting scent of pine needles and sap floated in the air, reminding me of Christmastime.

We kept up a quick pace, stopping a few times to check out the mountain views and sip water. Our conversation flowed naturally; we took turns telling each other about our families and our childhoods.

Christopher and I came from vastly different backgrounds. An only child, he grew up with a silver spoon in his mouth from a prominent Boston family. His father was a successful real estate tycoon, while his mother kept herself busy serving on the boards of many local charities. Half their summers were spent in their Nantucket home, the other half in Europe. I found his life fascinating compared to my simple upbringing, yet oddly, he was equally as interested in my family. He was brought up by nannies, and his parents were so busy keeping up with their social calendar that they didn't spend much quality time together. My parents, on the other hand, rarely went out to dinner without my sister and me, and we always ate home-cooked meals as a family. The one thing we had in common was that we both felt like we had ended up in the wrong family. He dreamed of home-cooked meals and a loving stay-at-home mom, while I yearned for a more sophisticated and cultured set of parents.

We finally made it to the end of the hike—a picturesque small body of water nestled in the snow-capped mountains. Christopher took a seat on a large rock.

"You hungry?" he asked, opening up his backpack. "I brought sandwiches from Shlomo's Deli."

I took a seat next to him. "Yes, I'm starving," I responded, a little embarrassed that I hadn't thought of bringing food.

"I have two sandwiches, turkey and corned beef. Do you have a preference?"

"I'm good with either."

"Want to split them?" he asked.

I nodded, and he handed me half of each sandwich.

"Thank you. I love how prepared you are," I said before biting into the rich and tender corned beef with a smattering of tangy, spicy mustard.

We sat quietly eating our lunch, taking in the tranquil surroundings and enjoying the serenity. The sun broke through the gray sky, shining its golden rays on the mirrored lake before us.

"This is incredible," I said, interrupting our meditative state.

"I know. Can you believe how lucky we are to live here? Rarely does a day go by that I don't appreciate this life."

"I feel so different when I'm out here—so calm."

"Me, too," he said.

Our eyes met for a moment. An energy radiated between us, making me feel lightheaded. "I want to hear more about your artwork," he said, breaking the spell.

"I've been drawing since I was old enough to hold a crayon. It's always been my way of visiting the world in my imagination."

"What do you like to draw?"

"Natural landscapes have always been my thing. Most of my sketchbooks are filled with scenes of oceans, mountains, rivers, and lakes."

"I'd love to look at them sometime, if you were cool with that."

"I'd love to show you," I told him, flattered that he wanted to see them.

He picked up the wax-paper wrappers from our sandwiches and put the trash in his backpack. When we stood up, I stretched my arms wide above my head.

"Wait," he said, stepping closer to me.

"Shit, I don't have food on my face again, do I?"

"No," he whispered. I could smell his sweet breath. His full lips parted slightly, and then he covered my mouth with his. I closed my eyes and let myself sink into the smooth wetness of his tongue. His strong arms wrapped around me, and as he pulled me in, I reveled in the heat of his body.

"I'm sorry," he said, stepping back.

"Sorry for what?" I asked.

"For kissing you."

"I'm glad you did."

He took my hand into his. "I guess we should probably head back now."

I didn't want the day to end. We were so caught up in conversation on the way back to the trailhead that I didn't pay much attention to my surroundings, and before I knew it, we were in the parking lot. On the drive home, Christopher asked when he could see me again.

* * *

After the hike, Christopher and I started hanging out with each other all the time. In the evening when he was working, Tracy and I went out for drinks and dancing. Christopher would join us after his shift. By then, Tracy had usually found some guy to hook up with for a night.

Richard and I mostly hung together at the Ranch. He and I often worked side by side in our free time. I would paint while he sketched furniture designs. We listened to classical music, discussed art, and let our creativity flow in the silence between us.

Winter was incredible. Aspen and the surrounding mountains transformed into a magical white wonderland. The energy in town was alive and vibrant, filled with tourists prancing around in their Bogner ski outfits, fur coats, and boots. Christopher and I skied together as often as we could, alternating between Snowmass, Highlands, and Aspen Mountain. Each mountain had its own personality. Snowmass was vast, with tons of terrain; Highlands was the local man's mountain, so it was less touristy than the others; and Aspen was my favorite. It was challenging, and, best of all, it was in town, so there was always a good time to be had at Ruthie's on the Mountain, or Schlomos at the base for après-ski. Christopher was a beautiful skier. Growing up, he had skied in Vail every spring break with his family. I struggled a little to keep up with him, but he was always patient and never made me feel self-conscious about my skiing.

* * *

As April approached, the snow was melting on the mountains and the buds were showing new signs of life on the aspen trees. With mild weather and ample sunshine, a new season was on the horizon. One afternoon I received an unexpected phone call that changed my sunny mood. My mother was crying hysterically when I picked up the call. "Hope," she said, sobbing. "Uncle Ralph..."

My heart skipped a beat. "Mom, what? Please, tell me."

"He had a..." More sobbing.

"A what?"

"He had a heart attack. He's gone."

"Oh, my God!"

"The funeral is this weekend."

A tear trickled down my cheek. When I got off the phone, I dialed Continental Airlines with trembling hands to book the next flight to Ohio.

Uncle Ralph was married to Aunt Myrna, my mother's younger sister. I adored them both. Unlike my parents, they were well-traveled and active. Since they had never had kids, they spoiled my sister and me with tales of their trips and keepsakes from around the world.

I made it home just in time for the funeral. Having rejected her Catholic roots, and fascinated by Buddhism, Aunt Myrna had asked her close friend, a Buddhist monk, to perform a funeral service at a nearby monastery. Following the ritual ceremony, complete with beautiful chants and poems about reincarnation, my parents invited everyone to our home. Old friends and family members showed up to pay their respects to Aunt Myrna, who was dressed in a multicolored African tribal dress. The day was filled with hugs and tears. "Such a good man," was echoed over and over, along with "I'm so sorry about your loss, Myrna" and "The two of you were so good together." Watching my aunt all day without Uncle Ralph beside her ripped my heart in half.

Bethany, my mother, and I cleared the dishes as soon as the final guests said goodbye. My father fell asleep on his reclining chair in the den, while Edward slouched on the couch, watching a baseball game with a can of Budweiser resting on his gut.

"Aunt Myrna, please, let me do that," Bethany insisted, reaching out to take a plate of spinach and cheese triangles from her hands. My sister's claw-like acrylic nails were painted the same shade of fuchsia as her lace dress.

"Honey, your uncle may have passed on, but I'm still perfectly capable of cleaning the kitchen."

I grabbed a few more dishes off the dining room table and brought them to the kitchen. Aunt Myrna was leaning over the table, spooning leftover food into Tupperware containers. Her short, spiked red hair usually gave her face a dewy look, but today, I noticed the glow had been replaced with a pallid complexion. I bit my lip in an effort to fight off my tears.

"Hope," my mom said over the loud stream of water running from the sink, "Bethany and I can finish up in here. Why don't you and your aunt grab a slice of pie in the dining room?"

"Let's go," Aunt Myrna said to me, snapping the lid onto a container of deviled eggs. "I want to hear about your life in Aspen." I followed her into the dining room, past the desserts, to the drink table. She picked up a bottle of Jim Beam and poured a generous amount into two plastic cups. "Here," she said, handing me one. "I think we could both use this right now."

She guzzled half her drink and then let out a big sigh. "I needed that. All right, now talk to me. What's going on with you?"

Even though I wanted to tell her about Christopher and Anderson Ranch, I couldn't get the words out. I couldn't share my happiness when her entire life had just been turned upside down. Ignoring her question, I took a hard swallow of alcohol. "Aunt Myrna, I'm so sorry about Uncle Ralph."

"Listen to me, Hope. I'm going to be fine. I had thirty blessed years with Ralph. All my memories are up here," she said, pointing to her head. "And here." This time she pointed to her heart. "Now, enough about me. Let's make a toast to the good times, and then I want to hear about my adorable niece."

I told her all about my life in Aspen, my work at the Ranch, and Christopher. She focused on my every word with a gleam in her eyes.

* * *

When I arrived back in Aspen, Christopher's parents were visiting. He had made reservations for all of us to have dinner at Piñons, an upscale restaurant. I was apprehensive about meeting them, but I didn't have too much time to dwell on it beforehand. I was determined to get to the post office on my way to dinner to mail one of my favorite paintings—four sets of colorful skis leaning on a wooden rack at the bottom of a snowy mountain—to Aunt Myrna. It was the least I could do for her.

As I left the post office, I glanced at my watch and panicked when I realized I was running late. I ran as fast as I could down South Mill Street. Trotting in high heels was not the prettiest sight. I sure as hell didn't look like a thoroughbred, more like a clumsy baby giraffe. Without warning, my ankle twisted in the wrong direction, thrusting my body onto the pavement. I landed face-down on the sidewalk right in front of the restaurant.

"Hope!" Christopher yelled, running toward me. "Are you okay?"

He leaned down to help me up. "I'm fine," I said, taking his hand. "Sorry I'm late. I had to run a quick errand before dinner."

"Don't worry about it," he said. "That was quite a fall. Are you sure you're okay?"

"All good," I told him, smoothing out my dress.

He gave my hand a gentle squeeze as we walked into the restaurant. "You look pretty," he said.

I thanked him with a grin. "I'm kind of nervous about meeting your parents."

"Don't be. They're going to love you," he said, holding the door for me.

"Mom, Dad," Christopher called out to the couple standing in front of the hostess's desk. They both turned around immediately. His mother wore a short mink coat draped over her shoulders, and she carried a black Chanel bag. Christopher's father looked like he had stepped out of a Brooks Brothers catalog with his blue-and-white striped button-down shirt and dark slacks. "I'd like you to meet Hope."

When I reached out to shake their hands, I realized I still had bits of gravel stuck in my palm. I tried to brush it off, but it was too late. "Mr. and Mrs. Whitmore, it's a pleasure to finally meet you." I caught Mrs. Whitmore casually trying to wipe the dirt off when I wasn't looking, which I appreciated, even though I was still embarrassed.

"The pleasure is ours. And please, dear, call me Donna, and this is Bill."

Christopher had clearly inherited his good looks from his father. Distinguished lines fanned out from his eyes when he gave me a warm greeting.

Soon after we sat at our table, Bill ordered a bottle of wine from the sommelier, who complimented him on choosing one of their finest bottles of Bordeaux. The first glass went down quickly, and I noted hints of black cherry and vanilla with a smooth finish. Never had I tasted anything like that before. My parents never drank much wine, or any alcohol for that matter, other than an occasional beer. At twenty-two, my liquors of choice were cheap bourbon and beer.

"This wine is lovely," Donna said to her husband, and then she looked at me. "So, tell me, Hope, which schools did you attend in Ohio?"

"Well, I started out at Mulletville School 16 for elementary, then went to Mulletville Middle School, and from there, I went on to our regional high school. And I graduated from Ohio State University." I took another sip of my wine, trying to swallow the embarrassment over my inferior education.

"And what kind of work does your father do?"

"He owns a car wash," I told her, and then added, "It's the only one around for miles."

Shit, I thought. I shouldn't have said that. Nothing could make a car wash sound glamorous. A moistness spread across my forehead. I was fighting the temptation to chug the rest of my wine, or better yet, chug the rest directly from the bottle. When I glanced at Christopher, he gave me a relaxed smile. I smiled back, wishing we were anywhere but here.

"Christopher tells us you're quite the artist," Donna said.

I blushed at the compliment.

"I'm not sure if he told you, but I sit on the board of Boston's Museum of Fine Arts, and I would love to get your input about our educational program."

Finally, we had a topic to discuss that didn't make me feel insecure. While Bill and Christopher spent most of the meal discussing business, Donna and I chatted about her involvement on the board. She gratefully accepted my suggestions about how to improve the museum's enrichment classes, and she asked me if I would mind helping her find a new piece of art for her home in one of the Aspen galleries before she went back to Boston.

"Have you put any thought into where you want to live when you move back to Boston?" Donna asked Christopher.

"No, Mom, it's only April," he responded in a stern voice. "I still have a month left before I need to start looking."

My mouth fell open, and I stared at Christopher in shock. He hadn't said anything to me about leaving Aspen so soon. I couldn't believe he would keep something like this from me.

Noticing the tension, Donna looked at Christopher and said, "I'm sorry," in a quiet voice.

Changing the subject, Bill mentioned that Donna had started taking golf lessons. For the rest of the meal, the conversation was all about their country club. I had a difficult time focusing on what anyone was saying and completely stopped engaging. Meanwhile, Christopher couldn't even make eye contact with me.

When we finished eating, the server placed the leather-bound guest check presenter on the table. Without even looking at it, Bill handed him his credit card.

On our way out of the restaurant, Donna reached over and gave me a loose hug, and then she whispered in my ear, "I'm glad Christopher found you. I've never seen him this happy before."

I forced myself to give her a half smile, even though I was seething and wanted to tell her that her son was a douche.

Before his parents turned toward their hotel, I thought I saw Donna slip something into Christopher's pocket when she kissed him on the cheek. *Fuck him*, I thought. He could have gone back to Boston to live with his parents right now for all I cared at that moment.

Once they were out of sight, Christopher turned toward me. "My parents can be a little intimidating, but I could tell they really liked you," he said, reaching his arm around my shoulder to warm me from the nighttime chill.

I pulled his hand off me and turned to face him. My blood was boiling. "When are you moving?"

He lowered his head. "Mid-June."

"June?" I said, raising my voice. "Why haven't you told me about this?"

"I was going to tell you."

"When?"

"Soon."

"You're leaving *soon.* Were you going to tell me as you were boarding the plane back to Boston?"

He had no response. I turned to leave, but he grabbed my arm.

"I was going to tell you about going back to Boston when I gave you this," he said.

Suddenly, he got down on one knee—and my heart skipped a beat. Christopher reached into his pocket, the same pocket I had seen his mother put something into, and he pulled out a black jewelry box. A two-carat oval-shaped diamond ring shimmered when he opened it. "Hope, will you marry me?"

A brilliant light reflected off the diamond. "It's spectacular," I said. Happy tears filled my eyes as I nodded. "Yes, I'll marry you."

"It was my grandmother's."

He stood up, took me in his arms, and kissed me, slowly and deeply.

"I love you," he said softly.

"I love you, too." I held up my hand to admire the ring again, and then it dawned on me. I took a hard swallow. "This means I have to leave Aspen, doesn't it?"

"I'm sure my mother can help you get a job teaching art classes at the museum."

"But if you love it here as much as I do, then why can't we stay?"

"Because I can't secure the same future for us living in Aspen. Give me time to build my career in Boston doing what I've been groomed to do my entire life, and one day we'll come back. I promise."

3

1997

AS MUCH AS I TRIED to enjoy every moment I had left before the big move, the final week slipped by faster than I wanted. Helen had insisted on throwing me a going-away party at the Ranch. Before heading over there, I tried to finish packing, but it wasn't going well. Clothes and shoes were splayed all over my bed and the floor. It looked like a war zone. Dust particles filled the air like snowflakes, tickling my nose when I pulled my duffle bag out from the back of my closet. My tennis racket was pushed into the far corner. I hadn't picked it up once since moving to Aspen. Christopher and I had discussed playing tennis a few times, but we were too busy with all the mountain activities.

My phone rang while I was shoving clothes into my bag. "Hey," Christopher said in a cheery voice. "I'm bummed I can't make it to your party tonight. I tried to get out of work, but my boss insisted I finish my last shift."

"Don't worry about it." I glanced at my watch. "Shit. I have to go. The party is starting in less than an hour, and I haven't showered yet."

Before hanging up, he said, "Wait up for me tonight. I'll come over after work."

After taking a quick shower, I dressed in a floral sundress with spaghetti straps and a cropped denim jacket. Dashing out of the house, I caught myself before tripping over a pair of black loafers near the doorway and ran as fast as I could to the bus stop, grateful I got on before it pulled away.

Seven of my paintings, sitting on easels, were displayed around the cafeteria at Anderson Ranch. Each painting had been completed while I was at the Ranch. I walked over to Richard, who was staring at one of my favorite paintings. The image focused on a series of large black spots that had formed after dead branches had fallen off a forest of aspen trees. It almost looked like a million crazy people were staring at you.

"They say the eyes are the windows to the soul," Richard said. "This is great. You really captured the mystery here."

I smiled at his compliment.

"Did you finish packing?" he asked.

"Not even close."

"I'm sure you'll get it all done." Nodding his head in the direction of the food, he said, "Let's grab something to eat. I'm starving. I haven't eaten all day."

I followed Richard to the buffet table, greeting my friends, colleagues, former students, and their parents. The hugs and well-wishes from everyone were heartwarming. Helen pulled me aside and told me how much she enjoyed working with me, and she encouraged me to continue my art. I hugged her and thanked her for the opportunity to work at the Ranch.

"Here," Richard said, handing me a plate of cheese and crackers. "I gave you an extra helping of Brie."

"You're the best." Before taking a bite, I noticed his almond-shaped green eyes behind the thick lenses of his glasses, realizing for the first time how striking they were. "Hey, have you seen Tracy?" I asked, sinking my teeth into the soft cheese.

"I think I saw her bum a cigarette off someone. She might be outside."

I headed outside to look for Tracy and found her sitting on the steps with a lit cigarette in her hand. The butt was covered in a ring of red lipstick. Her bare legs were crossed over to one side, pushing her short skirt up her thighs. Brilliant stars flickered in the darkened sky. A big smile washed over her face when I took a seat next to her.

She put her cigarette out on the steps and wrapped her arm around my shoulder. "I'm going to miss you, Hope."

"I'm going to miss you, too, and this ridiculous view."

In the distance, the rough-hewn mountaintops framed the night with a quiet power. A cosmic force settled inside me, filling up the pit at the bottom of my stomach.

"I get it," she said. "You know, there's a famous legend that the Ute Indians put a curse over this land. They said that anyone who leaves Aspen is destined to return."

I prayed she was right and that I would move back one day. We sat in silence for a few moments, marveling at the stars.

"And you're only a plane ride away," she added, trying to make me feel better about leaving, but her words only made me feel worse. It was a long fucking plane ride. Once Christopher and I started working full-time in Boston, I had no idea how often we'd be able to visit.

* * *

After the party, I crawled into bed naked and waited for Christopher to come over after work. I tried to stay awake, but despite the glow of the full moon shining through the window, my eyelids grew heavy and sleep was getting the better of me. Just when I started to drift off, the opening and closing of the door made a creaking sound. I could hear Christopher unzipping his jeans. His belt buckle made a clanking noise when it fell onto the hardwood floor. Pulling up the covers, he crawled into bed next to me. The sweet scent of his skin was a combination of sandalwood and vanilla. Wrapping his arm around me, he showered my neck with kisses. The heat of our bodies intensified when he pressed up against me. I turned around to face him, and, like magnets, our open mouths drew together, our tongues colliding fervently.

He pulled away for a moment and looked deep into my eyes. "I can't wait to spend my life with you," he said. Our hunger for each other was voracious. I needed him inside me. His lean chest pushed against my breasts, igniting my nipples. When he finally guided himself into me, my skin tingled and screamed out in pleasure. Unable to focus on anything but his movements, I suddenly lost full control, and violent shudders exploded from me like an earthquake. Seconds later, I felt his warm rush pouring into me. We were both breathless when he lifted his moistened body off me and lay on his back. Turning toward him, I rested my head on his chest, letting the soft beating of his heart lull me. All the anxiety I had about leaving Aspen faded away, as I fell into a peaceful sleep, snuggled tightly next to Christopher.

* * *

June 1998

Built in the late 1800s, Trinity Church was considered a historic landmark in Boston. The impressive stone-faced structure boasted cathedral ceilings, grand towers, and archways, along with ornamental details of expert wood craftsmanship on the walls, pews, floors, and ceilings. On either side of the altar was a large gold candelabra and an arrangement of orchids and calla lilies sitting on a tall pedestal. The elaborate artwork of murals and opalescent colors of the stained-glass windows added a mystical atmosphere to the ceremony.

Filling up only about ten rows on either side of the aisle, our two hundred and fifty guests looked scant in a space that could accommodate over fourteen hundred people. There was so much beauty and intricate design to admire inside the church that we chose to limit the flower arrangements to a minimum.

I want to believe that I floated down the aisle like a delicate snowflake performing a graceful ballet through the air—but that's not how it happened. Instead, I squeezed my father's right arm, almost cutting off his circulation, making my way down the red carpet between the wooden pews in stiff, robotic form. Every single step was calculated, as I concentrated on placing one foot in front of the other, choking on a fear that had been haunting me for weeks before the wedding—tripping. I was afraid that if I accidentally stepped on the flowing satin fabric sweeping the floor in front of me, I would pull down my strapless gown and flash my breasts for all to see.

Tiny beads of sweat laced my forehead by the time I was face-to-face with Christopher, standing regally in his black tuxedo. The shaking of my knees finally subsided when I looked into his eyes, his face beaming with joy. The reverend's words were heartfelt and touching as he talked about the spiritual union of marriage. When he finally pronounced us man and wife, I kissed my new husband so hard that I almost swallowed his tongue.

* * *

Immediately following the ceremony, shuttle buses transported everyone to the Four Seasons Hotel for the reception. Guests mingled during the cocktail hour, holding tall flutes of champagne as they wandered around the monogrammed ice sculptures, sampling food from carving stations filled with rack of lamb, beef Wellington, and baked Virginia ham, as well as seafood stations overflowing with cracked Maine lobster tails, colossal shrimp, and oysters. Servers passed around trays of blini caviar, puff pastries, chicken skewers, and spring rolls.

Aunt Myrna and Tracy spent the entire cocktail hour downing glasses of whisky and giggling like schoolchildren with one of the bartenders. I had known those two would hit it off. Back in her day, Aunt Myrna could party like a rock star. Even in her mid-fifties, she could keep up with Tracy, a woman half her age.

"Have you tried the smoked salmon on cucumber with dill cream?" my mother asked me.

I shook my head and took a sip of wine.

"It's delicious," she said. Swallowing her last bite, she added, "You know, it's making me wonder if I should add smoked salmon to my next batch of deviled eggs. I think the ladies from my crafting club would love it."

I rolled my eyes and wondered why my mother always had to mention her damn deviled eggs.

Donna approached us, carrying a martini. Her elegant Chanel skirt suit and single strand of creamy white pearls stood in stark contrast to my mother's watercolor floral print dress and the large silver armadillo brooch that was pinned above her breastbone on her purple cardigan.

"Oh, Donna, do you believe our wonderful children are married?" my mother gushed.

I noticed a smudge of hot pink lipstick on my mother's front tooth when she smiled.

"I know. We are lucky, aren't we?" Donna said.

"Jim and I really appreciate all you've done for our Hope."

I tried signaling to my mother to wipe off the pink stain, but she didn't notice and continued rambling.

"You know, I have a special surprise I want to show you two. Wait right here."

When my mother walked away, Donna turned to me. "I've been meaning to ask how everything is going at the museum. The education director sent me a lovely note telling me how fond they are of you."

I didn't have the heart to tell her how much I disliked it there. After all, if it weren't for Donna, I wouldn't have the job. My makeshift classroom was located in the windowless basement, next to the janitorial closet. Unlike Anderson Ranch Arts Center, where I had sweeping views to inspire me at every turn, the stuffy room sucked all the creativity out of me.

"It's going well," I responded, wondering if my nose was going to surge like Pinocchio's.

Thankfully, the conversation ended when we spotted my mother making her way through the crowd of guests, carrying a small brown bag.

"What do you think?" my mother asked, pulling out a brown crocheted cover with an owl face on one side. "Isn't it a hoot?"

I was stunned into silence as Donna looked at my mother's bizarre craft with genuine interest.

"It's a toilet roll cover. I crocheted it."

The owl's large white eyes were staring in my direction, almost like it was mocking me. A rush of heat lit my cheeks on fire.

"How adorable, Audrey. You're so creative. Now I know where Hope gets her artistic talent."

I couldn't believe Donna had said that. How could she possibly put my painting in the same category as my mother's juvenile arts and crafts projects?

In a high-pitched voice, my mother added, "And for a special surprise, my gals from the Mulletville Crafting Club helped me crochet one hundred and twenty-five of them—one for every couple to take home as a party favor."

Before excusing herself to get a drink, Donna hugged my mother, and actually thanked her for making the gift bags. How was she not mortified that all her snooty Boston blue blood friends were going to receive homemade toilet roll covers as wedding favors?

I was still on the verge of hyperventilating when my friend Marcy, looking chic in her black Gucci halter dress, walked over to us. It took a moment to recover from the shock of my mom's owl covers before I realized that I needed to make an introduction. "Mom, this is my good friend Marcy."

"Oh, it's so nice to meet you," my mother said. The lipstick mark on her tooth had finally dissolved. "How do you know Hope?"

"We met at a dinner party," Marcy said. "Hope and I moved to Boston around the same time. Both of us were forced to relocate because of our husbands' jobs." She winked at me. "Our friendship got us through our first year together."

"Do you live in Boston too?" my mother asked.

"I used to live near Hope, but my husband and I just bought a house in Concord. It's a suburb not too far from Boston."

"Oh, that sounds lovely," my mother said.

Marcy looked at me, her cute dimples indenting when she smiled. "There's a great house for sale down the street that I'm going to try to talk Hope and Christopher into buying when they come back from their honeymoon."

Just then, the large double doors to the ballroom opened and guests were ushered inside. Lush white floral centerpieces, surrounded by votive candles, sat on top of lace embroidered tablecloths. The grand space had a romantic and ethereal glow.

The rest of the evening flashed before me like a dream. Other than sitting down for speeches, Christopher and I spent most of the night on the dance floor. We looked like hot messes. A combination of foundation and sweat ran down the side of my face, and Christopher had large, wet pit stains on his white tuxedo shirt. When the band finally played a slow song, we hugged our bodies close together and swayed to the music.

"How am I going to get your dress off tonight with all those buttons?" Christopher whispered in my ear.

I gave him a sensual look. "You'll have to do whatever it takes."

"Mm. I can't wait," he said, nibbling on my ear.

When I glanced around the room, I noticed Aunt Myrna was sitting alone, eating a piece of cake. "Hey, would you mind asking Aunt Myrna to dance?"

"Of course," he responded.

I thanked him with a kiss on the lips. Aunt Myrna's face lit up when Christopher grabbed her hand and led her to the dance floor.

I made my way to the bar and ran into Tracy.

"Hey, you," she said. "Don't I get to hug the bride?" A fresh coat of glossy red lipstick matched her dark, lacquered nails.

We gave each other a tight embrace.

"So, who do you have your eyes on tonight? What did you think about Christopher's college roommate, Kyle Braxton?" Gazing at him from across the ballroom, I added, "He's single and really hot."

"Not for me. He's way too Harvard for my taste. Anyway, I already have late-night plans with the young bartender."

I laughed. "That guy looks like he's in high school."

"Close. He just finished his junior year at Boston College." With a big smirk, she added, "For the record, younger guys are more fun in bed."

"I miss you, Tracy. Christopher and I are going to try to come to Aspen to ski over vacation."

"You guys better come. By the way, with everything going on, I didn't get a chance to tell you my good news." She paused for a moment and took a sip of her cocktail. "My bartending days have officially ended. I just got my real estate license."

"That's awesome. I'm so proud of you."

"Thank you. I'm really excited." She took a sip of her drink. "Hey, are you still working at the museum?"

"Yeah," I told her, shrugging my shoulders. I wanted to tell her how much I pined for my old life in Aspen and my job at Anderson Art Ranch, but I didn't want to spoil the evening. Just when I was about to ask Tracy if she'd heard from Richard, who I was bummed couldn't make it to the wedding, the band started playing "Super Freak," and Christopher pulled us both onto the dance floor.

* * *

After saying goodbye to the last guest, Christopher and I rushed to the hotel elevator, excited to finally be alone and get up to our room in the penthouse suite. After pressing the button to our floor, I turned around and faced my new husband with lust in my eyes. With only a minute to spare before the doors opened, I knelt in front of him, unfastened his black pants, and opened my mouth over his hardness for a quick tease before we got to the room. He moaned while my tongue stroked the top of his shaft. Caught up in the moment, neither of us heard the ding of the elevator.

"Oh my," a familiar voice called out from behind. Fumbling, I stood up, while Christopher pulled his untucked shirt over his open pants.

"Oh my," the voice said again.

When I looked back, my mother was standing there. Her face was crimson. "I think I got off on the wrong floor."

"Hi, Mom," I said, unable to meet her eyes.

Christopher let out a fake cough. "What floor are you on?"

"Oh, shoot. I'm not quite sure. Ten, I think," she said, stepping into the elevator.

He pushed the button for her, and an uncomfortable silence filled the small space as we waited for the elevator to move.

Finally, my mother spoke. "What a wonderful party. You kids must be exhausted."

I stared at the elevator buttons, desperate for number ten to light up. When the door finally opened on my mom's floor, we both yelled out "Good night!" and then burst into uncontrollable laughter.

4

2007

"MOMMY, PLAY 'FRUIT SALAD' AGAIN," Bobby yelled from the back seat of the car.

Ever since I had bought the kids a Wiggles CD, it was all we listened to—over and over again. "How about I play some of Mommy's music next?"

"No," Bobby whined. "I want 'Fruit Salad.' "

I took a deep breath. "Okay, one more time, and then we're going to play something else."

Glancing in the rearview mirror, my heart warmed as I watched my adorable three-year-old shake his overgrown strawberry blond hair back and forth to the beat of the music. Even though he had my hair color, he looked like Christopher, with his dazzling blue eyes and a galactic smile that lit up a room.

Christopher and I had moved out of our Boston apartment when I was three months pregnant with Megan. Marcy had convinced us to buy a house around the corner from her in Concord. At first, our four-bedroom Colonial-style home seemed too spacious for the two of us. We took our time adding furniture to the family room and dining room, but soon after Megan was born, plastic baby toys began flooding our house. The bouncy seat, activity saucer, toy kitchen, toy vacuum, toy walkers, puzzles, musical instruments, and dolls were expanding at a rapid pace. No matter how many times I tried to clean them up and pile them neatly somewhere, toward the end of the day, they were scattered everywhere. Three years later, I gave birth to Bobby. When he started walking, we added a Thomas the Train set to the unfurnished living room, increasing my odds of tripping over one of the trains that were constantly rolling around from room to room on our polished hardwood floors.

I adored my children, and I loved being a mother to them, but the first few years were challenging. Not to mention, my tits had deflated, and I had acquired an extra flab of skin around my midsection. My days were filled with changing diapers, feeding, cleaning, and stealing ten-minute naps whenever the kids happened to be on the same sleep schedule, which wasn't often.

The sound of the garage door opening at around 6:30 p.m. during the week would make me salivate like one of Pavlov's dogs, anxious to see Christopher walk in the door after work with a glowing smile. After we put the kids to bed, we relished our few hours of alone time. Often, we would open a bottle of wine and enjoy a quiet meal together. He was always interested in what I had to say, but all I could contribute to our conversations were daily trips to Star Market, Gymboree class, or running to the mall to return a onesie to Baby Gap. Hanging on his every word, I listened to him enthusiastically discuss work, reviewing acquisitions, new tenants, building plans, and lease renewals.

When Megan finally started school, I had a little more time in my day, although not much, since I still had an active boy in tow. The only respite I had was during Bobby's two-hour naps. Every now and then, I thought about pulling out my old box of art supplies, but with trying to straighten up the house, wash and fold laundry, and prepare dinner, I never felt like I had enough time. *Soon*, I promised myself. *Soon, both kids will be in school a full day, and then I'll have more time to start painting again.*

Before Bobby had a chance to ask me to turn on "Fruit Salad" again, we pulled into the garage. The school bus was expected to arrive within the next five minutes. I unbuckled Bobby from the car seat and held his little hand in mine while we sauntered over to the bus stop at the end of our driveway. We played a quick game of I Spy until we spotted the bus coming around the corner and heading toward us.

The bus driver opened the door, and Megan came bouncing down the steps with her long pigtails swinging back and forth. Wrapping my arms around her, I gave her a hug and kissed the top of her head. Her hair still smelled like the sweet berry shampoo she had used the night before in the bathtub.

"How was your day?" I asked, taking her Cinderella backpack and throwing it over my shoulder.

"Guess what?" Megan flashed me a wide smile. "I lost my tooth at lunch!"

"Oh no! How are you going to eat dinner tonight?"

"Very funny, Mom. When's Daddy coming home? I want to show him."

"How about we meet him for an early dinner after ballet?"

"Yay!" Megan jumped up and down.

Bobby followed suit, jumping and shouting "Yay!" along with her.

* * *

Christopher and I were taking the kids to Aspen for Christmas vacation, and they needed truckloads of crap. We had spent three hours at The Sport Loft renting ski equipment and buying long underwear, neck gaiters, gloves, hats, and ski socks. The kids were miserable. I was miserable. The employees were miserable from helping impatient customers with their Christmas shopping. By the time we left the store, I was sweating and exhausted.

Before I started packing for our trip the following day, I went into the garage to grab the bag of new clothes from the trunk of the car. The skis, boots, and poles were still there, but the bag of clothes was missing. For the life of me, I couldn't remember what I had done with it. I ran back into the house and circled the bedrooms and closets, to no avail.

The doorbell rang at the exact moment I picked up the phone to call the ski store to find out if I had left the bag there. When I looked through the peephole in the door, I saw Marcy standing there, bundled in a chocolate brown shearling coat with a powder blue cashmere scarf wrapped around her neck, holding a bottle of wine.

A gust of blustery wind blew into the house when I opened the door. "Hey," she said in a cheerful tone. "I'm glad you're home. We have some celebrating to do."

"Hi," I responded, confused. I racked my brain for a moment, trying to remember if there was something important I had forgotten. "Let me get the bottle opener," I said.

Marcy followed me into the kitchen. The kids were in the family room watching *Cars*. I probably had a good hour before the movie was over, and then I would have to think about dinner.

"Before I share my news, I need to use the bathroom," Marcy said, removing her coat and throwing it over one of the barstools that were tucked under the center island. I poured two glasses of chardonnay while I waited for her to come out.

"Why do you have this big bag from Sport Loft in here?" Marcy said, as she returned from the bathroom.

Laughing to myself, I shook my head. "I'm such an idiot. I've been ripping the house apart looking for that bag." Thinking back, Bobby had gone potty when we got home from shopping the day before. I must have left the bag in there after I wiped his ass. I breathed a sigh of relief.

"All right, what's up?" I asked, handing her a glass of wine.

"First of all, it's official: I signed my divorce papers today. Dave and I are done." A wide grin spread across her face. That was good news. He was a schmuck, and Marcy deserved better than him. "And..." She paused for a moment, adding to the suspense. "I signed a two-year lease for a store on Newbury Street. I'm finally going to open up a woman's clothing boutique!"

"That's amazing!" I reached out and hugged her. "You've been talking about opening a store for so long. I can't believe you finally pulled the trigger, and on one of the most high-end streets in Boston."

"I know. I'm still in shock myself." She raised her glass and said, "To new beginnings."

"I'll drink to that."

For the next hour, we polished off the wine while Marcy talked about her exciting plans for the new store, beginning with a trip to Paris for the spring fashion show. After the holiday, she was going to New York and Los Angeles to check out the showrooms of some of her favorite designers. She threw out ideas for logos, how she envisioned the layout of the store, and possible names. A gnawing sensation tugged at my gut as I listened. Finally breaking away from her bad marriage, and with her only son in school full time, she was putting her life back together, following her dream. Meanwhile, I had put my career on hold and had stopped painting cold turkey after I had kids. Granted, I had an ideal marriage and healthy, wonderful children, but my brain seemed to be turning to mush from running mundane errands, cleaning the house, and contemplating what to make for dinner. I hated myself for being jealous of Marcy.

* * *

Standing at the base of Buttermilk Mountain, I watched Megan ski down in her pink-and-white Spider jacket, her legs wide open, her hands out in front of her, and a proud smile spread across her face. Not too far behind, Christopher was holding Bobby between his legs in a snowplow position, heading toward me. Bobby looked so cute with his long hair sticking out of the large gap between his black goggles and helmet. Smacking my gloves together, I clapped like a crazed seal, and called out, "Good job, guys!" When Christopher was only a few feet away from me, he let go of Bobby so he could ski into my arms. "Look at you, sweetheart. You're skiing," I said.

"I want to go again," Bobby said, as I hugged his little body into mine. Pulling out a tissue, I wiped his runny nose before the snot could land in his mouth, and then I kissed his rosy cheek.

"Megan, you rocked it, too." I beamed with pride.

"Can I get poles now?" she asked, her voice pleading.

Christopher knelt in front of her. "You were awesome today." He gave her a fist bump. "I think next time we ski, you'll definitely be ready for poles." He looked at me with questioning eyes. "One more run?"

Grinning, I said, "Yes," and then pointed my pole toward Megan. She grabbed the end, and I glided my skis toward the chair lift, pulling her behind me. Christopher did the same with Bobby. The lift operator slowed the chair down when it was our turn to load. The other attendant lifted Bobby onto the seat. Once we were all on, Christopher pulled the safety bar down. The late afternoon sun had started its descent, and a thin layer of gray clouds lined the sky above the snowy mountain peaks, adding a chill to the air. None of us seemed affected by the dropping temperature. Tomorrow we would be heading home, back to a long, bone-chilling New England winter.

"Did you guys have a great vacation?" Christopher asked.

"Yeah," both kids called out in unison.

"Can we take one more family picture when we get to the top?" I asked.

"Mom, you've taken so many pictures of us," Megan said, sounding annoyed.

"I know, but we'll want to remember this. It's our first family ski vacation."

Spotting the sign that said, *Prepare to Unload,* Christopher lifted the safety bar before calling out, "Okay, everyone, what do we say?"

Together, we shouted, the same way we did before getting off every single lift during our week-long vacation, "Tips Up!"

We took our final picture and then skied down to the bottom.

That evening, Tracy joined us for dinner. I drank more champagne than I probably should have, but we were celebrating her latest and most profitable closing, earning her a reputation as one of Aspen's top real estate agents.

Sadly, we had both lost touch with Richard over the years. I'd heard he moved out of Aspen. Even though Tracy and I didn't get to see each other that often, we spoke on the phone every few days. Listening to her Aspen stories allowed me to live vicariously through her, and, of course, she still loved to party.

After dinner, we said goodbye to Tracy, packed up for our departure the following morning, and put the kids to bed. Christopher and I made love in front of the orange flames that danced behind the glass doors of the fireplace.

"I wish we didn't have to leave," I lamented, snuggled in his arms. "Tracy said the schools are great in Aspen, and lots of young families are moving here."

He kissed the top of my head. "I know. I heard her. Give me another few years, and then we can try to make it happen."

My eyes lit up. "Really?"

"Yeah," he said. "I want to live here as much as you do. I'm just not ready yet."

* * *

March 2008

Nibbling on bites of macaroni and cheese, Megan and Bobby's eyes were glued to the *Power Rangers* on the small television that was nestled in the corner of our kitchen. I didn't make a habit of allowing the kids to watch television during mealtime, but since it was the weekend, I had made an exception. Our Aspen vacation was already a distant memory, and Christopher had been working late for the past few weeks. I'd been dreaming about our Saturday date night all day, looking forward to being alone with him and not having to put the kids to bed.

"I'm back," Christopher called out when he walked into the kitchen after his run. He was wearing Nike running pants with his tight-fitting maroon Harvard Business School T-shirt underneath an unzipped windbreaker. Messy strands of hair stuck out of his ski hat. His face was flushed, and sweat was dripping from his forehead. His stale body odor mixed with his Gillette deodorant came wafting toward me. In a sick way, his smell turned me on—pheromones were powerful. He chugged water from the Poland Springs bottle in the refrigerator and then went over to the kids to give them kisses.

"Daddy, you stink," Megan said in a sing-song voice.

"So I can't kiss my sweet girl?"

"Kiss me, Daddy!" Bobby called out. Christopher gave him a big, wet kiss on his cheek, and Bobby belly laughed. While he played around with the kids, I ran upstairs to shower and get ready for dinner. Marcy had convinced me to splurge on a pair of black knee-high boots when they were on sale a month earlier, and I hadn't worn them yet. I rarely dressed up during the week, because I was always running around in my workout clothes with my hair in a ponytail and no makeup. I threw on a pair of jeans, a royal blue silk blouse, my new boots, and then I spent a little extra time blow-drying my hair and adding a touch of makeup to my washed-out, winter face. After Christopher stepped out of the shower, he spotted me admiring myself in the mirror.

"You look hot," he said.

Christopher stood beside me with a towel wrapped around his waist. His hair was wet, and sculpted muscles protruded from his arms. A delicious scent of Irish Spring soap emanated from his body.

"So do you," I replied.

Christopher had always been a runner, but with his busy schedule, he could only fit it in on weekends now. He liked to wake up early before work and do a set of push-ups and sit-ups. For a while, I'd been trying to talk myself into running, but there never seemed to be enough time in the day—at least that was the excuse I told myself. Lucky for me, love was blind, and Christopher never noticed my extra belly pooch or the dimples of cellulite underneath my ass cheeks.

When Lynn, our sixteen-year-old babysitter, finally arrived, dressed in ripped jeans and an oversized black sweater, I told the kids that I expected a good report. After stating their bedtime, I caught Lynn winking at Megan, a signal that she could stay up a little later. As long as they were sleeping by the time we walked in, I didn't care what went on. I jotted down the name and phone number of the restaurant in downtown Concord on a yellow sticky note. The kids were so busy planning their evening with Lynn that they barely looked up when Christopher and I kissed them goodbye.

Driving through the tree-lined streets of our suburban neighborhood, a light drizzle of cold rain hit the windshield. Christopher drove cautiously, staying within the twenty-five mile-per-hour speed limit. Soot-covered snowpack still lingered along the roads in early March. He grabbed my hand, and we rested our intertwined fingers on the console. It was hard to believe that after nine years of marriage, I was still infatuated with my husband. We drove up and down Main Street for a few minutes until we found a parking spot a few blocks from the cozy Italian restaurant, Mama Rosalita.

A biting wind mixed with rain blew in my direction when I stepped out of the car. I pulled the hood of my coat over my head. Christopher draped his arm around me, warming me from the cold and holding me so I wouldn't slip on the black ice. We waited a moment at the crosswalk until it was safe to cross the street. Midway through the busy intersection, I was laughing at something Christopher had said, when suddenly, the sound of screeching tires reverberated through the air. Snapping my head around, I turned to see blinding headlights shining in my eyes. Within seconds, the car slammed into us.

5

MY BODY WAS STIFF and immobile, lying on the pavement. I was floating in and out of consciousness. Loud sounds enveloped me. The swooshing of cars. Thumping of footsteps. Voices. "Ma'am, can you hear me?"

Words were stuck in my throat. I couldn't respond. Someone yelled out, "Call the paramedics!" A bolt of pain shot up my left leg. I tried to move it and cried out in pain, wincing. A tickling sensation crept up my esophagus, begging me to cough. But I couldn't. It hurt. It felt like something was crushing my chest. My breathing was labored. Turning my head slightly to the side, I forced one eyelid open and saw people hovering over Christopher. I wanted to call out to him, but the heaviness was taking over again. Someone covered me with a puffy down coat. It didn't help. I was shaking. The blaring sounds of sirens were increasing in intensity as they drove closer to us.

"The ambulance should be here soon," a woman said. Squinting for a brief second, I could see flashing strobe lights in the background. Every one of my senses was on overload, until eventually, the world around me turned black.

* * *

My vision was blurry when I woke up. Excruciating pain, like throbbing tentacles pinching my leg, caused me to moan. Bright florescent lights were shining above me. Machines were beeping. Men and women, dressed in blue scrubs, were walking in and out of the room, writing on clipboards. Hands prodded my body, and a nurse took my blood pressure. Someone inserted a catheter in my urethra, while someone else hooked me up to an IV. A doctor was standing next to me with his white coat wide open and a stethoscope hanging around his neck. "Hope," he said, "can you hear me?"

I mumbled something back, indicating that I had heard him. Words still wouldn't form from my lips.

"I need to ask you some questions about what happened this evening."

I nodded.

"What do you remember?"

Using all my strength, I forced the words to come out. "Car. Hit. Us." That was all I could say for now. I remembered the sensation of flying through the air. I remembered lying on the street. I remembered Christopher near me. I didn't remember any more. The doctor told me the nurse was going to wheel me to radiology. He said he needed to get X-rays of my chest, legs, and pelvis.

"Wait," I said, sounding hoarse. I felt like I was pushing through a pile of bricks that were flattening my chest in order to get the question out: "Where's my husband?"

In a gentle voice, he said, "I don't know right now." He turned and walked away.

"Please," I pleaded, willing him in my mind to come back.

Another nurse made her way toward me, her pink sneakers squeaking against the floor. She had short, bleached-blonde hair that was pulled back into little pigtails, like a little girl. "I'm going to take you to radiology," she said, lowering the gurney.

I wanted to ask her if she knew where Christopher was, but she was too busy checking something off her clipboard to notice that I was trying to get her attention. She pushed me down the long hallway, passing doors, passing people dressed in white lab coats and scrubs, passing three nurses standing behind a U-shaped counter. They would know. The heavyset woman sitting behind the desk would know what happened to Christopher. I needed to ask her. Someone back there had to have information about him.

Soon enough, I was in another room. More pain infiltrated my body as I was lifted onto the steel bed underneath the X-ray machine. The radiologist looked like Howdy Doody with his bright red hair and cheeks dotted with freckles. A shower of spit sprayed from his mouth as he explained what he was going to do. I couldn't focus. And I didn't care.

"Please, Doctor, can you tell me where my husband is?" It was the first time my voice sounded stronger.

Flashing his large white teeth, he said, "I'm sorry. I don't know. I don't have any of that information." The unknown was making it difficult for me to breathe.

Every minute that passed with no news about Christopher was far worse than the physical distress I had to endure. A female doctor spoke to me after the X-rays. Her face was pinched, and she was matter-of-fact in her delivery. She told me I had a broken rib and an open fracture of the tibia and fibula. She would fix my leg by putting a plate and pins in me.

Pigtail nurse came back to wheel me to the operating room. Alone in the elevator, I begged her to tell me something about my husband. Softly stroking my arm with her left hand, she said, "You need to relax before surgery."

I noticed a small diamond engagement ring on her finger. She continued to wheel me down the hall, pushing the double doors open with her backside. I wanted to grab her, rip her fucking ring off, and insist that she give me some information about

Christopher. Inside the cold, sterile operating room, an IV tube was inserted into my arm. Within seconds, the general anesthesia took effect, and I was out cold.

* * *

I was disoriented and groggy when I woke up. It took a few minutes for my eyes to focus and my brain to register my surroundings—the white walls, the sterile room, and me lying in a hospital bed. My mother was sitting on a chair in the corner, knitting. Gripping the long needles, her trembling fingers worked frantically to create loop after loop with the multicolored yarn that rested on her lap.

"Mom." I didn't recognize my scratchy voice.

Her face looked startled when she heard me. "Hope, honey." She dropped the yarn and rushed toward me. "You're awake." When she kissed my forehead, I noticed dark, heavy bags under her eyes. "How do you feel?"

Memories came flooding back: the accident, the emergency room, and the questions that nobody would answer. "Where's Christopher?"

"Oh, honey." Tears filled her eyes.

"Mom, what?"

She shook her head.

"What? Please tell me."

"Oh, honey." The tears rolled down her cheeks.

My heart was closing in. I knew. I just knew. "Say it," I implored. "Where is he?"

"He didn't...." She was sobbing now. "He didn't make it."

Her words were slicing me in half. "What do you mean, he didn't make it?" I could feel myself drowning, being sucked down by a violent undertow.

She took a deep breath. "He's in heaven now."

"No, no!" I screamed. I was hysterical. "Please, no."

My mother tried to calm me down. She couldn't. I was thrashing my head against the pillow. The grief was overbearing, swallowing me whole, eating me alive.

A nurse walked in when she heard me shrieking. She said something about giving me a sedative to help me relax. After she administered it through the tube connected to my vein, I continued to call out, "No, no, no," until I had nothing left.

* * *

I was awake, but I didn't want to be. I wanted to fall back into my heavy, dreamless, drug-induced sleep so I wouldn't have to face my life-altering nightmare. My body wouldn't listen to my mind. It was rejecting sleep. Staring at the tiny black holes in the ceiling tiles above my bed, I imagined myself being pulled inside one of them, just like the black holes in outer space that hold a gravitational force so powerful that light can't even penetrate.

"Sweetheart," my mom called out in a gentle voice.

I couldn't answer her.

She held my limp, cold hand in hers, and rubbed the back of my thumb.

"Are you thirsty?" she asked.

My mouth tasted like cotton balls, but I didn't want to move.

Reading my mind, she picked up a Styrofoam cup. "Take a small sip," she said, placing the straw against my mouth. Reluctantly, I swallowed the tepid water, moistening my dry tongue.

"Good girl. Would you like me to get you some ginger ale? Soda pop always made you feel better when you were younger."

Is she fucking kidding me? My husband just died, but sure, that sounds great—a soda pop will make everything better.

"Where are the kids?" I asked in a raspy voice.

"They're with your father in the cafeteria."

"Do they know?"

She was silent. A single tear fell down her face.

"Answer me. Do they know?" I demanded.

Her voice cracked when she spoke. "Yes, sweetheart, your father told them that Christopher is in heaven now."

He's in heaven, while the rest of us have to stay here on Earth—in hell.

"I want to see them."

"Are you sure you're feeling up to it?

I nodded my head.

"Okay, sweetheart, I'll go look for them." She kissed my forehead. "And I'll bring you that soda pop."

I was glad she left. I needed to be alone for a few minutes to gather my thoughts before she brought the kids back. None of this felt real. I thought the universe was playing some kind of sick and twisted joke on me. Christopher couldn't be gone. He would never do this to me— leave me alone to raise the kids—leave me alone, period. Someone was going to walk through the door and tell me it was a big mistake, and Christopher was alive and well. Maybe they brought him to another hospital. Maybe they confused him with a John Doe. When the truth came out, *Dateline* would definitely want to feature us in a story. Better yet, Barbara Walters would interview us. I had always wanted to meet her. "It was a case of mistaken identity," she would tell her viewers in her famous lisp. Sitting across from her, Christopher and I would be holding hands, emotional and teary-eyed as we told her how lucky we were to be given a second chance.

My dry, cracked lips were irritating me. I wanted more water, but I was afraid to reach for the cup. Using the bed control, I pushed the button to raise the bed and snagged the cup off the tray table. The sudden movement left me feeling like I had been stabbed in the chest with a fork. Once the soreness subsided, I drank the rest of the water, while I waited for someone to walk into my room and give me the good news.

* * *

As soon as my father stepped through the door, I knew from his drooping shoulders and downturned lips that he wasn't bringing good news. Suddenly, I felt trapped. The oxygen in the air was thinning, and all I wanted was to escape from the hospital bed—escape from my doomed reality.

"Hey, honey," he said in a soft voice. His heavy feet moved across the shiny, waxed floor, and when he leaned over to kiss the top of my head, I smelled coffee on his breath. "How're you feeling?"

"Pretty shitty." I bit the inside of my lip so hard that I nearly ripped the skin off.

He blinked back a tear. The only time I'd ever seen my father cry was when my grandmother had passed away. I was too young back then to understand what death meant, but I'll never forget how much it hurt watching my father sob like a little boy.

"I can't even imagine how difficult this is for you." A small droplet trickled out of his eye. "I love you, honey, and I'm here for you."

My mouth felt like it was glued together, restricting my ability to speak. A strong urge to shut my eyes came over me, but my gaze drifted once again to the black holes in the ceiling.

"Mom should be here any minute with the kids," he said. "Bobby had to use the bathroom."

Hearing him talk about the children was like a slap across my face, a swift reminder that I needed to snap out of my despair—for them. I had to be stoic. I was all they had left. Over and over, I repeated the words: *Stay strong. Stay strong. Stay strong,* continuing my mantra until Bobby came waltzing through the door.

"Mommy," he sang out when he saw me. His bulging blue eyes studied my appearance. I could only imagine what I looked like, lying in bed with a tube connected to my arm, my left leg in a cast elevated on a pile of pillows, and greasy, untamed hair surrounding my gray complexion.

Stay strong, stay strong. "Hi, sweetie," I said with every ounce of fake enthusiasm I could muster.

"Mommy, Grandpa said you have a bad boo-boo on your leg."

Before I could respond, Megan walked into the room holding my mom's hand. One look at her rigid body and ashen face, and I knew she understood. At four years old, Bobby didn't know. At seven, Megan did. Her mom was here, but her dad was gone forever. I swallowed hard, forcing the lump in my throat to sink back down. *Stay strong.*

"Don't be frightened, love. Come to Mommy, both of you." Bobby moved in closer. Megan took her time, hesitating at first like I was a stranger, and then gradually making her way toward the other side of the bed. I reached my hands out for them to hold, ignoring the achy pressure in my chest. *Stay strong.* But I couldn't. The dam broke when I gently squeezed their warm little hands into mine, releasing a waterfall of tears. I told the kids that I was going to be okay. I told them that *we* were going to be okay, and that I loved them so much. Inside, I was screaming. I was lying to them. I was saying one thing, trying to reassure them, but I wasn't okay—we weren't going to be okay. Their father was dead. I needed my Christopher back, the love of my life, my rock, my missing piece.

6

MY PARENTS WERE LIVING IN my house, taking care of the kids while I was in the hospital. It had been four days since the accident. Even though I was feeling better physically, the emotional wound was wide open and raw. I continued taking the little pink pills the nurse offered me for the pain, hoping they would ease the unbearable suffering inside of me. They didn't help. All they did was make me lethargic and cause my nose to itch.

I was having a difficult time wrapping my head around everything, desperately trying to process my husband's death. Whenever someone walked through the door, I still expected to see Christopher's thick feathered hair and radiant smile. As sorry as I felt for myself and the children, I also felt sick for Bill and Donna. My heart had been shattered into pieces, while their hearts were pillaged from their chests. Children were supposed to bury their parents, not the other way around. Somehow, despite my mother-in-law's devastating sorrow, she managed to feign a smile when she came to see me.

"You have a visitor coming," pigtail nurse said as she entered my room to pick up the orange tray filled with a half-eaten bowl of chicken noodle soup. I was happy she was taking it away. It looked, smelled, and tasted like urine. Noticing the empty bag of oyster crackers, she offered to get me some more before she left, but I told her I wasn't hungry.

"Hello, dear," Donna said, entering the room. I could barely see her face behind the massive bouquet of flowers she was carrying. They looked like they weighed more than she did. "Someone sent these to you. The nurse asked me to bring them in."

She placed the flowers on the table and handed me the card. When she gave me a light kiss, I noticed her sunken cheeks and the deepened frown lines around her mouth. Clearly, she and I were both struggling to eat. We were trying to be stoic for one another, but when she affectionately pushed my hair off my forehead, I broke down—and so did she. For the next few minutes, neither one of us could speak as tears spilled onto our cheeks. Melancholy filled the space between us, swallowing the oxygen in the room, until finally she cleared her throat, looked at the flowers, and asked, "Who sent you these gorgeous flowers?"

Wiping away my last tear, I read the card and released a much-needed chuckle.

Dear Hope,
I really wanted to get you a bottle of Belvedere Vodka, but I didn't think that would be appropriate in the hospital. First chance I get I'll come out there with the biggest bottle I can find, even if it requires traveling to Poland to locate it. I'm here for you. Distance will never keep us apart. I love you.
Love,
Tracy

"They're from my friend Tracy, in Aspen," I said.

"She was one of your bridesmaids, wasn't she?"

"Yes." I wondered if Donna remembered Tracy slamming shots all night with the bartender.

Donna sat in the chair across from me. We spent the next hour chatting about Christopher. She shared funny stories about how mischievous he was when he was younger. I had heard many of the stories before, but I loved hearing them again.

"Did I ever tell you about the time I tried to wash Christopher's mouth out with soap?" Donna asked.

"Yes, but tell me again. I love that story."

For a brief moment, I felt like a little kid, listening intently to a bedtime tale.

"I came home from a charity luncheon, and our nanny, Elsie, told me that Christopher, who was eight years old at the time, had used the f-word. Needless to say, I was mortified."

While Donna spoke, an itchy sensation tickled my nose, which I rubbed a few times.

"I ran into his room, grabbed him by the arm, and asked him to tell me what had happened. He admitted point-blank that he had told Elsie to fuck off."

Hearing my proper mother-in-law use the word *fuck* in a sentence made me want to giggle.

"I made him apologize to her, and then I took him into the bathroom to wash his mouth out with soap. I tried to put the bar into his mouth, but he grabbed it from my hand, bit off a piece, chewed it up, and swallowed it. With a devilish grin, he told me it was delicious." Donna shook her head and smiled at the memory.

I laughed out loud and rubbed my nose at the same time. "Do you need a tissue?" she asked, pulling one out of the box and handing it to me.

I blew my nose, but it didn't help. "I think I need to stop taking the painkillers. For some reason, they make me itchy."

Donna placed her hand on my arm, the expression on her face turning solemn. "I just want you to know that you're a wonderful mother, much better and more present than I was with Christopher." Her voice cracked. "As difficult as this is for me to say, I believe that if God had to take one of your lives, it's better that he took Christopher's. Of course, children need their father, but a mother should be a constant presence in her kids' lives." Pausing for a moment, a tear fell from the corner of her eye. "I wish I could turn back the clock, so I could have been a better mother. He was my golden boy. I should've been there for him."

I took her hand and squeezed it to let her know that I loved her. I also wanted her to believe that I was strong and could handle raising my kids alone. But, in reality, I was weak, and I had no idea how I was going to go on without him.

Donna gently wiped her smudged mascara and wet, stained cheeks with a tissue. "I also want you to know that Bill and I would like to help you financially. We don't want you and the children to have to worry about money."

"Thank you," I responded, grateful for her offer, but at the same time caught off guard. I hadn't thought about what would happen to us without Christopher's salary. He had once mentioned that he had a life insurance policy, enough money so I could get by for the next few years without working. Since I had married young and regretfully lived like a 1950s housewife, I had never dealt with our finances. I was by no means a spendthrift, but without Donna and Bill's help, I didn't know how I would be able to afford my children's college educations.

* * *

A knock on the door startled both of us.

"Come in," I called out.

A young man wearing a black robe and a clerical collar entered the room. He was carrying a Bible and a cross in his hand.

"Hope?" he said. "I'm Father Hannigan. May I come in and speak with you for a moment?"

"Of course," I said. "Father, this is my mother-in-law, Donna."

He greeted us with a kind smile. "Pleasure to meet you both." His mouth turned downward. "I'm terribly sorry about your loss."

"Thank you," I said, wondering how he knew my name and why he was here.

"I want you to know that God is with you, and the Almighty himself is praying for your healing." He spoke with a heavy Boston accent. "I've also come to speak to you on behalf of Patricia Murphy, the young woman driving the car the evening of your accident."

The muscles in my neck and shoulder clenched tightly.

"Patricia is only nineteen years old. She didn't see you on the road."

The blood in my ears hissed and pulsed, tuning him out.

"I was hoping you would grant Patricia absolution for this tragedy."

In a deep, steely tone, I replied, "Patricia was careless. She killed my husband. My children have to grow up without a father." I turned my head toward Donna. "Christopher was her only child." I raised my voice one decibel below screaming. "And you want me to forgive this woman's stupidity. Really, Father?" My heart pounded so hard I thought it was going to pop out of my chest.

"I hope you will find it in your heart to release your anger. May God bless you," he said, and then he turned and walked out of the room.

Shaking my head in disbelief, I looked at my mother-in-law. "Do you believe the nerve of that guy? I know she didn't kill Christopher on purpose, but I can't find it in my heart to forgive. She ruined my life."

Donna spoke with a reassuring tone. "You don't have to forgive anyone right now. Focus on your own healing, so you can go home and mother your children. They need you."

* * *

My father picked me up the day I was released from the hospital. I hadn't been home in two weeks, but it felt like an eternity. I balanced a set of crutches on my lap as my father pushed me in a wheelchair toward the hospital parking lot.

I was apprehensive about going home to face the reality of my situation. Once outside, I squinted my eyes to block out the blinding rays streaming from the sun. The official start of spring was a week away. Usually I welcomed the warm weather, excited for the frozen earth to wake up, so I could spend more time outside. But instead of feeling joy for the changing season, I was numb and cold on the inside.

We drove in silence. I stared out the window, focusing on the Massachusetts license plates speeding past us. Concord was a charming town, famous for its rich colonial history. One of the first battles of the American Revolution was fought here, where, despite the Minutemen's victory, countless men lost their lives. Husbands, fathers, sons, and brothers had died fighting for a cause they believed in. Unlike those brave soldiers, my husband was killed for no reason—killed because that woman was careless.

"Would you like me to turn on the radio?" my dad asked, interrupting my thoughts.

I shrugged my shoulders and watched him flip through the radio until he found music he liked on a golden oldies station. The song playing in the background sounded like static in my ears. I was tempted to shut it off, craving the uncomfortable silence again. I had nothing to say. I was empty.

When we turned down my street, an acrid feeling rose from my belly, worsening as we pulled into the driveway. After shutting off the ignition, my father got out of the car and grabbed my crutches out of the trunk. I took a few deep inhalations before opening the car door with trembling hands. Placing all my pressure on my right leg, I held my broken leg in the air and then gradually stepped out of the car. My dad tried to help me when he handed me the crutches, but I signaled to him that I could do it myself, and then I hobbled up the front steps.

* * *

"Mommy!" Megan yelled when she heard the door open. She ran into my arms, almost knocking me over. Bobby shuffled behind her, but his face lit up when he saw me.

I squeezed both kids, hugging them to me with a desperation I had never felt before.

"Be careful," my mother cautioned. "You don't want your mom to fall over."

She leaned in and kissed me hello. "Let me help you into the living room." She was wearing an apron stained with brown spots.

"I'm fine. I can do it."

I made my way inside, clenching the bars on the crutches so tightly my knuckles turned red. Sweet smells of sugar and cinnamon wafted through the house. Under normal circumstances, I would have been salivating over the scent, but my belly had no interest in food.

By the time I hobbled into the living room and took a seat on the couch, I was exhausted. My mom rushed over and pushed the ottoman toward me so I could keep my legs elevated. Megan and Bobby wanted to play with my crutches and bickered over who would get them first. They were acting as if our lives were perfectly normal. But how could they understand the depth of our loss? They were just kids.

"I want them," Megan screeched, forcefully pulling the crutches out of Bobby's hands.

"They're mine," Bobby whined.

A slack expression covered my face while I watched their aggressive game of tug-of-war. I didn't have the energy to discipline them. My mother intervened before the fighting took a turn for the worse. In a soothing voice, she told them that the crutches were not a toy. Then she suggested they relax before dinner.

Obeying her orders, the kids crawled to either side of me, pushing into my body like they were trying to force their way back inside my womb. I stroked their heads while they watched *Hannah Montana* on the large television screen that was mounted above the fireplace. Bobby was sucking his thumb so hard I was afraid he was going to pull it off. Christopher and I had been talking to him over the past month about how he was a big boy now and needed to stop his thumb sucking. We had been making headway, noticing that he was doing it less frequently, but with everything going on, he had clearly resorted to his full-time habit.

The words and images coming from the television sounded like a foreign language. I couldn't focus on the show because my eyes were glued to a large framed photo of the four of us posing in our ski clothes on top of Buttermilk Mountain in Aspen. It was our last family picture, taken during our last family vacation, our last family—everything. I wondered if we would ever smile again like we had smiled in that photo. We were so happy that day—that entire week—without a care in the world. I had nagged Christopher about moving back to Aspen. His words were still fresh in my mind. "One day we will, I promise," he had said.

Well, fuck you, Christopher! Fuck you for leaving me here without you!

Later in the evening, we sat around the kitchen table, surrounded by my mother's elaborate meal of honey-glazed ham, cheesy potato casserole, and creamed spinach. The rich food tasted like cardboard in my mouth. I pushed the meal around on my plate and took bites only when the kids were looking at me. My mom rambled on about dyeing her deviled eggs different colors for Easter, and then she proceeded to discuss my Tupperware cabinet, talking about how messy it was and how she couldn't wait to clean it. "Every lid should have a proper home," she said. I didn't give a shit about her fucking deviled eggs, and I didn't give a shit about the Tupperware cabinet. I could feel the heat rising. I wanted the meal to end, so I could go to sleep and shut her out—shut everything out. I wanted to take an Ambien for dessert. The little white pill was powerful. It would let my mind drift off to nowhere, unnaturally forcing me into a deep sleep.

"Honey," my dad said, "you look so tired. Why don't you get into bed? The doctor said you need a lot of rest."

He excused me from the dinner table like I was a little girl. Only I wasn't. I was a grown woman with children of my own. I covered my mouth to hide a yawn and told the kids I wasn't feeling well and that Grandpa was right, I should probably get some sleep. After kissing them goodnight, I grabbed my crutches, hobbled toward the staircase, and made my way to my bedroom.

The door to my room appeared larger than usual. Holding my breath, I turned the knob slowly, entering the darkened space.

I flipped the light on, stood motionless for a moment, and gazed around the room. The windows were shut, but it was cold. The white duvet cover was pulled neatly over the bed. Without blinking, my eyes narrowed in the direction of Christopher's side. A faint dent was still there, as if it was left over from the last time he had sat on it. I moved toward the bed and let my fingers brush over the spot. A hardcover book, *The DaVinci Code*, sat on his night table with a ripped piece of paper wedged in the pages to keep his place. He had been enjoying the book and told me I should read it when he finished. A pile of coins and crumbled receipts sat on top of our dresser, left over from the last time he had emptied his pants pockets. I felt his presence wherever I turned.

Biting the inside of my cheek in an effort to fight back the tears that had been building inside me all day, I hobbled toward our shared closet. His button-down shirts and pants hung neatly from their respective hangers. Piled in the corner, next to the hamper, were his dirty running clothes. I hated when he left his clothes on the floor. I picked up his Harvard Business School T-shirt and hugged it, inhaling the fetid odor.

If only I could bottle the scent, I thought. I ripped off my shirt and replaced it with Christopher's.

Next I went into the bathroom and generously applied his Gillette deodorant under my arms. The bristles on his toothbrush were dry and haggard. I wet it and brushed my teeth with it. I considered using his razor for a second, but since I had no facial hair, I decided against it. I thought about using it on my armpits and legs. Then again, what would be the point of shaving? What man would see me? After we were married, I had stopped worrying about my body hair, only shaving once a week in the winter, more often in the summer. Sometimes Christopher would make fun of me, and we'd laugh about my gorilla legs.

I loved his freshly shaven face and the feel of his smooth, soft skin against my flesh. When he shaved before bedtime, it was his way of telling me that he wanted to have sex. He had shaved the night of the accident. A few glasses of wine in his wife was a sure sign that he was going to get lucky in bed. Not that night. Not ever again. I had slept with two men in my life. Christopher was the only man I ever made love to. I couldn't imagine making love to another man or loving another man as deeply as I loved my husband.

Back in the closet, I grabbed a pair of Christopher's J. Crew boxers, the ones with sailboats all over them. I put them on, and then crawled into his side of the bed. His scent lingered on the pillow. Wrapping my arms around it, I squeezed it for warmth. I squeezed it because I was afraid that in time, I would lose his scent forever. The finality of his death was hitting me hard. How many times had I lain in this bed wanting to hit him in an effort to stop his harsh snoring sounds that kept me up at night? Or tell him to shut the fuck up when he had violent sneeze attacks, blew his nose like a trumpet, or released a fart so loud and stinky that I thought he had burned a hole in our bed? What I would give to get it all back.

Our large king-sized bed was too big for one person. Despite curling up under the heavy down comforter, my body was chilled. The man who was always available for cuddling and warming me was no longer there. We had the perfect snuggle position: my head nestled in his neck, one arm over his chest, one leg in between his, our hearts beating as one.

I could no longer hold back. The depth of my sorrow soared, collapsing the levee with a thunderous roar. I cried and cried, saturating the pillow with my salty tears, until eventually, I had nothing left and sleep got the better of me.

7

IF IT HADN'T BEEN FOR Marcy, who forced me to wear an elegant black knit sheath dress from her store, I would have gladly worn Christopher's smelly Harvard T-shirt to the funeral. I hadn't taken off his clothes since I had come home from the hospital three days earlier.

"I don't think I can do this," I told Marcy as she brushed my hair in front of a mirror. The reflection staring back at me looked sickly. There were dark circles under my eyes, and my sad face was sallow.

"I brought you a Xanax. You'll take it on the way to the church," she said, pulling a tinted moisturizer from her makeup bag. I sat unmoving in the chair, while she tried her best to make me look human again, even though I didn't want to look or feel pretty. I wanted my appearance to match the ugliness I felt on the inside. She painted my lips with a heavy coat of lip gloss.

"Much better," she commented, admiring her work.

I fought the temptation to wipe off the makeup, rip off the uncomfortable dress, and crawl back into bed, but I knew it wasn't an option. After Marcy finished working her magic on my face, she helped me downstairs. Megan was dressed in an adorable purple dress, and her hair was pulled back in a headband with a big bow on top. Bobby looked handsome, wearing a royal blue button-down shirt with dark blue pants. Dressed in our Sunday best, we should've been heading out for Easter brunch, instead of attending their father's funeral.

Before Marcy left, she slipped the small yellow pill into my hand. Wedged in between my children in the backseat of the car, with my father driving and my mother in the passenger seat, I swallowed the pill without water and waited patiently for it to ease the anxiety that was penetrating my core.

The knot inside my stomach twisted so tight I thought my organs were going to squeeze out when we arrived. My mother helped me out of the car, and then my father drove around to find a parking space. Clutching my crutches with a death grip, I moved unsteadily up the stone steps of Trinity Church. Megan stayed next to me and Bobby bounced ahead, holding his stuffed bear in one hand, like he was racing us to the playground. Once inside, familiar faces, attempting to hide their damp eyes, hugged and kissed me. Many of the same people standing before me had sat in these pews nine years earlier to watch my nuptials.

A slow, woozy wave settled over me, making me feel like I was inebriated. The Xanax was finally kicking in. This was not good. Old friends, relatives, and Christopher's colleagues offered me their condolences, but I couldn't respond coherently. I wanted to say thank you, but my mouth was having difficulty forming the proper words.

Soon enough, we were ushered into the sanctuary. Despite the warm glow coming through the stained-glass windows, there was a rawness in the air. The uplifting painted images of heaven that had symbolized light and new beginnings on my wedding day appeared dark and somber. A heavy emotion circulated through the church. My eyes remained dry as I staggered down the aisle toward the front row, afraid that once I started crying, I wouldn't be able to stop. I could feel everyone watching me—the widow—make her grand entrance.

Right before I took my seat, Aunt Myrna stepped in front of me to give me a hug—and that was when I lost it. Not even the warm rush inside my capillaries from the Xanax could stop my sobbing. She was the only one who understood what I was going through. Crying in her arms, I looked straight ahead toward the altar and a massive portrait of Christopher. His big, beautiful body had been cremated. A man with so much more living to do had been pillaged from the earth, leaving us with nothing more than a pile of ashes. Why? Why did this have to happen to me, to our family? Nobody answered me that day—not in the eulogies, not in the sermon, not even a voice from above. Somehow, I would have to understand how to live with this tragedy, but I was far from ready.

* * *

"Mommy, are you up?" Bobby's cute face was right up against mine. I could almost taste his stale morning breath.

"I am now, sweetie. Come in bed with me." I lifted the covers, and he crawled inside. "I love you, my sweet boy," I whispered in his ear. He sucked his thumb, making loud smacking noises with his mouth while I held him in my arms. A minute later he pulled his wet, slimy thumb out and asked me to turn on the television. While he was busy watching, I tried to fall back to sleep, but as soon as I was about to drift off, I heard a soft knock on the door.

"There you are, Bobby," my mom said, poking her head through the doorway. "I was looking all over for you. Breakfast is ready." When he made no effort to move off the bed, she walked toward us, holding out her hand for him. "Come with Grandma before the food gets cold."

Shaking his head back and forth, he said, "No, I want Mommy."

"I think Mommy wants to sleep some more. Do you want me to carry you downstairs?" she asked, reaching both arms out.

"No, I want Mommy to take me."

"It's fine," I told her. It had been two weeks since I was released from the hospital. Other than the funeral, I hadn't left the house, and I spent most days hiding in my bed. I could tell the kids missed me. "I'll take him down."

"Do you want me to grab your crutches and help you get dressed?" she asked.

"No," I snapped, and then, feeling guilty, I lightened my tone. "Thank you, but I can do it myself."

"Okay, kiddos, I'll meet you downstairs."

When she left the room, I rolled out of bed and threw on a pair of Christopher's sweatpants.

"Mommy?" Bobby asked as we followed the scent of bacon frying in the kitchen. "Why do you always wear Daddy's clothes?"

"I don't know," I told him. "I guess they're just more comfortable than my clothes." The only time I'd taken off Christopher's smelly T-shirt was for the funeral.

We headed downstairs and to the kitchen, where Megan was standing on a chair in front of the stove, dressed in her Barbie nightgown and helping my mom flip pancakes.

"Morning," I murmured as I made my way toward the kitchen table. My father was sitting at the table, sipping coffee and reading *The Boston Globe*. He greeted me with a smile.

"Mommy," Megan said, her bright eyes widening when she saw me, "I made pancakes. Look." She lifted the plate to show me. "I made an M for my name, and this one is an H. I made it for you."

"Wow, I'm impressed," I told her. "I can't wait to try it."

My mother helped Megan off the chair, placed a stack of pancakes and a platter of bacon on the table, and, after serving the kids, she filled my plate.

"I have a B for me," Bobby sang out before taking a bite of his breakfast. His pancakes were drenched in a pool of syrup. I forced myself to swallow a piece and almost choked on it when Bobby called out, "This one looks like a C for Daddy's name."

"I can't believe how well you know your letters," my mom told him.

I pushed my plate away, and Megan asked in a soft voice, "Don't you like the pancakes?"

"I do. I'm just not that hungry this morning."

"Hope, you should eat," my mother chimed in. "What else can I make you?"

"Nothing, I'm fine," I told her.

"Mommy, do you want cereal?" Megan asked.

Before I could respond, my mother asked, "What about French toast? Or how about a toasted bagel with butter?"

"Stop! Please! I'm not hungry," I snarled, silencing the room with my anger.

Megan put her fork down and stopped eating. "Can I be excused?" she asked, her voice barely audible.

I hated myself in that moment. "Do you want to lie on the couch with me and watch TV?" I asked.

She nodded her head and pouted her lips. I gave her a reassuring grin before we got up from the table and made our way into the family room. A few minutes later, my father and Bobby, who was holding a stuffed animal, entered the room. My father sat on the club chair and buried himself in a crossword puzzle, while Bobby eagerly climbed onto the couch next to me.

After my mother finished cleaning the breakfast dishes, she turned on our screechy vacuum. The screeching noise grew louder as she pushed it into the family room. Other than Megan turning up the volume on the TV, nobody else seemed bothered by the noise. The harsh sounds were making me crazy. I started scratching my arm and couldn't stop—back and forth—over the same spot. Back and forth with the pushing of the vacuum. Back and forth with my father's pencil movements. I was losing my mind. I wanted my mom to stop. I wanted Bobby to stop picking his nose and sucking his thumb at the same time. I wanted him to go outside and play, maybe play catch with my father or kick the soccer ball around. My son no longer had a father to teach him to play sports or coach his little league team.

Back and forth, back and forth I scratched, until finally, I called out, "Mom," but she didn't hear me. "Mom!" I yelled again. This time I was so loud that everyone looked at me. "Shut the damn vacuum off!"

"Oh, I'm sorry," she said, and then she turned off the vacuum and started coiling the cord around the handle. "Hope, what happened to your arm?" Her voice was panicked.

"It's fine. It's nothing. Just a rash." I covered my self-inflicted wound with my hand. "Dad, do you think you can drive me to CVS? I need to get some calamine lotion."

I told the kids I would be back in a little while and grabbed my crutches, following my dad toward the garage door.

"Honey," my mom said, "do you want me to get you some fresh clothes to wear?"

I was still wearing Christopher's dirty clothing. I didn't have a bra on, and his sweatpants were sagging down my ass. "No, thanks. I'm good," I told her on the way out the door.

* * *

On the way to CVS, my father took a longer route to avoid Main Street, the scene of the accident. Neither of us spoke on the drive. I had nothing to say. And after the ear-splitting sounds in the family room, I appreciated the peace and quiet in the car. The rash on my arm was burning a little, but in a sick way, I liked it. The pain was distracting me from the pain in my heart. Even though I knew how fucked up it was, I understood why people cut themselves intentionally.

"Would you consider talking to a therapist about what you're going through?" my father asked, interrupting the silence.

"No, Dad. There's nothing to discuss." I brushed my fingers through my unkempt hair, catching them in a large knot at the back of my head. "What's a therapist going to tell me? Christopher's dead. I'll be fine." I released my fingers from the tangles, and considered buying some trashy magazines while I was there.

The parking spaces closest to the entrance of CVS were filled. My father offered to go inside for me, but I told him I could do it myself. He pulled in front of the store to let me out. I balanced on my good leg while sliding my crutches out from the backseat. Once they were securely under my arms, I took a couple of steps through the automatic glass doors into the store.

Feeling stronger on my crutches than I had in days, I wandered down the greeting card aisle. Running an errand was actually making me feel human again. When I turned the corner, I spotted two mothers, whose children were in Megan's class, chatting with each other. They were dressed in skin-tight designer jeans and ballet flats. I wasn't fond of either of them. Susan, the mousier-looking one, didn't bother me as much Kelly, who was probably cheerleading captain back in high school. As PTA president, she bounced around the elementary school, her blonde ponytail always swinging in sync with her tiny hips, like she owned it.

Spinning my head around, I walked as fast as I could in the opposite direction and into the next aisle, praying they hadn't seen me.

"Was that Hope Whitmore?" Hearing my name, I froze in front of the hair care products and leaned in closely with my ears perked up.

"Yes, I think that was her."

"Is she wearing her husband's clothes?" The voice sounded like Kelly's.

"Poor thing. She looks awful. I always thought she was a little out there, but this has probably thrown her over the edge," Susan said.

"It's so tragic. I actually knew Christopher when I was younger. He went to Phillips Andover Academy with my brother. I used to have a huge crush on him. I never understood what he saw in Hope. He was such a catch."

Susan moaned in agreement. "How is she going to find anyone as great as Christopher?"

My blood pressure was rising rapidly.

"She's certainly not going to find anyone dressed like that," Kelly said, chuckling.

That was the final blow. Gritting my teeth, I stormed back into the aisle to face them. Kelly saw me first, and her body tensed up. When Susan noticed her friend's wide eyes and closed-lipped smile, she looked in my direction, and all the color drained from her face.

I gave off a high-pitched laugh, sounding like a deranged psycho. "No, she probably won't ever date again." I was seething, and my knees were trembling inside my baggy sweatpants. "She will sit in her house and hide in her bedroom, wearing her late husband's clothes for the rest of her life. Better yet, she will turn into a slut and fuck both of your husbands." Continuing my icy stare-down, I raised my voice and said, "Fuck you, ladies. Fuck you," and then I hobbled toward the exit.

By the time I reached the car, I was still breathing fire. Ignoring my dad, I flung myself onto the seat, shoved my crutches over the console and into the back, and then slammed the door shut.

"Everything okay, honey?" my father asked.

"Please drive," I commanded.

Obeying my orders, he put the car in reverse and backed out of the parking spot.

"Why didn't you get the stuff you needed?"

I mumbled something about the line being too long.

The roaring anger eating my insides was soon replaced with a massive lump in my throat. I swallowed hard before it had a chance to rear its head. Where was my life going? I hated to admit it, but those bitches were probably right. I would never find anyone as great as my husband. What man would find me attractive? I sure as hell didn't stand a chance dressed like a vagabond in Christopher's clothes, but the truth was that I didn't really care. They made me feel closer to him. With his death, my entire identity had transformed, officially turning me into the pathetic widow people whispered about.

"Do you want to stop somewhere else?" he asked when we got onto the main road.

"No, I just need to get home."

Not another word was uttered for the rest of the drive.

* * *

"Dad," I said, after he pulled into the garage and turned off the ignition. I turned toward him. "I appreciate everything you and Mom have been doing for me and the kids." Inhaling deeply, I forced the lump in my throat down. "I think it's time for you guys to go back to Ohio at the end of the week. I need to start mothering my kids again. I need to try to move forward."

His forehead crinkled. "But how are you going to deal with your broken leg?"

"I'll be fine. Marcy will help out with the driving, and the cast should be coming off in a few weeks. We'll find a way to manage."

Wrapping his arms around me, my dad hugged me tightly. I hugged him back as tears streamed down my face.

"I love you, Hope."

"I love you too, Dad."

8

I WOKE UP TO THE loud buzz of my alarm clock and hit snooze three times, desperate for a few more minutes of sleep. Every minute I stayed in bed would only add to the morning stress of getting the kids off to school. Since Bobby was the classroom helper this week in his preschool, I had to get him there a few minutes early, but clearly that wasn't going to happen. When I finally peeked at the alarm clock, it read 8:25 a.m. *Shit.* I only had ten minutes to get the kids dressed, fed, and out of the house. I opened the window blinds to a gray sky and a blanket of snow. Great—snow at the end of April. I had had enough of this long winter. It was time for spring.

I ran around the house like a crazed animal, hurrying the kids out of bed and making a quick batch of oatmeal for them to eat.

"I don't want oatmeal. I want waffles," Bobby cried.

"We don't have time for waffles. Please don't be difficult this morning, honey. Just eat the oatmeal. We need to move quickly, otherwise we're going to be late for school."

Bobby pouted, pushed the oatmeal aside, and refused to touch it. I didn't have the time or the energy to deal with him. I didn't know why I did this to myself. Had I gotten up when I was supposed to, I could've avoided all the stress and yelling. Tomorrow I would wake up earlier. Tomorrow I would be better. I was like a broken record. I knew myself well enough to realize that tomorrow would be the same shit.

"All right, kids. You need to get in the car," I commanded.

"My tummy hurts," Megan whined. "I don't want to go to school."

I wasn't in the mood for this. "Sweetheart, you've been complaining about your stomach for two weeks." I picked up her empty bowl of oatmeal. "Do you need to go to the hospital?" It had only been seven weeks since the accident, and our wounds were still raw and open.

"It's okay," she said. "I'm fine." With slumped shoulders, Megan walked toward the mud room to get her backpack.

I reached out to grab Bobby's hand. His thumb was in his mouth, and his fingers were clenched to the paw of his stuffed bear. "Do you want to leave bear home with me today?"

He shook his head. I didn't even know why I bothered to ask. He had grown more attached to the bear in the past few weeks, and his thumb-sucking had only gotten worse. We were all drowning from the weight of our loss.

* * *

I was planning to get back into bed for a few more hours after I dropped the kids off, but first I needed to clean the kitchen. It was a mess from the morning hustle. Standing at the sink, I stared out the window while I washed the dishes. I had to admit the snow looked beautiful piling up on the trees, pushing the branches down with its weight. A symphony of large snowflakes tickled the earth beneath. If we were living in Aspen, we would have been running for the mountains, screaming, "It's a powder day!" In the suburbs of Massachusetts, it was just an inconvenience. Had I convinced Christopher to stay in Aspen, maybe my life wouldn't have turned out the way it did. Maybe there wouldn't have been a fatal car accident.

I let the warm soapy water run over my hands and gazed into the abyss of white. Out of the corner of my eye, I noticed the top of someone's head on the patio. I couldn't make out the person's face. I could only see the outline of his body. A man. A tall man about Christopher's height. I was fixated on the image, desperately trying to process what I was seeing. *Christopher?* My pulse started to accelerate to full speed. I ran to the back door, opened it, and yelled, "Christopher! Christopher!"

Nobody responded. There wasn't a person in sight. He was gone. The vision had disappeared into thin air. It was him. I was sure it was him. It had to be. Unless, of course, I was delusional, which would make sense.

I took the dish that was in my hand and threw it on the ground, shattering it into pieces all over the tiled floor. My body slid down against the side of the center island. Hugging my knees, I burst into tears. I could feel him. His presence was near me. Nobody would believe me, but it was him. I was sure of it.

The loud braying of the phone startled me. I wiped the tears from my face, cleared my throat, and answered the phone.

"Hello?"

"Hope, I'm so glad you answered," my sister said in an enthusiastic tone.

"Hey, Bethany."

"You haven't returned any of my calls."

I rolled my eyes. "Sorry, I've been kind of busy."

"How is everything?"

Everything fucking sucked. My life sucked. I was lonely, sad, depressed, and hallucinating. "All good here," I responded in my most pathetic, fake voice.

"Have you made any plans for summer?"

"I haven't thought about it."

"Well, Eddie and I would like to drive out there with the kids and spend some time with you guys."

I picked up a piece of the shattered plate and held the pointy edge in between my fingers. It was razor sharp. "I guess that would be fine."

"Great," she said, and then she rambled on about her plans, but I tuned her out and focused on what it would feel like to puncture my skin with the shard. It would hurt. I would bleed.

"Hope, are you there?" Bethany asked, distracting me from my deranged thoughts.

"Oh, yeah, sorry."

"Okeydoke. Please give Megan and Bobby a kiss for me," she added before hanging up.

Looking at the mess on the floor, I wondered if I had spoken too soon. I wasn't sure if I could handle visitors. I could barely handle myself at this point. My sister meant well, but she certainly couldn't understand what I was going through. On the other hand, maybe having them around would help us get out of our funk.

The days and weeks blended together, and before I knew it summer had arrived. I had always loved this time of year, spending time outside, carefree. Sitting outside on the front steps, I watched the kids playing, getting lost in their imaginary worlds. Megan was drawing pictures with sidewalk chalk, while Bobby rode up and down the driveway on his Radio Flyer tricycle. It was the perfect summer day, the kind you dreamt about all winter—the smell of fresh-cut grass, basking in the sunlight, the smoky scent of barbecue wafting through the air, laughter humming through the neighborhood. Yet the radiant sunshine did nothing for the darkness I was carrying around inside of me. Christopher's death was weighing me down, occupying my head space. It was as if the joy was drained from my life, and the heaviness was taking hold of my mind.

"Bobby! Stop it!" Megan screamed. "Mommy, look what he did."

"Stop fighting," I called out in a flat tone.

Five seconds later, Bobby ran toward me, crying in a loud voice that sounded like a hyena.

"What happened?" I pulled him into my arms and hugged him.

"Megan," he said, gasping for air, "pushed me off my bike."

"Oh, sweetie, are you okay? Where does it hurt?"

He pointed to his scraped knee. I gave his boo-boo a gentle kiss.

"Megan, get over here," I yelled.

She walked toward me with a satisfied smirk plastered on her face.

"What's the matter with you?" I said. "Why did you push your brother?"

"He ran over my purple chalk with his stupid tricycle and smashed it into pieces. He's a jerk."

"Is this true, Bobby?"

He shrugged his shoulders.

Megan's lips pouted when she looked at me, and her voice cracked when she spoke. "You didn't even care. I asked you to tell him to stop and you just ignored me."

"Well, that doesn't give you the right to hurt your brother."

The three of us turned our heads when we heard the humming of a motor turning into the driveway. It was Bethany's minivan. Perfect timing. We needed the distraction. "No more fighting, you two."

We walked toward their car to greet them. Bethany jumped out first. "Well, that sure was the longest car ride ever." She was wearing a hot pink bowling shirt. Her name was written in cursive above her breastbone. "Hope, it's so good to see you," she said, hugging me. "Oh my, you're all skin and bones. Have you been eating?"

"I haven't had much of an appetite lately." This was probably the only good thing that had come out of mourning. I finally lost my extra pregnancy weight, and then some.

When she turned to hug Megan and Bobby, I noticed the back of her shirt read "Mulletville Bowling Babes."

"Isn't your sister's shirt great? She designed it herself," Edward said when he stepped out of the car. His tight-fitting Cleveland Browns tank top accentuated his round belly. The stench of his body odor hit my nose with ferocity when he gave me a bear hug. "Hope, we gotta put some meat on you. Too bad I can't give you some of this." He pointed to his jiggly stomach.

"Seriously, Ed, what are we going to do with that?" Bethany laughed and rubbed his roll of fat. He playfully smacked her ass, and for the first time, I was actually envious of their relationship.

After we all greeted one another, both my kids ran off with Nicholas, my eight-year-old nephew. Since he was only a year older than Megan and preferred to play with girl toys, they loved spending time together. Bobby liked to follow them around. At thirteen, my other nephew, Kevin, wasn't as interested in hanging with his younger cousins.

"Kevin, would you put that damn book down already," Ed reprimanded him. "And go grab my cooler of beer from the back and bring it inside." On the way into the house, Edward said, "Do you believe my kids? My older son is a dork, and my younger son only wants to dress up like a fairy princess. What the hell did I do wrong?"

What the hell did you do wrong? At least you have a fucking wife who loves you, along with two healthy kids.

"Oh, Ed, get over yourself. We got good kids," Bethany said.

"Maybe it's time we think about making another one." He winked at her, and then she giggled when he pinched her ass.

Their public display of affection was no longer making me jealous. It was starting to give me the same irritation as a mosquito buzzing in my ear. Was I going to have to listen to this all week?

Inside the house, Edward secured his spot on the couch in his favorite position—remote in one hand, can of beer in the other hand, resting on his gut. Kevin sat on the other side of the family room, and buried his head in the latest Harry Potter book. Bethany and I unloaded their snacks from the cooler and placed them in the refrigerator.

"You never commented on my new bowling shirt. What do you think?" Bethany asked, pulling out cans of beer one at a time.

"It's nice."

"I'm the president of our women's bowling league. It's a lot of fun. And it gets me out of the house once a week."

"That's great."

She snapped open a Budweiser and sucked the fizz off the top. "I think you should consider joining a league too. It's a good way to be social and meet new friends."

"I'm not looking to make new friends."

"It'll give you a break from the kids," she said after taking a sip of her beer.

"I'm fine."

"What about dating?"

"What about it?" I asked, annoyed that she would even suggest that.

"Have you considered it?"

"Bethany, please. I don't want to have this conversation." I grabbed a beer off the counter, opened it, and took a large gulp.

"How about you and I head over to the mall this afternoon? Maybe we can buy you some cute summer dresses." She popped open a can of Pringles and ate a handful, cramming them all in her mouth at once. "You're so skinny. I can't imagine your clothes fit anymore."

Going to the mall was the last thing I wanted to do, but I said yes anyway. Bethany was trying, and she certainly meant well. I had always had a difficult time relating to her. Growing up in Mulletville, she had spent most of her free time wandering around the mall with her friends, which was never something that appealed to me. I preferred escaping to the basement and losing myself in front of my easel, squeezing and mixing tubes of paint, trying to create the perfect colors and shades, and turning blank canvases into scenes that spoke to me.

After we were both married and had kids, we finally had something to talk about—but now that I was a widow, our lives had once again veered off into opposite directions. Tragedies had that effect on people, differentiating them into separate categories. It was almost as if the sufferer spoke a new language, which non-sufferers couldn't understand. No matter how hard friends and family tried to help, their words never infiltrated.

Macy's department store was like a drug for Bethany. She was all fired up, walking around and looking at everything. On the way to the women's department, she stopped to inhale the perfume scents in the makeup section like she was snorting cocaine. She tried to convince me to buy some new eye shadow and bronzer, but after looking at the bright blue on her lids, I adamantly refused.

In the shoe department, she caressed the vibrantly colored sandals that lined the shelves until we finally made it up the escalator to the second floor, where she sifted through dozens and dozens of garments hanging on circular racks. The dizzying array of merchandise was making me lightheaded. I sat in a white leather chair near the entrance of the dressing room while she held up maxi dresses, baby doll dresses, and T-shirt dresses in floral prints, geometric block prints, and stripes.

Bethany held a smocked crinkle dress in her hand. "What about this one?"

"I don't wear red."

"Hope, you're impossible. You say no to everything." She huffed. "At least try it on. The color will brighten up your skin tone."

"All right, fine," I said, just to appease her. "Do you mind if I run to the bathroom first?"

"Go ahead. I'll pull a few more dresses for you to try on."

This was torture. I would have preferred hanging at home with my brother-in-law, while he guzzled beers and farted on the couch, rather than be forced to buy a dress I was never going to put on my body. The sooner I agreed to one or two, the sooner we would get out of there, though. Shuffling my flip-flops along the glossy floor, I made my way toward the women's lounge, located next to the customer service department.

"Hope," a man's voice called out. I looked up and stopped dead in my tracks.

"Kyle?" I could feel my face heating up. A perfect wave of dirty-blond hair fell over the bronzed skin on his forehead. "What are you doing here?"

He held up a Macy's shopping bag. "My parents are celebrating their fortieth wedding anniversary. I needed to buy a gift."

Kyle had been Christopher's college roommate. The last time I remembered seeing him was at our wedding, or maybe it was the funeral. I couldn't remember. He must have been there.

"Wow, forty years. That's a long time."

"Yeah," he said, casually. "How are you?" He touched my shoulder with his left hand, shooting a warm sensation through me. "I've been thinking about Christopher a lot lately." When he pulled his hand away, I noticed he wasn't wearing a wedding ring. He was such a catch, I was surprised he was still single. Then again, he reminded me of Tracy, always out for a good time, never wanting to be tied down by anyone. "I miss him," he said.

"Me, too." I sighed. An uncomfortable silence fell between us. We were both trying not to cry.

"Well, it was great seeing you."

"You too, Kyle." Pulling himself closer, he wrapped his strong, masculine arms around me in a tight embrace. I could smell his earthy scent. It was different from Christopher's. Goose bumps laced my skin from the sensation of his body against mine. We pulled away from each other awkwardly.

"Take care," I told him, and then I bolted toward the bathroom.

Standing in front of the sink, I ran tepid water over my trembling hands, washing them repeatedly. When I looked at my reflection in the mirror, I was frightened by what I saw. My face was gaunt, my hair was straggly, and there were dark circles under my eyes. Bethany was right. I needed something to help my appearance. Maybe after I purchased a new dress, I would stop in the makeup department after all.

9

MEGAN WAS LUCKY TO HAVE landed in Miss Winter's third-grade class. She had a reputation for being one of the best teachers in the school. Watching her during back-to-school night, I understood why everyone loved her. She was an attractive woman with long blonde hair and dewy white skin, and she spoke in a melodic voice.

Glossy posters lined the walls with classroom rules, punctuation marks, parts of speech, timelines, the solar system, writing tips, and maps. Parents sat at their children's desks, which were pushed together in small clusters around the room. Miss Winter handed out sheets of paper, asking for volunteers for class parties, beginning with Halloween, which was only a month away.

I had no idea what the kids were going to wear, and worse than that, it would be my first Halloween without Christopher. He loved dressing up and taking Megan and Bobby trick-or-treating. The previous year, when he came home from work, he had hidden in the laundry room and jumped out at the kids, dressed in a goth punk rocker costume, complete with a face of black makeup.

At the end of Miss Winter's presentation, we were asked to write letters to our children and place them in their desks. When I finished mine, I drew a small picture in the corner of Buzz Lightyear, and I wrote, "I love you to infinity and beyond" underneath it. By the time I finished, most of the parents had already walked out the door. *Perfect*, I thought to myself. I could probably sneak out to my car and avoid having to make small talk with anyone.

I threw my coat on, grabbed my handbag, and started toward the door. I considered introducing myself to Miss Winter, but she was talking to another mom.

"Mrs. Whitmore," Miss Winter called out just as I was about to leave.

I turned to look at her. "Do you have a minute?" she asked.

"Sure," I said. The other mom said goodbye, leaving the two of us alone.

"Thank you for coming in tonight," she said.

"Of course."

"I wanted to talk to you about Megan. I'm a little concerned about her, socially."

My heartbeat sped up as Miss Winter continued.

"She doesn't interact much with the other students. During recess, she sits by herself on a bench reading a book, and when the other girls ask her if she wants to play with them, she always refuses."

I could feel a tightening in my chest. "Well, it's been a difficult couple of months for us."

"I know." Her hazel eyes were filled with sorrow. Of course, she knew. The entire school knew about us. Last year, Megan's second-grade class wrote cards and sent baked goods to our house.

"I thought maybe it might help if she met with the school counselor," she said.

Her suggestion blindsided me, spurring a tangled mix of emotions. Was this Miss Winter's way of telling me that my daughter was broken? I could feel heat rising in my face.

"Oh. I suppose that might be a good idea," I mumbled, as I fought back the urge to weep.

"Megan is a sweet girl. I want you to know that I'm here to help in any way I can."

"Thank you. I appreciate that."

After I said goodbye, I raced out of the school. I felt like such an asshole. I had been so caught up in myself that I hadn't even realized how much Megan was suffering. Or did I know, but chose to ignore it? Either way, I needed to do what I could to help her. Although I wondered how I could help her when I could barely function myself. What if I surprised both kids with Halloween costumes that would earn them prizes for the most creative ensemble? Winning the award might boost Megan's confidence. I could even plan a small party with the kids' friends at our house before we went out to trick-or-treat. Then again, I was probably getting ahead of myself. I decided to set up an appointment for Megan to meet with the school counselor first, and in the meantime, I could work on something spectacular for both kids to wear on Halloween.

* * *

For the next few weeks, I kept myself busy while the kids were in school, designing and buying the material to make their costumes. I made daily trips to Michael's, Target, JoAnne's Fabric, and our local arts and crafts store, purchasing hundreds of peacock feathers, a leotard, tights, spray paints, sequins, tulle, gems, and boas. I painted, hot-glued, and sewed until my fingers were numb. Before picking the kids up from school each day, I hid the supplies in a bin, which I kept stashed in a closet, so I could easily take it out when they were sleeping or out of the house. The kids complained when there was no food left in the pantry or the refrigerator, and Megan was annoyed when I dragged them to the supermarket after school, rather than run my errands while she was in school. For the first time since Christopher had passed away, I was so focused on my projects that I stopped feeling sorry for myself.

When I finally finished the costumes, I couldn't wait to show them to Megan and Bobby. On the way home from school, I told them I had a surprise waiting at home. Both costumes were displayed in the kitchen. Megan's was hanging over the pantry doorknob and Bobby's was standing in the middle of the room.

"Thomas the Train!" The wide smile and large eyes on the face of the blue and black painted cardboard box matched Bobby's excitement. "Yay!" he screamed, running toward it to try it on.

"What is that?" Megan asked in a snotty tone, looking at the leotard with the large cluster of feathers spreading out from the back.

"It's a peacock," I said.

Her face contorted. Her forehead wrinkled. And she burst into tears.

"Why are you crying? Doesn't it look like a peacock?"

The crying grew louder.

"Why did you do that?" she asked.

"Do what? I wanted to surprise you with a costume. I thought you would love it."

"But I don't want a homemade costume. I want to buy something from Party City. That's what all the girls in my class are doing." Her voice grew louder. "They're not wearing some dumb costume that their mom made." She ran upstairs to her room.

Bobby was thrilled with his costume, prancing around the kitchen in it. I knew Megan's reaction wasn't about me. She didn't want to stand out from her classmates. We'd had a lot of that over the past few months—looks of pity from everyone—teachers, friends, and strangers feeling sorry for us.

I'm doing the best I can, I told myself. I poured a glass of wine and drank it in three gulps. Feeling a little better, I went upstairs to Megan's room and offered to take her to Party City tomorrow after school.

She hugged me, and in her sweet little voice, she said, "Thank you, Mommy."

I wanted to tell her that I was trying, that raising two kids on my own wasn't easy, but she was too young to understand. Our pain was the same, yet it was also different. I had lost my partner. She had lost her father. The common thread was that we lived with a perpetual sadness that lingered through our household at all times.

Somehow, the kids and I survived our first Halloween without Christopher. Heavy rain poured down from the sky like teardrops, saturating the streets and ruining the usual holiday excitement and sugar high the kids typically felt. For us, the weather was kind of a gift. We grew tired of stepping in large puddles while lugging around bags of candy and umbrellas, so we decided to call it quits after half an hour of trick-or-treating. Once we were back in the warmth of our house, I shut off the outside lights, signaling to the other trick-or-treaters to skip our house, and then the three of us got into my bed, binged on candy, and watched a movie.

* * *

American consumerism was so out of control that stores hit us in the face with holiday decor months before the date. Star Market, Target, CVS, and the like were pushing Christmas on the first day of November. *Give me a fucking break already.* Couldn't we at least get through Thanksgiving? This was bullshit. The last thing I felt like doing was buying Christmas shit.

My parents invited us to Ohio for Thanksgiving, but I declined. My in-laws also invited us to their house for Thanksgiving, but I declined. Marcy invited us too. I tried to decline, but she insisted. Since she was an excellent cook, I filled the void in my belly with her juicy turkey, starches, creamy vegetable dishes, and pies. By the end of the night, the snap on my pants popped open, refusing to close again. All the weight I had lost had come back twofold, but at least I slept well that night, rocking my food baby to sleep.

As much as I wanted to skip Christmas, I had to find a way to face it, and all the annoying rituals that went along with it. Christopher and I had always taken the kids to a local nursery to pick out a tree. Afterward, we would go out for a special brunch at the Inn at Hastings Park in Lexington, not too far from our home. But this year I couldn't do it. I didn't want to buy a real tree. A real tree symbolized life. I wanted an artificial one, because it symbolized how I felt on the inside—lifeless.

Megan called me out on it when we pulled up to the Target parking lot. "Why are we getting a tree here?"

Dreading the task, I replied in a snappy voice, "Because we're doing something different this year."

"Do they sell the same kind of trees as the nursery?"

"The trees here come in a box, but when we put it together, you won't be able to tell the difference."

Megan kept her downturned eyes on the pavement as we walked toward the entrance of the store.

"How about you both pick out a gingerbread kit while we're here and we can work on it when we get home?"

Bobby's eyes lit up. "Can we get extra candy to put on it?" he asked.

"Sure," I told him. "How does that sound, Megan?"

"Fine," she said in a monotone voice.

Bobby kept his thumb in his mouth, while we strolled up and down the aisles. "I want that from Santa." He pointed to a blue bicycle.

"But that bike doesn't have training wheels," I told him.

"I don't want training wheels anymore," he said.

"I'll tell you what...if you stop sucking your thumb, I'll make sure you get a new bike for Christmas."

He pulled his thumb out of his mouth. “Okay,” he said. “Can I suck it in my bed?”

“Start by giving it up during the day, and then you can work on giving it up at night.”

Would this work? Could he stop that easily? I’d let him get away with sucking his thumb for too long, not having the energy to deal with it since Christopher had died. Ignoring his thumb-sucking was my coping mechanism; sucking it all day every day was his. At five years old, he needed to break the habit, and he needed to learn how to ride a bike without training wheels. Christopher had taught Megan how to ride a bicycle in an empty parking lot when she was four, while I stayed home with Bobby, who was napping at the time. Afterward, they ran into the house, screaming with excitement, and then I went outside to watch her ride. It was one of those milestones that made us all proud. Since I wasn’t there, I didn’t know how Christopher taught her, so, of course, I had no idea how I was going to teach Bobby.

* * *

The kids woke up early on Christmas morning, chomping at the bit to open their presents. I had stayed up late the night before to finish wrapping their gifts, numbing the pain of our first Christmas without my husband by drinking three glasses of cheap red wine. Stupid idea. My head was pulsating when I dragged myself out of bed in the morning. Trying to ignore the throbbing, I plastered on my fake smile, while the kids opened the gifts that were piled underneath our fake tree.

“Here, Mommy,” Megan said, handing me a wrapped present.

“Thank you, sweetheart.” I ripped open the paper and pulled out a colorful, handmade beaded bracelet. I was about to put it on, but the ringing of the phone distracted me. When I picked it up, my parents cheerfully sang Merry Christmas on the other end. I spoke to them briefly, then put the kids on the phone and went into the kitchen to pull out the ingredients to make pancakes. After the call, the kids stood on step stools in front of the center island to help me make breakfast.

"I want to crack the eggs," Megan demanded.

"No, I want to do it," Bobby whined.

"I'm better at it than you," Megan said in a snooty voice.

"Enough, you two. You need to take turns. Megan, you crack one egg and Bobby can crack the other." I handed each of them an egg, and they took turns cracking them into the bowl.

"You dummy. You got shells everywhere. I told you, you can't crack the eggs." Megan's nasty words made Bobby cry.

"Megan, what is wrong with you? Stop acting so nasty. Apologize to your brother this instant."

"No! And you can't make me."

I could feel my veins becoming engorged. I grabbed Megan's arm, pulled her off the stool, and glared at her with a death stare. "How dare you talk to me like that! It's Christmas, and you should be grateful for all the presents Santa brought you. Stop acting like a brat, or you'll sit in your room for the rest of the day."

"I hate Christmas, and there is no Santa. And I hate your pancakes. You don't even make them right. Dad made them better. I wish Dad was here to make pancakes, not you." She ran upstairs and slammed her bedroom door.

Her words were like an arrow that shot right into my heart. I was speechless, frozen, unable to process her biting remarks.

"Mommy, is there really no Santa?" Bobby asked in a sweet voice.

"Of course there is. Don't listen to your sister. Can you do me a favor and watch TV in the other room for a little while?"

Bobby walked into the family room with his head down. Sitting at the kitchen table, I stared blankly outside. The gray sky and barren trees mirrored my mood. I had to deal with Megan, but I didn't know what to say to her. The last time I had spoken to Miss Winter, it sounded like Megan was doing better in school. She had been spending time with a new girl in her class. The school counselor had suggested that Megan invite her friend over to our house. The playdate went so well that a week later, the girl came back for a sleepover. But over the past few weeks, I had been so consumed with my own sorrow over the holidays that I hadn't thought about how it would affect my kids.

Forcing myself out of the chair, I went upstairs to Megan's room. I knocked softly on the door, and when she didn't answer, I opened it slowly and peeked my head in. She was lying on her bed, hugging her American Girl Doll with tears rolling down her face. The sight of her weakened me.

"Honey, can I talk to you?" I asked, tiptoeing inside. I sat on the edge of her bed and started to rub her back. "Sweetheart, I know you miss Daddy. We all do. It's hard, especially during the holidays, when he's not with us. I love you with all my heart, but we're still a family, and we need to work together and try to make the best of it."

"Make the best of it? You're not. You're always snapping at us, and you didn't even like the bracelet I made for you."

Another punch in the gut. She was right. I had been a bitch over the past few weeks.

I swallowed the lump in my throat, and my voice cracked when I spoke. "I have been kind of crabby lately. I'm so sorry, angel. Will you please forgive me? And you're wrong. I love the bracelet you made for me. I was planning to wear it to Grandma Donna and Grandpa Bill's house for dinner this evening. I'll tell you what... why don't we start over, and instead of making pancakes, let's make French toast from now on for Christmas breakfast."

"Okay," she mumbled under her breath.

"Can you give me a hug?" I pulled her into my arms and hugged her with urgency and desperation.

Then we walked downstairs, hand in hand, and started the morning over again.

10

2009

AFTER I MADE IT THROUGH the holidays, life started to become more manageable. The kids and I got into a good routine, waking up on time for school and filling our weekends with visits to the Boston Science Museum, Children's Museum, and indoor activity gyms. I had this manic goal to keep the kids moving at all times. One Saturday, we went ice skating, tubing, and bowling, and then we finished off the night with dinner at Chuck E. Cheese. By the time we got home, the kids couldn't move. I was running them ragged.

Everything changed when March rolled in. It was as if I hit a wall, and instead of moving at full speed on my hamster wheel, I lost all motivation to do anything. I was lethargic throughout the day, struggling to get out of bed in the morning. After dropping the kids off at school, I would drive home and either crawl back into bed or sit on the couch in the living room, staring off into space for hours on end. The breakfast dishes remained on the kitchen table, beds were left unmade, and the garbage overflowed. I couldn't figure out what was wrong with me. At first I assumed I was coming down with something—but I knew better. I wasn't getting sick. Nor was I premenstrual. My body was preparing me for doomsday—the first anniversary of the accident.

"Mom!" Megan screamed one morning. "What's for breakfast?"

"I don't know," I mumbled from under my bedcovers, but she didn't hear me.

She stormed into my room. "Mom!"

"What?" I snapped back. "What is it?"

"Aren't you going to get out of bed? I'm starving."

"You're eight years old. Why can't you pour yourself a bowl of cereal?"

The entire bedroom shook when she slammed the door on her way out. I forced myself out of bed and went into the bathroom. I had to face the day. I had to face the next couple of days, even though I didn't want to.

I stood in the shower, trying to wash away my despair. Lathering soap all over my body, I scrubbed and scrubbed until my skin turned pink and raw. The tears streamed down my face in sync with the water flowing out of the showerhead. When I had nothing left in me, I turned the water off, wrapped myself in a towel, and stepped out of the shower, drained and empty.

I could hear Bobby making *vroom vroom* noises in my bedroom. I opened the bathroom door, and my heart started to race when I saw him playing with his toy car on top of my dresser.

"What are you doing?" I screamed. A pile of coins and wadded-up receipts from Christopher's pocket had been sitting in the exact same spot for almost a year. Bobby had scattered the items all over the dresser, destroying the messy little pile—my shrine to Christopher. Every single day I glanced at it, imagining him standing there sorting through his stuff.

Bobby looked at me, his blue eyes filled with innocence. "I made a race course," he said.

"You ruined everything," I told him, gritting my teeth.

The corners of his mouth turned down. He dropped his car on the floor and ran out of my bedroom. When he left, I swept the pile back to the corner of the dresser, desperately trying to remember how it was. Suddenly, it dawned on me that I was losing my mind. What the hell was I doing? Leaving that shit there, along with all of Christopher's clothes in the closet, was not going to bring him back. I picked up the loose change, threw the garbage away, and ran into Bobby's room.

He was curled up in the fetal position on his bed, with one arm wrapped around his bear.

"Sweetheart, I'm so sorry for yelling at you."

He turned to me with his tear-stained face.

"Please forgive me," I said. "Sometimes moms act a little crazy for no reason."

"I didn't know I wasn't allowed to do that," he said.

"No, it's okay. It's my fault. That was Daddy's garbage. For some silly reason, I was saving it, but I don't need it. Here." I held out my hand. "You keep the coins. Go put them in your piggy bank."

Smiling, he took the change from me, got up, and hopped toward his dresser.

"Do you want to help me clean out Daddy's closet? I bet we can find more change in there for you to keep."

He nodded, delighted at the prospect of collecting more money. After grabbing a box of garbage bags, we made our way into the closet, where Christopher's clothes had remained untouched for the past twelve months.

"How about I hand you some of Daddy's clothes and you can put them in the big bag?"

"Okay," he said. I shook open the trash bag and gave it to him to hold. Starting with his dress shirts, I pulled Christopher's clothes off the hangers one at a time, passing them to Bobby so he could shove them into the bag.

"Do you think Daddy is going to be mad that we're giving away all his stuff?"

"No, sweetie. Knowing your dad, he'll be happy that his clothes will go to someone who might need them."

He pushed another shirt inside the bag. "Where is Daddy right now?"

"He's in heaven."

"Where is that?"

"Well, when someone dies, their body doesn't work anymore, but their spirit goes to a special place where they can look after all the people they love back on Earth." I felt like I was talking out of my ass. Truth was, I didn't understand death, and I wasn't even sure what I believed.

"Is he in outer space?"

"Yeah, I guess you could say that."

"What if he comes back to Earth to see us? He won't have anything to wear."

And that was exactly why death hurt so much. "Honey, he can't come back. He doesn't have a body anymore."

"Why did he leave us?"

"He didn't have a choice. He left because—"

I wanted to tell him that life was a pile of shit and unfair, but I couldn't say that. I couldn't poison his mind any more than it already had been with our tragic situation.

"Sometimes we don't have any control over our lives. Things just happen, and we don't know why."

When we finished with the dress clothes, I moved on to Christopher's casual clothes. I unfolded a gray raglan-sleeved Red Sox baseball shirt with blue sleeves.

"Daddy loved this shirt. I think he wore it the night you were born."

There was a red stain on the top corner that brought back a funny memory of that evening, when Christopher had dripped marinara sauce all over himself at the exact moment my water broke.

"I bet your dad would want you to keep this shirt," I told Bobby. "It has a lot of special memories."

Nodding, he said, "Can I wear it now?"

"Sure."

He held his hands up in the air and let me take off his Thomas the Train pajama top, and then I helped him into the shirt. His little body was swimming in the oversized garment, but he looked adorable. Grabbing my pint-sized Christopher into me, I hugged him as tight as I could. My son—this living, beautiful being—was created out of the purest kind of love. I squeezed my tears back like I was winding the handle of a Jack-in-the-box, afraid that at any moment the weight of the emotions battling inside me was going to burst out.

Drawing in all the air I could manage, I took a deep breath. "Okay, let's finish up in here," I said.

We spent the next hour clearing out Christopher's side of the closet. Afterward, we dragged the bags downstairs and into the trunk of my car so I could take them to Goodwill.

Megan had spent the morning watching cartoons in the family room. I apologized to her for not getting up to make her breakfast. She forgave me right away, especially after I promised the kids we could go to the market and buy tons of ingredients and have a lazy Sunday in the house, baking cookies, cupcakes, brownies, and muffins.

I ran back upstairs to finish getting dressed. Standing in the closet, I felt unbalanced. Christopher's side was empty, while my side was overflowing. I started to rearrange my clothes, pushing them into my newfound space on the racks and in the drawers. When I finished, I admired my organized closet and realized for the first time since we had moved into this house, I could actually see all my clothes, and I had discovered pieces that had been lost and suffocating in the bunched-up mess. I stretched my arms wide above my head to release the tension from my body, and I exhaled.

Out of the corner of my eye, I noticed a drawer had opened slightly. Inside were two neatly folded stacks of Christopher's boxer shorts. I guess it would be kind of weird to donate his boxer shorts. I mean, other than a pervert, who would want someone's used underwear? I thought about throwing them away, but then a brilliant idea popped into my head. I would cut each pair open and sew them together to make a shawl—my own sacred prayer shawl made from the same cotton that had held my husband's magical pleasure- and life-giving organ intact.

That evening, after the kids and I spent the entire day listening to loud music while we baked, licked batter, fingered frosting, baked some more, and overdosed on sugar, they eventually passed out, and I pulled an all-nighter. Working tirelessly, I patched Christopher's preppy J.Crew underwear together. I sewed his colorful patterned boxer shorts, a mismatched array of sailboats, dogs, polka dots, stripes, and checkered designs, into a long shawl. When I finished my masterpiece, I covered myself with it, and before the sun's orange glow rose from the horizon, I crawled into bed, allowing a warm heat to radiate through my chest, and I finally fell into a peaceful sleep.

* * *

Ever since I had become a widow, people had been taking a vested interest in giving me a makeover. First it was Bethany, forcing me to buy the ugly sundresses. Next it was Marcy, who brought over some sexy designer outfits from her store. My beloved fashionista friend could rock a high-waisted pencil skirt with Christian Louboutin pumps like a runway model—but I sure as hell couldn't. And anyway, where would I be going dressed like that, particularly with my fat ass? I hated to sound ungrateful, because I did appreciate Marcy's attempt to turn me into a blonde, white-skinned, freckle-faced, alien version of J. Lo, and even though she insisted I looked good, it just wasn't me. Not to mention, showing up at school pick-up in something like that might not bode well with the other moms. Dressing like J. Lo was Marcy's speed, not mine. I'd always been more of a sneakers-and-jeans kind of girl.

Donna was the next one who tried to save me from getting arrested by the fashion police. Just like Bethany and Marcy, she tried to impose her own style on me. As much as I hated to admit it, I understood why she felt the need to change my appearance. One afternoon, while the kids were in school, she invited me to the grand opening of a new restaurant near her Victorian brownstone in Boston's prestigious Back Bay. Ignoring the funny stares from the other patrons, I proudly walked in wearing my new shawl.

"You and your mother are so creative," she said after I explained to her how I had made my new design. Even though she wasn't trying to be condescending by comparing me to my mother, hearing her say that made me realize that I probably shouldn't have worn my shawl in public.

About a week later, Donna showed up at my house. "I have a big surprise for you," she said in a giddy voice when I opened the door and found her standing there, holding an enormous box from her favorite store in Nantucket. Her small, bony frame could barely carry the oversized box into my house. I took it from her and brought it into the living room.

Donna had bought me various articles of clothing over the years—cardigans, floral scarves, and Lily Pulitzer dresses. After she gave me these generous gifts, Christopher would mock me, telling me that I could have won an Academy Award for my overzealous appreciation. Every present she bought me was left tucked away in the back of my closet, never to be worn.

I bit my lip, avoiding eye contact with her while I opened the box. Inside there were about fifteen white gift boxes, each with a pink whale on a blue sticker that said, "Vineyard Vines." I stole a quick glance in her direction and watched her eyes light up. It was the high one gets from the joy of gift giving. Unfortunately, it would be a more pleasant exchange if the gift giver was in tune with the recipient's style.

I was the daughter Donna never had, and she finally had an opportunity to dress me as a miniature version of herself. I swallowed hard and opened each box slowly, pushing away the tissue paper to find an array of tank dresses, collared shirts, and drawstring shorts. The pastel-colored garments were embellished in various designs, some of which included pineapples, nautical stripes, paisley, and small whales. Donna insisted that I try them on so she could see how they fit. It no longer felt like Christmas or my birthday, but rather a Halloween horror show. I tried on one outfit after another, showing off my preppy clown attire while Donna clapped with joy, priding herself on picking out the perfect summer wardrobe.

"I don't feel comfortable accepting all of this," I told her.

"Don't be silly. It was my pleasure. I'm happy to do it for you, and I plan to do the same for the children as well."

I gave her a small peck on the cheek, thanking her for her generosity.

"Bill and I were hoping you and the kids could spend some time with us in Nantucket this summer."

"Oh, um, sure. I guess so. I haven't put any thought into our summer plans."

"Wonderful," she said. "You and the kids haven't been out there in a number of years. The renovations have finally been completed, so of course, there's plenty of room. I will sign the children up for day camp at the country club, and there's a terrific women's tennis clinic for you as well."

Spending time at the beach did sound kind of nice, and a change of scenery would probably be good for us. I thanked her again before she left, and then watched her head to her car with a light step. I looked at the mess that was scattered on the floor of my living room and thought, *Am I really going to have to wear this stuff all summer?*

I could almost hear Christopher laughing at me from heaven.

11

THE DAY AFTER THE KIDS got out of school at the end of June, I packed up the car, and we drove to the Hyannis Port Ferry. As soon we got on the highway, a feeling of release came over me. It was a perfect day— a balmy eighty degrees with a cloudless sky, filled with abundant sunshine. I turned up the Jonas Brothers on the radio for the kids, singing the lyrics in my head as I looked forward to a summer on the beach. We were making great time, having left early enough that we avoided the usual bumper-to-bumper traffic that plagued drivers heading toward the beach.

The ferry pulled into Nantucket harbor around lunchtime. The steamship man signaled for me to disembark. I drove off the ramp and onto the cobblestone streets, welcomed by the summer energy that permeated the ice cream shops, boutiques, souvenir stores, and seaside restaurants. American flags stood proudly on many of the homes we passed. Through the open windows, we drank in the fresh ocean air as we drove down the bumpy dirt road toward my in-laws' home.

We finally pulled into the long driveway, which was made of crushed seashells that led to a massive gray-shingled house with white trim and a wraparound porch, overlooking the ocean. The sight of the spacious home made my palms sweaty against the steering wheel. After Christopher died, Donna had decided it was time to gut their summer home, pouring her energy into redoing the dilapidated house and knocking it down to the studs. She had shown me photos during the year-long renovation, but they didn't do it justice. The sight of the palatial home was intimidating.

Christopher and I had taken the kids to Nantucket when they were toddlers, but since the house hadn't been baby-proofed, particularly the wide-open pool, we were too on-edge to enjoy ourselves. At eight and five, the children were finally at the perfect ages for a Nantucket getaway; however, we were missing a vital member of our nuclear family—trudging through life lopsided.

"Mommy, is this Grandma Donna and Grandpa Bill's house?" Megan asked. "It's so big."

"Yes, it is. Now remember, I want you guys to be on your best behavior. Both of you grab a bag, and let's go in."

On the outside, we looked like the perfect Nantucket preppy family. I was wearing my pink whale-covered shorts with a matching pink collared shirt, and Megan looked adorable in her blue-and-white embroidered shift dress. On our way up the wide stone steps, which led to the front door, I tucked Bobby's gingham shirt into his belted khaki seersucker shorts.

Soon after I rang the bell, a four-foot-ten Filipino woman wearing a dark gray uniform answered the door. "Hello, Mrs. Whitmore. Please come in. May I help with your luggage?"

"You must be Winnie. Please, call me Hope, and this is my daughter, Megan, and my son, Bobby."

Winnie greeted the kids with a friendly smile. She grabbed the children's bags, and then we followed her into the house.

"Right this way. Mrs. Whitmore is out on the patio," Winnie said.

Donna was always in the market for the perfect housekeeper. She had been raving about Winnie since she had hired her two months ago, convinced that she had finally found a keeper. We walked cautiously on the glossy, hardwood floors as we followed the petite woman through the wide-open, light-filled hallways, taking in the oversized matching white furniture. The formal rooms were filled with pricey Cololonial-era antiques and expensive artwork.

Donna stood up when we stepped onto the patio and came over to greet us, pulling off her enormous sun hat.

"What a pleasant surprise. I wasn't expecting you for at least another hour. Look at all of you." She flashed us a big smile. "I'm so pleased your clothes fit. You look darling."

"Grandma Donna, can I take these clothes off now? Mommy said I have to wear the stuff you bought us."

My face turned a crimson color. I should've known better than to tell Bobby something that wasn't to be repeated.

"How about you two get your swimsuits on, and then you can go for a dip in the pool?" Donna asked, and then the kids ran off behind Winnie to get changed.

"The house is gorgeous, Donna," I said.

"Thank you." She pushed her black sunglasses on top of her head. "Come inside, let me show you around."

I followed her through the house, complimenting her on the tasteful decor.

"I would love to get your opinion about a painting my decorator brought over," she said as we made our way through the double-entry foyer and up the swooping staircase. A large oil canvas of a lone dinghy floating in ripples of blue water hung on the wall. There was a sad emptiness in the image, almost as if the boat was stranded, desperately waiting for someone to return.

"It was painted by a local artist," she said.

"It works well here. I mean, it adds interest to the white wall," I told her.

"She wants almost ten thousand dollars for it."

I nearly gasped at the price tag. *What the fuck?* I could have painted it, and I would have been happy if someone paid me five hundred dollars, although my painting career was just as lost as the dinghy in the picture.

"That seems like a lot," I confessed. "But I suppose if you love it, then you should keep it."

"Hmm," she said. "I'll give it some more time."

The high-pitched sounds of Bobby and Megan giggling echoed through the house as they raced each other toward the pool.

"I'm glad you agreed to come out here. I think we could all use the distraction," Donna said.

After touring through the five spacious bedrooms with en suite baths on the second floor, we went back outside, took a seat on the Adirondack chairs, and watched the kids playfully swim.

Staring out at the deep blue ocean and the golden sand, surrounded by the tall dune grass, I watched the wild irises sway in the gentle breeze. White seagulls made screeching sounds as they flew over us. For a fleeting moment, I wished that I could be a bird with the freedom to soar through the sky and release the heaviness that I'd been carrying with me.

* * *

When my father-in-law came home from playing golf, he opened a bottle of Harlan Estate, welcoming me and the kids to Nantucket. More wine flowed throughout dinner, which I appreciated, although I wasn't sure if Bill was celebrating our arrival or drowning away his sadness with alcohol. It was probably a little of both. At first the wine helped me forget my pain, but when I got into bed that evening, the hurt that I was trying so hard to mask started to boil again.

Tossing and turning in the luxurious cream-colored Frette bedding, I remembered the first time Christopher brought me to Nantucket, before we had kids. Donna and Bill were away in Europe and told us we could use the house. We spent the entire weekend sipping rosé on the deck and feasting on lobster, clam chowder, local cheese, and fresh fruit in between marathon lovemaking sessions.

The memory was keeping me awake. Through the open window, the cool night breeze blew salty air into the room. I could hear the calming sounds of swooshing waves as they crashed against the shore. Nature was playing relaxing music, yet my mind was ill at ease, and instead of allowing myself to melt into the sounds, the songs of the ocean were adding to the cacophony in my mind. I got out of bed to close the window, and when I looked up I could see the same subtle glow of the crescent moon that was reminiscent of the blissful weekend that I had spent with my husband years ago on this island. I had once found balance in nature, but it no longer soothed me. Coming here was a mistake. It hurt to be in Christopher's parents' home without him by my side. The later it got, the more anxious I felt. In a few hours, the sun was going to rise, and I would need to get out of bed, put on a fake, cheery smile, and head off to the women's tennis clinic that Donna had signed me up for. I didn't have the energy to socialize with a bunch of snooty housewives I didn't know.

* * *

At some point, I fell asleep, because the ringing of the alarm startled me out of bed at 8:00 a.m. When I first opened my eyes, it took me a minute to reorient myself and remember where I was. *Shit*—day one of the tennis clinic at the club.

I went to the dresser and pulled my new L'Etoile tennis outfit from the bottom of a pile of workout clothes. I glanced in the full-length mirror—I didn't even look like myself in a sleeveless V-neck white top and matching pleated skirt. The last time I had played tennis was with Christopher, and I had been wearing a Nike running ensemble. If only he could see me now. I put my hair in a ponytail, and when I took a closer look at my face in the mirror, I could see heavy bags under my eyes. A tan would probably make me feel better. I added a light pink gloss to my lips and headed downstairs for breakfast.

Bill and the kids were sitting at the kitchen table. Bill was sipping coffee and reading *The Wall Street Journal*, while Bobby and Megan were eating cereal.

"Good morning. You look ready for tennis," Bill commented.

"As ready as I can be."

I kissed Bobby and Megan goodbye, promising them we would build a sandcastle on the beach when I got home.

As much as I wanted to play tennis, I was dreading the idea of spending time with snooty housewives who send their kids to fancy private schools and spend half their summers in Europe and the other half on Nantucket. By the time I reached the entrance of the club, there was a tightening in my abdomen, which steadily increased as I passed a small, unassuming sign that read, "Nantucket Country Club." I drove up the long driveway toward the massive colonial style clubhouse. The vast property, located on a hill and surrounded by acres of lush green grass strewn with roses and hydrangeas, overlooked the harbor. I pulled the car up to the valet, took a deep breath, and handed my keys to the parking attendant.

When I arrived at the tennis court, four women were taking turns hitting with a twenty-something version of Brad Pitt. His dirty blond hair was cut short, and he had a strong, muscular build. I couldn't take my eyes off him.

"Are you Hope?" young Brad Pitt called out to me.

I nodded.

"I'm Scott. Why don't you get in line and join the group? We're just doing a warm-up exercise."

I ran over to get in line. A tall, brunette woman with full lips painted with shiny hot pink gloss introduced herself to me, and then the other women shook my hand and said their names, which all went in one ear and out the other. Beads of sweat were dripping from my forehead, and I hadn't even begun hitting yet.

"Hope, you're up," Scott yelled.

I pounded the first ball he hit to me so hard it hit the fence on the other side of the court.

"Take it easy," Scott told me, before hitting another ball in my direction. This time I swung with the same force and missed the ball.

"Oops," I said a little too loud.

"Relax, Hope. You're thinking too much. Just free your mind and let go," Scott instructed.

He was right. I was thinking too much. My heart was still racing, and I could have filled a bucket with my sweat. I wanted to hit the ball hard and with the same finesse I once had back in high school, when I was on the tennis team. *Focus, Hope. Focus and release,* I told myself. This time I whacked the ball in the sweet spot of the racket, and it landed perfectly inside the far-right corner of the box.

"Great one. Now repeat what you just did."

Each time I swung the racket across my body, I willed it in the exact location I had been targeting. It was coming back to me. The adrenaline rushed through my veins as I soaked up the power after each perfect hit. When my turn was up, I got back in line, grinning with satisfaction behind one of the women.

"Do you play a lot?" a red-headed woman asked. "You're really good."

"Honestly, I think the last time I picked up a racket was about ten years ago. I used to play competitively when I was in high school."

"Wow, that's impressive."

"I apologize, but what's your name again?" I asked.

"Melanie, but most people call me Mel."

"Mel, you're up," Scott called out.

Each time I made contact with the ball, I was releasing pent-up anger that I had stored in my core, and for the first time since the accident, I wasn't thinking. I was letting go.

About an hour into the drills, I started to feel a churning in my tummy. My bowels were screaming that it was time to release a shit. It must have been all that jumping around; my body had forgotten what it was like to exercise.

As soon as we stopped for a water break, I excused myself and ran to the restroom. I usually didn't like shitting in public toilets, but this was an emergency. I covered the seat with toilet paper and let it all out. When I finished, I pulled up my skirt and peeked at the prize I had just deposited, happy to see that it was a long, wrap-around-the-toilet poop, which was a sign of optimal health. My entire body was feeling lighter, as if I had lost five pounds. I washed my hands and looked at myself in the mirror. Instead of my usual pale, ghostly face, I looked like I had been kissed by the sun. *Not bad*, I thought. I looked pretty good. I skipped out of the bathroom, feeling invigorated. I was genuinely grateful that Donna had signed me up for this clinic.

Scott was reviewing the proper grip with everyone when I got back to the group. I had this odd feeling that they were all staring at me. Had they noticed that I looked skinnier? It was possible they were jealous. After all, I was smoking them on the tennis court. I grabbed my racket and placed my hands in the correct position and waited for Scott to come over and check.

Mel leaned over and whispered in my ear, "Hope, you have toilet paper hanging out of your tennis skirt."

I quickly reached behind my back and pulled out a wad of toilet paper. A rapid fire rose from my neck through my face and my ears. I walked over to the trash and threw it in the garbage.

Now what? They had all seen it. I didn't want to go back to the court. I was fighting the urge to make a fast getaway, although I knew if I did that, it would make me look more ridiculous. I took a cup from the dispenser, poured myself some cold water, and sipped slowly.

Scott yelled out, "Hope, you're up."

I walked cautiously over to him and placed my hand on the lower end of the racket.

"That's exactly what I'm looking for. Does everyone see this? You just need to loosen up. Don't hold the racket with so much force. Ladies, tennis is about clearing your mind, becoming one with your racket. You need to have a quiet head. Stop thinking. Be free and let go, and I promise you'll see a vast improvement in your game. Okay, now let's get out there again and hit some balls."

Easier said than done, Scott. What does this guy know about letting go? He's a baby. I guess if I were a hot tennis instructor surrounded by bored housewives, I probably wouldn't have much on my mind, either. All right, I'm going to try to free myself from my erratic thinking, forget about how mortified I was a few minutes ago, and get out there and do my best.

For the next hour, I got into the flow. Every time I made contact with the ball, I went deeper into a meditative state. Time melted away, and I lost my sense of self. The zone broke when the clinic ended. Scott thanked us for coming and said he looked forward to seeing us tomorrow. One of the women asked if I wanted to join the group for lunch, but I politely declined.

When I got back to the house, Donna was sitting outside on a lounge chair, reading a book.

"Hi," I called out. I noticed Bobby's stuffed bear sitting on a chair. "Where are the kids?"

"Bill took them fishing," she said, putting her book down.

"Bobby didn't take his bear?"

"No, Bill told him to leave it home."

"Really? He didn't get upset?"

"No, not at all."

I couldn't believe it. Bobby never left home without his bear.

"How was tennis?" Donna asked.

"It was great." Looking out toward the ocean, I spotted three seagulls, one ahead and two behind, soaring through the air. "I'm going to take a quick shower before the kids get back."

Before I walked away, Donna told me she had made reservations at the club for dinner, which I wasn't too thrilled about. I had already had enough socializing for one day.

"It'll be great for the kids. There's going to be a bounce house, a clown, a tattoo artist, and a magician," she said, trying to make it sound more appealing.

* * *

I sat in the back of Bill's Mercedes between Megan and Bobby on the way to the club. As soon as we stepped out of the car, the charcoal scent of the barbecue grills came wafting through the air. My mouth was salivating, and I realized that I had forgotten to eat lunch. The loud screams and laughter of happy children grew stronger as we walked toward the event. The weather was idyllic—the bright sun was still ablaze against an azure sky. Food stations were set up all over the large patio. The aroma of sizzling steaks, burgers, and fries were torturing my rumbling tummy. Tables with red-and-white checkered tablecloths and chairs were scattered around, and the children's entertainment was spread out on the grassy area.

Bill and Donna chatted with their friends, while I took the kids over to watch a magician performing on the lawn. Once they were settled, I made my way toward the bar and ordered a margarita. The tangy, sweet, and refreshing drink was like a symphony of flavors dancing through my parched throat. I drank it quickly and then ordered another. I sucked the second one down and waited a few minutes until I could safely order a third without embarrassing myself. The tequila went directly into my bloodstream, whisking me to a world where everything felt lighter. I complimented the bartender on the delicious beverage and asked for another one. I grabbed my third drink and unsteadily walked toward the salad bar. My stomach was begging me to eat, and my head knew that it was a good idea—food would help absorb some of the alcohol.

I sauntered over to one of the large food stations, stopping dead in my tracks when I spotted three of the women from the tennis clinic. I quickly pivoted and staggered around the other side of the clubhouse. Somehow, I ended up in front of a small building with a sign in front that indicated it was the pro shop. I opened the glass door and was immediately drawn to the stillness, the quiet escape from the overstimulation of the party. I walked to a rack of women's tennis clothes and started to weed through the neatly arranged outfits.

"Hope, is that you?" a man called out from behind the cash register.

When I looked up, I almost jumped back. "Hey, Scott," I said in an awkward, slurring tone. "Um, I, um, just came in to check out the tennis rackets."

"I was getting ready to close the shop, but I'd be happy to stay a little longer and help you. The rackets are over here in this corner."

I followed behind his perfectly sculpted iron-clad body.

"Any idea which one you wanted to look at?"

When he turned around, I noticed his enchanting seafarer-blue eyes. He had been wearing dark sunglasses during the tennis clinic. Seeing his eyes up close and personal gave me a strange sensation.

"No, I, uh, was hoping you could help me figure it out," I told him.

"You did great today at the clinic. Have you been playing tennis long? You seem like a natural."

"No, actually, I can't remember the last time I picked up a racket. I played a lot in high school and sporadically in college, but not much since then." I flipped my hair back in a pathetic attempt to make myself look better. "So, where are you from?" I asked, expecting him to say somewhere in California.

"Aspen."

"What?" I asked in shock.

"Aspen," he repeated. "Colorado. Have you ever been?"

"Yeah, actually, I lived there for a little while after college."

"No way. Small world, isn't it?"

He started to tell me how he had ended up in Nantucket, but I had trouble focusing on what he was saying. As I stood next to him, a fiery feeling came over my body, almost like an electrical current was burning inside of me. And then it just happened; the liquor flushed away my inhibitions, and I leaned in close to him, turned my head to the side, opened my mouth, and kissed him. Our tongues pushed together in a deep, carnal hunger. A warm rush shot through every inch of my skin. His body was responding to my needs, and the intensity was moving rapidly. Then suddenly, as if being awoken abruptly from a dream, I stopped and stepped back.

"I'm so sorry. I shouldn't have done that," I said.

He shook his head and grabbed me gently by the neck and took me back in. His hands lightly caressed my ears. Our bodies were screaming with desire. I wanted him. I wanted more. I wanted to stop, but I couldn't resist his touch. I was ravenous. I had forgotten how it felt to be held and kissed by a man. A man? Shit. He was a boy. I was almost double his age. What the hell was I doing?

I broke away from his hold. "I gotta go," I said, and sprinted out of the pro shop as fast as I could.

I ran back to the barbecue and found my mother-in-law sitting at a table, nibbling on a piece of chicken.

"Hope, where have you been?" she asked in a concerned voice. "Are you okay? Your face is awfully pale."

"I'm fine," I replied.

"Here, sit down. I have so much food here."

I took the empty seat next to her, and she put some chicken and ribs on my plate. I picked up a sticky rib smothered in barbecue sauce and ripped off pieces of meat with my teeth, eating every last bite until there was nothing left but the bone. Just as I was about to pick up another one, a woman paused at our table to greet Donna.

"Hope, do you remember my friend Carol?" my mother-in-law asked. The woman had a bright orange Hermès scarf wrapped so tightly around her neck, I couldn't help but wonder how she was breathing.

"It's lovely to see you, Hope," Carol said, sitting down next to me. I almost fainted when I caught a whiff of her Chanel No. 5 perfume.

"You too," I said, even though she didn't look remotely familiar. I picked up my napkin and tried to wipe the red stains off my fingers.

"Donna tells me you joined the women's tennis clinic."

"Yes, today was my first day."

"Is Scott your instructor?" she asked, winking at me. "All the ladies have crushes on him. Isn't he just delicious?"

"Excuse me," I said as I let out a small cough. The heat in my face turned up a notch.

"Don't be bashful. We spend hours gushing over him during our bridge game. He's such a catch."

"Yeah, he is good-looking, but he's also great instructor," I said, trying to steer away from this uncomfortable conversation. I picked up another rib and took a big bite.

"You know," Carol said in a barely audible voice, "there's a rumor going around that one of the women in your group was caught making whoopee with him in the pro shop."

A piece of rib got stuck in my throat, and I started to choke on it.

"Waiter, over here! She's choking!" Carol yelled out.

A server put his tray down, rushed over to me, and patted my back a few times. On the final hit, I coughed up a piece of rib into my napkin.

"Hope, are you okay?" Donna asked, handing me a glass of water.

I took a sip. "Yes, yes, I'm fine. The food must have gone down the wrong way." I turned toward the waiter and thanked him for saving me.

Before the waiter walked away, Carol asked him to fill our wineglasses. "So, Hope, speaking of men, have you been dating?"

No, not this again, I thought to myself. "I'm really not that interested at this time," I replied.

"Well, you let me know when you're ready. I just love matchmaking. Come to think of it, my nephew recently got divorced. His wife was cheating on him. The nerve. I mean, after all, she totally married him for his money. She came from nothing. My nephew is a wonderful man." She turned toward my mother-in-law. "You remember John, don't you, Donna?"

I drank my wine as beads of sweat began to form on my forehead.

"Yes, of course I remember John. I'm sorry to hear he's getting divorced," Donna said, and then took a sip of wine. She looked toward me and spoke in a monotone voice. "Hope, maybe you should consider dating."

"You just let me know when you're ready, and I'll ring my nephew and give him your number," Carol said with a big grin on her face. I don't know why, but I suddenly had this urge to strangle her with her orange scarf.

Could this night get any more awkward? My mother-in-law was encouraging me to go out on a date. I guess we all knew this would be coming at some point. This conversation was like a pimple embedded deep in the skin's surface. Soon enough it would rise to the surface and rear its ugly white head—and tonight it had appeared.

* * *

Scott and I were alone on the court, hitting the ball back and forth. I was wearing my short white tennis skirt, no underwear. Every shot I hit was hard and fast. When it was my turn to serve, I threw the ball up and tried to slam it, but it went into the net. I tried again, and this time the ball landed in the court next to us. Scott came running over to me. "You're doing it all wrong. Let me show you," he said.

He got behind me and wrapped his arms around my body, while I held the racket in my hand. He placed his warm hands over mine, hugging them into the handle. "Hold it like this," he whispered in my ear with his sweet breath. I could feel every inch of his tight body, his strong muscles. He turned me around, his eyes blazing. The look on his face—the salacious ferocity—weakened me, made me feel faint. He enveloped me in his arms and kissed me with intensity. My body was raging with goosebumps.

Scott gently placed me on the clay court, lifted my skirt, and brought his head down underneath it, touching my naked flesh with his tongue.

"Oh, yes," I cried out with pleasure.

When he lifted his head from my skirt and looked into my eyes, I screamed out in shock, "Christopher!"

"Do you like it, Hope?" he asked.

"Yes!" I called out. I looked again, and this time I saw Scott. His deep blue eyes were glowing. "Scott!" I said.

"No, Hope. It's me, your husband, Christopher." It was Scott's face and Christopher's voice.

I woke up gasping for air and drenched in sweat. I checked the time on my cell phone—3:00 a.m. My mind was flooded with guilt.

The sex in my dream had felt real. It had felt good. I wanted it to continue, but with whom? I got out of bed. I needed some water.

When I got downstairs, I saw a light on in the kitchen and found Donna sitting at the marble counter, holding a cup of tea.

"Donna," I said, "what are you doing up so late?"

"I couldn't sleep. I should ask the same about you."

"I couldn't sleep either," I told her.

"Can I make you some tea?"

"No, thanks. I just need some water." I walked to the sink in the middle of the island, closest to where Donna was sitting. I noticed her eyes were red and blotchy. "Are you okay?" I asked.

She shook her head and put her hands over her eyes. "I just miss him so much. Not a second goes by when my heart doesn't ache for my son. I fake it every day. Every single day, I fake it."

Tears started to stream down my cheeks. "Me too, me too." I walked over to Donna and hugged her. Together, we sobbed, hugging and crying.

When she pulled away from me, she placed her hands on my shoulders. "Listen to me, Hope. Carol Johnson was right. You need to start dating again. You need to find someone to love again. I know you'll always love Christopher. That will never change, but you need to move forward. You can't be single forever. Go out there and find a man to love. I give you my blessing."

"I appreciate that. I really do. I'll date again, in time...when I'm ready."

"Well, then, we need tissues. Let's blow our noses and get back to bed." Donna opened the junk drawer and pulled out a small pack of tissues and handed me one. We blew our noses and giggled a little at how ridiculous we sounded.

"By the way, I really appreciate that you signed me up for the tennis clinic, but I'm just not sure I'm feeling motivated to continue playing right now."

Truthfully, I was embarrassed about what had happened with Scott and couldn't bear to go back there and face him and all the other stuck-up women at the club.

"Of course, dear. I totally understand. To be honest, ever since Christopher died, I have no patience for some of those people myself."

I was glad she had said that.

"And that Carol, she's a piece of work. Do yourself a favor and stay far away from her nephew John. He's a dirty creep and a notorious philanderer."

I was blessed to have Donna. Even though we were so different, she understood me.

12

SEPTEMBER ROLLED AROUND QUICKLY, and as soon as I got the kids settled in school, I signed up for a gym class. All the drinking and eating in Nantucket had rolled right into my midsection. Dating was somewhere in the back of my mind, but I wanted to get in shape and feel good about my body before I put myself out there.

Since tennis had left a bad taste in my mouth, I was determined to find a new exercise regime. A friend of mine told me about an intense fitness program called Jolly's Boot Camp, conveniently located by my local Starbucks. She warned me that the instructor could be intimidating, but it only added to the thrill of the workout. The class focused on cardio and core training. It sounded ideal—I could get an entire body workout in one hour, a few days a week.

After drinking a triple-shot Iced Venti Latte from Starbucks, I walked into class fired up on a caffeine buzz. Four women and two men were standing around the stale, sweat-infused gym, stretching while they waited for class to begin. They looked fit, dressed in their tight-fitting gym attire, but their appearance was in no way intimidating. I could take them on—or so I thought.

It was a minimalist gym with a large open floor in the center of the room. Medicine balls, kettle bells, and ropes were lined up neatly on three of the surrounding brick walls. How bad could it be? I was happy to see there wasn't any strange exercise machinery. I had never been a gym person, and the few times that I'd been to one, I could never figure out how to work any of the equipment properly.

I made my way toward the office at the back of the gym. Before I had a chance to knock on the door, a six-foot-three, cut-to-shreds Rambo lookalike walked out. He had a crew cut and bushy black eyebrows. This guy could have lifted me with his pinkie and spun me around the room.

"You new?" Rambo asked.

"Yes, sir." I had to throw the *sir* in. "I signed up online for the trial class."

"What's your name?"

"Hope Whitmore."

"Good to meet you," he said, reaching out his large hand to shake mine. "I'm Jolly. Are you ready to get into the best shape of your life and turn your flab into steel? Check in with me after class, and we'll discuss whether or not this class will suit your needs. Now, move your jiggly ass and get over there with the rest of the group."

I couldn't believe he had called my ass jiggly and my body flabby. *I'll show him,* I thought. *I'm ready, Jolly. Bring it on.*

"Okay, let's begin. Everyone find a space on the mat for stretching."

There were only six people in the class, so there was plenty of room. Jolly led us through a five-minute simple stretching routine. My body was tight, and I could barely touch my toes. When the pre-exercise routine ended, loud heavy metal music echoed throughout the gym. Within minutes, the intensity of the class grew exponentially. Jolly had us doing sit-ups, crunches, jumping jacks, burpees, and the worst—push-ups. I could barely handle three. My arms were shaking violently.

"Keep going, Whitmore. Don't give up. Giving up is a sign of weakness," Jolly screamed.

I glanced around the room. How the hell were the others doing so many push-ups? I could barely lift myself off the smelly black mat. My body was begging me to stop. Part of me wanted to keep going. The other part wanted to get the hell out of this damn class.

Jolly turned around to yell at Jacob, a tiny man wearing spandex shorts that accentuated his crotch. "Where's your Aspen?" was written on the buttocks of his shorts, which I assumed he had purchased in a souvenir shop in Aspen. I wanted to ask him about it, but I was too tired to speak. When nobody was looking, I collapsed my arms, turned my head to the side, placed it on the floor, and inhaled the fetid odor of smelly feet. I didn't care that my cheek was rubbing up against the dirty mat—I was so relieved to have a second to breathe.

"On your feet. Find a partner. We're doing the leap-frog exercise," Jolly commanded.

I looked around the room, frantically trying to find someone to pair up with me. A tall brunette with heart-shaped lips nodded when we made eye contact. All we had to do was alternate jumping over our partner while they were in a crouching position. I think the last time I had done something like this was in second grade.

We started off slow, but then we were told to increase our speed. The faster I went, the harder it was. The crouching movement was turning my legs into spaghetti. Just when I thought I couldn't do any more, Jolly told us to do another round. *NO!* I screamed in my head. The next thing I knew, I fell on top of my partner. My legs were straddling the back of her neck, and I was suffocating this poor woman with my vagina.

"Oh, no," I mumbled as I somehow managed to roll off her. "Are you okay?"

"Yes, I'm fine," she said in an annoyed voice.

I continued to apologize until Jolly called the next exercise. We swung kettle bells and then jumped rope. I was about to faint from exhaustion, praying the class was almost over. I looked at the clock, thankful there were only a few minutes left. We finished the class with sprints.

"Go, go, go! Faster, faster! You can do it! Whitmore, you're falling behind. Get back in the game."

I wondered why he was always picking on me. I had nothing left. I was empty, depleted of all the energy I could muster. I was fighting with myself to finish. When he called time, I collapsed on the gym mat like Jell-O, broken into pieces, drained.

"You okay, Whitmore?" Jolly asked quietly in my ear.

"I'm good. I'm good," I replied, forcing the words out.

"Then get off your ass and get up." He grabbed my hand and lifted me to my feet. "Class is over. Get yourself some water and come into my office."

I hobbled over to the fountain. Jacob was filling his water bottle when I got there.

"I know how you feel. The first class is the worst. I promise if you stick with it, it gets better. Jolly is the best. He's abrasive, but he's a great guy, and he'll get you in the best shape of your life."

"Thanks," I said. I appreciated his words of encouragement, but I was so dehydrated that I could only focus on getting water into my mouth. My lips were stuck together, my tongue was dried out, and my insides resembled the desert. I had no fluids left in me. I stood at the fountain sucking in as much water as I possibly could, until I could feel it sloshing around my insides. Then I walked languidly over to Jolly's office.

When I got to the door, he was sitting at his chair, feet up on the desk. Jolly was kind of sexy in a young Sylvester Stallone way. For a second, I had a flash of what sex would be like with him. If his dick was anything like the size of his bulging, muscular body, I imagined it would hurt, badly. Then again, maybe he would whip me around the room, tie me up with the exercise ropes, and show me how rough and soft he could be at the same time—it might be great.

"You did good out there, Whitmore," Jolly said, interrupting my perverted thoughts. "What did you think of the class?"

"It was hard, real hard, but I liked the hardness."

When he smirked, I realized how ridiculous that sounded.

"I mean, I liked the workout."

"Do you want to sign up? I offer a few different packages."

I took a quick glance at the form and chose the three-month unlimited package. I thanked Jolly and told him I would see him tomorrow. If, of course, I could move. He suggested I drink plenty of fluids and eat a lot of protein.

After class, I drove to a D'Angelo sub shop and ordered a large steak and cheese sub. I inhaled the sandwich and a bag of salt and vinegar chips, hoping the food would fill my belly and take away the throbbing, achy pain that was penetrating every muscle in my body.

After a few weeks, I was an addict, hitting Jolly's class five days a week. It was sixty minutes of hell, but hell was making me strong, stronger than I had ever been in my life. I would collapse in bed every night, falling into a deep sleep, hearing Jolly's voice playing in my ear, "Harder, Whitmore. You can do it, Whitmore. You're almost there, Whitmore."

Every class ended with sprints. Jacob, who attended as many classes as I did, was by far the fastest in the group, but I was determined to beat his tight little spandex ass. Finally, my glory day arrived. Playing the theme song to *Chariots of Fire* in my head, I ran like the wind, stepping over the white line one second before Jacob.

"Whitmore, you rock!" Jolly called out. He ran over and hugged me with his hard body. Even Jacob congratulated me on the way out. Feeling like a superstar, I left class, owing my new strength to Jolly.

He believed in me, and he made me believe in myself. Every night before bed, I imagined him clasping my hands over my head with the rubber exercise bands and placing me in titillating positions, awakening my sexual prowess and moving my body in ways that I never thought possible. But I was growing tired of the fantasy. I was ready for the real thing. If he wasn't going to ask me out, then I would have to ask him.

The following morning, I arrived thirty minutes before class. The lights were on, but there was no sign of Jolly. I walked across the gym toward his office. Strange noises were coming from behind the closed door. It sounded like moaning.

"Oh, yeah. That's it. Right there."

I froze. It was Jolly's voice. My heart sank.

"Jacob, baby. Yes! Yes! Yes!" he screamed.

Holy shit, I thought. Jolly was gay. I bolted out of the gym as fast as I could. I couldn't believe it. How had I missed the signs? I was such an idiot.

I called Marcy as soon as I got into the car and told her about Jolly. When she stopped laughing, she offered to take me to Sculpt Barre. I agreed to give it a try, thinking I could use a more feminine exercise, because instead of losing weight, boot camp was bulking me up, turning me into a not-so-sexy female Rambo. At least that's what I told myself, but deep down, I knew the real reason was Jolly. The sexual chemistry I thought we had was nothing more than a facade—something I had clearly made up in my head. And now that it was gone, my motivation had been killed.

* * *

Sculpt Barre was the antithesis of boot camp. Where boot camp smelled like dirty feet, barre class had a clean, inviting smell. The small studio had mirrors along one wall, a ballet barre along three walls, and a slight chemical scent of polyurethane coming from the shiny hardwood floors. A few women dressed in fashionable body-hugging workout attire, with their hair pulled back in headbands and brightly colored lipstick, were stretching in the middle of the room when Marcy and I walked in. Before finding a space on the floor, we made our way over to the shelves in the back and picked up four-pound weights, elastic bands, and small medicine balls. *What a joke.* Coming from boot camp, this already seemed lame.

I sat up against the wall next to Marcy and waited for class to begin. Within a few minutes, a woman came bouncing in the room, her high blonde ponytail swinging in sync with every step. A microphone headset was strapped onto her head and she sang out, "Okay, ladies, let's get started!"

One look at the instructor's face and I wanted the floor to swallow me up. I prayed for an earthquake, a tornado, or a fire—anything that would get me out of this class. Kelly—the PTA president, the woman I had told to fuck off in CVS, my sworn enemy—was teaching this class.

Tucking myself behind Marcy, I did my best to avoid eye contact with her. Kelly sashayed her perfect little body over to the stereo and turned on the music. The class started off with a few easy warm-up exercises that included leg, arm, and ab movements—and then it got progressively harder. She told us to do some pelvic thrusting, twist our bodies into unnatural pretzel shapes, and lift our legs and move our feet in small circular motions. Every woman in the room seemed to understand these strange movements—except me. I was so busy trying to hide behind Marcy and at the same time figure out what to do, that as soon as I had some idea of how to move my body, Kelly called out the next instruction. Meanwhile, my legs were shaking so violently I could barely hold a position for a few seconds.

Over and over, Kelly called out in her high-pitched cheerleader voice, "Tuck, squeeze, tuck, squeeze."

I thought boot camp was challenging, but this shit was taking exercise to a whole new level of difficulty. There was so much pelvic thrusting that I felt like I was training to be a stripper. What had happened to the simple days of "Let's Get Physical" in step class? Glancing at the clock every five minutes, I prayed this torture would end soon.

It got worse when we were asked to put one leg up on the barre and reach for our toes. *Is she fucking kidding me?* There was no way I could raise my leg that high. I looked around the room. Every woman had her leg resting up there as if it were no big deal. *You're better than this, Hope,* I told myself, forcing my stiff leg on top of the barre. Somehow, I managed to get it up, and then suddenly a pain stung the back of my leg, like an arrow had plunged through me. I started to lose my balance, and my leg vibrated uncontrollably, which in turn caused my own inner bodily earthquake.

That was the last thing I remembered. When I opened my eyes, I was lying on the floor, and all the women were gathered around me. They had looks of horror in their eyes.

"All good. I'm all good," I said, getting up slowly. The room was still spinning.

"You poor thing," Kelly said. "Are you sure you're okay?" she asked in a voice that sounded like she was talking to a toddler. I gave her a half smile, and then she whispered in my ear, "Honey, you may want to shave your armpits before the next class."

I bit my tongue in an effort to restrain myself from lashing out at her. I could barely concentrate during the last few minutes of class. As soon as it ended, I told Marcy I would meet her in the parking lot, and then I ran out of there, never to return.

* * *

After that horrific experience, I took some time off from exercise, until one afternoon, while I was standing in the checkout line at Whole Foods, I picked up a health magazine and skimmed an article about the miraculous benefits of yoga. Whenever I spoke to Tracy on the phone, she was always raving about her yoga class in Aspen and how it was the perfect complement to skiing and hiking.

A few days later, I signed up for a beginner class at a yoga studio, located in a strip mall not too far from my house. A powerful scent of patchouli floated through the room when I entered and was greeted by a woman named Blossom. She had long, light brown hair that reached her lower back, and she spoke in a soothing voice.

"Please remove your shoes before entering the studio, grab a mat from the back room, and then find a space on the floor," Blossom instructed.

The class began with Blossom asking us to close our eyes and repeat a few chants. Then she moved us through different poses. Lifting her arms high in the air, she proudly revealed her dark armpit hair, which resembled a ball of steel wool. Clearly, this woman had never met a razor. At least I didn't have to be self-conscious about my own stubble in this class.

"Open your heart center, my friends," Blossom said, as she talked us through different poses. "Feel your heart being lifted as you place your left foot on your right thigh."

I was beginning to feel like I was playing a game of Twister. Over and over, Blossom told us to "open our hearts," but as I struggled through the poses, I wondered if my heart had been shut for too long and if it would ever reopen. With a few minutes of class left, Blossom turned off the lights and asked us to lie down on our mats in Shavasana.

"Now close your eyes and relax every muscle in your body," Blossom said in a tranquilizing tone.

I listened intently, as she instructed us to mentally let go of our toes, our feet, our legs, our thighs; she talked us through every organ, continuing until she reached our heads. My body responded to her every command, growing heavier and heavier and heavier, as I sank farther and farther into the mat.

I felt a tap on my shoulder.

"Hope," someone whispered in my ear.

Slowly, I opened my eyes.

"Hope, it's time to get up." Blossom was leaning over me. "I have another class coming in soon."

I sat up and looked around the room. All the other students had left. Startled, I jumped up. "What time is it?"

"It's a few minutes before three. You fell asleep for about an hour." Blossom looked at me with a gentle kindness in her eyes. "You must have needed it."

"Shit. I'm so sorry. I need to get my kids from school."

A rush of heat warmed my face. I thanked Blossom, grabbed my shoes, and left.

* * *

On the drive to school, I noticed the bright and boldly colored leaves blowing off the trees, dancing through the air. The angle of the sun's rays highlighted the spectacular array of yellows, reds, and oranges as they piled onto the earth's surface. As the weather changed, the tiny seed of dread at the pit of my stomach began to rise, reminding me that winter was right around the corner—and so was the anniversary of the accident. I was ready to try a new type of exercise, one that took me outdoors and into the fresh air.

Christopher had been a runner. He ran all year long, even in inclement weather. A few weeks after passing out in yoga class, I bundled up, laced my new running shoes securely on my feet and stepped outside. A cold, wet, and angry wind blew in my direction. I could see the sun trying to peek through the overcast sky. Starting off slow, I placed one foot down and then the other. Every step forward was an effort at first. My heart rate steadily increased, and as I picked up the pace, my breath struggled for air. Despite the brisk chill, small beads of salty sweat burned my eyes.

Every exercise class I had tried over the past few months had been led by an instructor who taught and motivated us. Running was solitary. Running was about perseverance. It was up to me; going faster, slowing down, and deciding when to stop. Some type of gravitational force was pulling me forward, increasing my speed until it hurt. The physical pain was taking away the emotional pain that had been wedged inside me. I ran and I ran and I ran, mile after mile, until I couldn't run any more. When I stopped, I fell on the ground and looked up at the sky. The sun was breaking through the clouds, shining its golden ray of light on me. I finally understood why Christopher loved to run outdoors—it made him feel as free as a bird. For that one hour, I was able to run away from my wounded heart, and at the same time, running in nature connected me to my husband in a way that I had never experienced.

13

2010

RUNNING BECAME MY OBSESSION. I ran outside all winter, overcoming the harsh, biting extremities of the cold weather. I welcomed spring with open arms, dazzled by the blooming flowers, the lush grass, the shimmering sunlight, and the chirping birds. Everything was coming alive again following a long hibernation. I was itching to get out and do something, so when Marcy invited me to the Hamptons for a weekend with her friend from New York, I accepted. Other than running a few errands and taking the kids to and from school, I had nowhere to go. No job. No nothing. And the desire to pick up a paintbrush had died a long time ago. At least I could look forward to a weekend getaway. I had never been to the Hamptons before, and I figured it would be nice to get out of town and hang with single women for a change.

* * *

Soon after my parents arrived at the house to take care of the kids, I was ready to leave. Bobby gave me a big hug, but Megan was full of tears when I said goodbye to her. I promised I would call her often and that I would only be gone for a few days. All my guilt about leaving them melted away as soon as I stepped onto the Hampton Jitney from downtown Boston. The six-hour bus ride didn't bother me one bit. For the first time in years, I didn't have to listen to whining and fighting. It was just me, alone, heading to the beach for a good time.

Marcy and Erika picked me up from the bus station in a white BMW convertible. They looked like teenagers with their tanned skin and brightly colored beach cover-ups. Marcy jumped out of the car to greet me, and then helped me with my luggage before I hopped into the backseat.

"Finally," Marcy said, beaming. "My two favorite friends get to meet."

About twenty-five gold bracelets dangled from Erika's arm when she reached out to shake my hand.

"It's great to meet you, Hope," she said. Perfect, shiny golden strands highlighted her long, pin-straight hair. Sitting behind these two attractive, well-dressed women, wearing my baggy, ten-year-old shorts from the Gap, made me feel self-conscious about my appearance.

On the drive to the house, Erika filled me in on her life. She'd never been married, and although she dated a lot, she hadn't been able to find the right guy to settle down with. As editor-in-chief of a major fashion magazine, she worked with some of the most famous designers in the world. Erika's life was radically different from mine, and I found it fascinating.

We pulled up to the sleek and modern home, located at the end of a cul-de-sac on a wooded street. Erika gave me a tour of the house, while Marcy mixed vodka drinks.

The ranch-style house had a big, open floor plan with four comfortably sized bedrooms. I liked the black-and-white decor, although it reminded me of a bachelor pad. After Erika showed me to my room, I quickly threw on a bathing suit and went outside. By the time I got there, Marcy and Erika were sitting on lounge chairs next to the oval-shaped pool, drinking their cocktails. A forest of dogwood and pine trees surrounded the backyard.

"Let's make a toast," Marcy said, handing me a tall glass filled with lemonade and vodka. "To a fun girls' weekend."

"With lots of liquor, lots of laughs, a little weed, and if we're lucky, we'll all get laid too!" Erika added.

Smiling, I took a sip of the strong drink, thinking how much Erika reminded me of Tracy. We spent the next few hours talking, drinking, and giggling. When the sun went down, we went into the kitchen and nibbled on leftover prepared foods from Citarella, a local gourmet market.

After we cleaned up the kitchen, Marcy pulled out a joint. Lighting the end, she took a deep inhale before passing it to Erika.

"I've only been with two guys since my divorce," Marcy said, letting out a cloud of smoke. "I think it's time I find a third."

"Hell, yeah," Erika said, taking a drag and then passing it to me. "We're all going to find someone," she said, winking in my direction.

Whatever happened this weekend didn't really matter. I didn't come here to manhunt; I came here to let go and have fun—and so far, that's exactly what we had been doing. That evening, I slept better than I had in long time—of course, the weed and vodka helped, but I woke up late, hangover-free, to bright and radiant sunshine.

Erika suggested we drive into town to get breakfast. With the roof down on the convertible and our hair blowing back in the open breeze, we drove through the tree-lined neighborhood toward the village. Stopping at a cute take-out restaurant called Marty's Marvelous, we ordered large coffees and muffins and then wandered around, checking out the small boutiques that lined the streets. Pausing at a small furniture shop, I admired an interesting end table through the window.

"How cute is that bikini?" Erika asked, pointing to a bathing suit on display in the store next door.

"I love that," Marcy said. "Let's go try it on."

"I'll meet you guys in a few minutes. I want to look at something in this furniture store first," I told them.

Inside the gallery, unique pieces of wooden furniture were scattered around. Every item was made of various types of wood. There were coffee tables, end tables, dining tables, and chairs. Some were made with large slabs, some with thin slabs, some had a glossy finish, and some had a natural, refurbished look with distinct markings. The furniture was handcrafted by someone who took pride in their work, treating each piece like a distinct, one-of-a-kind work of art.

"Can I help you?" a man's voice asked as I ran my hand over the top of a table made from reclaimed antique wood.

I looked up, startled by the familiar voice. Standing before me was a man with a long ponytail.

"Oh, my God." My heart was racing wildly. "Richard!"

"Hope!" We embraced. "What are you doing here?"

"I'm here with some girlfriends." The lines on his forehead and around his eyes were more distinguished, and he was no longer wearing thick glasses. "What about you? Is this your store?"

"Yeah, I moved out here a few years ago."

"How did you end up here?"

"It's pretty random, actually," he said. I gave him questioning eyes, wanting to hear more. "I just needed a change. I tried living in New York City for a year, but city life was a little too claustrophobic for me. A friend of mine owns a large estate out here with an empty barn he doesn't use. He let me live there and convert the barn into a woodshop. I was making a living selling custom furniture until this space became available, and then a few months ago, I signed a lease and opened this store."

"Richard, that's amazing. I'm so happy for you."

"What about you? How is everything? Christopher? The kids?"

Taking a long, deep breath, I filled Richard in on my life. We hugged. We cried. We laughed. Nothing was more heartwarming than seeing a friend from my old life back in Aspen.

"Excuse me," a woman called out. "How much is this?"

"I'll be right there, ma'am," Richard said. Before he helped the customer, we exchanged phone numbers. I hugged him goodbye and left the store feeling lighter.

Erika and Marcy were standing outside, waiting for me. "Who was that cute guy you were talking to in there?" Marcy asked.

"An old friend from Aspen," I replied. "It's so weird running into him. I haven't seen him in years."

"You're blushing," Erika said, raising her eyebrows.

"No, it's not like that. He's just a good friend."

* * *

We spent the rest of the afternoon relaxing at the beach, heading back to the house early to get ready for our night out. Since we all wanted to drink, we called a cab to take us to the restaurant for dinner, which was about twenty minutes away. The cab driver was a sinewy man with thick white hair, who made friendly conversation with us throughout the drive.

"I just want to warn you that it might be difficult to get a cab home tonight. This is one of the busiest nights in the Hamptons," he warned us when we got out of the car. Anxious to get inside, we heard him, but didn't listen.

The expansive restaurant resembled the interior of a yacht with whitewashed walls, shiny mahogany wooden floors, and a series of French doors that opened to a spacious deck overlooking the harbor. We were seated at a table outside, where the fiery sun tucked into the horizon with strokes of pink and orange hues that dazzled the blue ocean. Right away, we ordered a bottle of rosé. The sky grew darker as we sipped our drinks, and the restaurant started to fill up with patrons.

"Do you think that guy over there is hot?" Erika asked, pointing to a man sitting at the end of the bar.

"If you like an older man with salt-and-pepper hair," I said. "But he's not my type at all." Finishing my glass of wine, I added, "And I think he just put his hand on his friend's inner thigh."

"Shit, really?" Erika shook her head. "Why are the best-looking guys gay?" Signaling to the waiter, she ordered another bottle of wine. "Wait a minute, check out that hottie who just walked in," she said.

A middle-aged guy with a massive nose and nostrils that pointed upward, wearing faded jeans and a white linen shirt, took a seat at the bar. Clearly, Erika and I didn't have the same taste in men, unless she was drunk or needed glasses—or was just really desperate.

Pulling a tube of berry-colored lip gloss from her Christian Dior handbag, Erika applied a heavy coat and then stood up. "I'll be back. I'm going over there to talk to him."

We watched her strut toward the bar in her short dress and high wedge sandals.

"She's hilarious," I told Marcy as the waiter opened a new bottle of rosé, pouring us each a generous amount.

"Let's play a game. It's called, *Who Would You Rather Fuck?* I'll name two celebrities, and you choose the one you'd rather sleep with." I grabbed a piece of bread off the table, smearing it with creamy butter, and ate it in two bites, while I waited for her to begin. "Okay," she said. "Jerry Seinfeld or Jim Carrey?"

I took a sip of wine, and said, "That's a hard one. I guess I'll say Jim Carrey."

"Rob Lowe or Brad Pitt?" Marcy asked.

"Rob Lowe, hands down. Your turn. Robert Downey Jr. or Johnny Depp?"

Without hesitating, she said, "Robert Downey."

When the waiter appeared, we ordered a sampling of appetizers to share and continued playing the game until the alcohol began clouding our ability to think of celebrities.

"Okay," she said, slurring. "Would you fuck that guy?" She pointed to a five-foot-six man with jet-black hair that was gelled back. He wore a paisley button-down shirt that revealed a chest full of hair. "Or the guy with the receding hairline sitting across from him?"

"Really? They're both awful," I told her, narrowing my eyes toward the men.

The server placed our food on the table, and we both dug in.

"You have to pick one," she said with a big grin, taking a bite of shrimp cocktail.

"I guess the guy with the greasy hair. He looks like he would be better in bed."

"Is that Erika over there making out with the silver-haired man at the bar?" Marcy asked, wide-eyed.

"I guess he wasn't gay after all," I said, and we both laughed.

"Hope?" she asked. "I'm wondering if a night of casual sex would be good for you. Maybe it would loosen you up and open you to meeting someone down the line."

"Maybe, but after mistakenly falling for Jolly, I'm not even sure how I could make that happen. Plus, I've never been good at flirting."

"It's not that hard, Hope. You just need a little practice."

I had never thought of flirting with guys as something I needed to practice. But then again, I didn't have much experience in the dating department. The thought of having to work so hard to meet someone was draining. I looked over at Erika, who was throwing her head back as she laughed at something a man said to her. Clearly, she had mastered the art of flirting.

Marcy and I polished off the second bottle of wine and cleaned our plates. Yawning, I suggested we pay the bill and call a cab.

Marcy agreed, but when she dialed the number, a recording said all signals were busy. She tried a few more times, but couldn't get through. We decided to head over to the bar for another drink before trying again.

"Hello there, beautiful ladies," the greasy-haired guy said to us. "Can I buy you a drink?"

"Sure," Marcy said. "I'll have a gimlet."

"And you?" he asked, turning toward me.

"I'll have the same, thanks."

While he ordered our drinks, I called three different cab companies, getting the same frustrating busy signal every time.

"I'm Tony," he said as he reached out to shake our hands. I noticed a thick skull ring on his finger. We introduced ourselves, and then I asked him if he knew any cab companies or a car service that could pick us up.

Cackling, he said, "Hon, you ain't getting a cab tonight. Next to July 4, it's one of the busiest nights of the summer."

I took a large gulp of my drink after he handed it to me, trying to alleviate my anxiety about getting out of here.

"Don't you want to thank me for the drink?" Tony asked, leaning close to me. His aftershave made me gag slightly, and his hot breath made my nose hairs curl.

"Thank you," I said, and then I flashed Marcy a desperate look that plainly communicated how desperately we needed to try to get out of here.

"Mar-ceey! Hop-e-y! Come meet my new friend Josh-ey," Erika slurred from across the bar. She was getting drunker by the minute, and I was beginning to lose my shit every time the busy signals stung my ear.

"Who's your hot friend?" Tony asked us. "She's got a nice set of tits."

Gross. This guy was creeping me out.

"Hey, baby," he said to Erika when she wobbled toward us.

"I just love your shark-tooth necklace," she said, pointing one of her dark lacquered fingernails at his chest.

"My girlfriend gave it to me when I got out of prison."

Marcy and I froze when he said the word *prison*.

"Check this out," he said, unscrewing the pointy end of the tooth from the clasp. "I store some of my candy in there. You ladies want a bump?"

"No, thanks," I called out before Erika could respond.

"What were you in prison for?" Marcy asked.

"I got busted for dealing cocaine."

I could've guessed that.

"But I'm all good now. I promised Ma that I'd get a respectable job working in my buddy's garage."

Someone turned up the volume of the music in the restaurant, and when I turned around, my eyes almost popped out of my head when I spotted Erika dancing on top of the bar, gyrating with another woman.

"Damn," Tony commented as we watched the performance.

Next thing we knew, the two women started to make out. Tony was gawking. "My cobra is getting hard," he said.

Marcy turned to me. "We need to get out of here before Erika hooks up with the entire bar."

"Where are you ladies headed? I can give you a ride," Tony offered.

After one last failed attempt to get through to the cab company, Marcy and I reluctantly agreed.

We pulled Erika off the bar and followed Tony to his red Mustang, which was parked in front of the restaurant.

"Uh-oh," Erika cried out before opening the car door. "I'm going to puke."

"Not in my car, you're not," Tony said.

Erika coughed a few times, and then she retched next to Tony's car. Green puke splashed onto the car door.

"What the fuck?" Tony screamed angrily. He jumped into his car, revved up the engine, and sped off, leaving us in the dust.

"I feel so much better," Erika said, wiping her mouth with the back of her hand.

"Now what are we going to do?" Marcy asked, walking over to a big rock. She sat on the edge and buried her face in her hands. "Does anyone know someone we could call?"

Suddenly, it dawned on me—Richard lived nearby. Scrolling through my contacts, I dialed his number. He answered after the first ring. When I told him we were stranded, he said not to worry. He'd be there shortly.

"We're getting rescued!" I sang out, giving Marcy and Erika high fives.

A few minutes later, Richard pulled up in his pickup truck. I hugged him after I climbed into the cab. We shared the details of our wild night on the drive home. As soon as we pulled into the driveway, Erika ran to puke again. Marcy thanked Richard, and then she followed behind Erika to help her.

I gazed into Richard's iridescent green eyes. "I can't thank you enough. You saved us tonight."

"Of course, Hope. I'm happy I could help an old friend."

My hand rested on the door handle. I was about to pull it, but then the words tumbled out of my mouth before I could stop them. "Do you want to come in?"

His lips turned upward, and he said, "Yes."

We got out of the car, made our way into the house and into my bedroom. I was finally ready.

14

I WOKE UP, NAKED, LYING next to Richard. While he slept peacefully, I watched the rhythmic movement of his chest rise and fall. My mind was spinning with mixed emotions. I had enjoyed the sex. It felt good to be physical with another man. The same gentle hands that Richard used to create masterful pieces of furniture had caressed every inch of my body, satisfying a much-needed desire. I loved Richard, but not the way that I loved my husband. My heart wasn't ready for that kind of love. Richard was a friend—a good friend—and that's all he could be to me.

His eyes opened, and he caught me staring at him. "Good morning."

"Good morning," I said, giving him a weak smile.

"Are you okay?"

"I don't know. I feel kind of weird about last night."

"Hope, don't overthink it. We had fun."

"It was fun, but I guess I'm feeling a little guilty."

He brushed my hair back with his long fingers. "You have nothing to feel guilty about."

"What's going to happen now?" I asked.

"I don't know. Maybe we'll meet up again someday, but for now, you're going home to your kids, and I'm going to remain here in East Hampton."

Sighing, I said, "But other than my children, I have nothing, and one day soon, they're going to grow up and leave me. In the meantime, I have no husband, no career, and I feel like I'm drowning in my boring suburban town."

"I can't help you with the husband part, but what happened to the Hope I once knew, who loved to paint, loved the mountains, and dreamed about becoming a successful artist?"

I turned my head away from him. "She's lost."

"Well, find her. Dig deep and find her. Nobody is forcing you to stay in Massachusetts. Get out, like I did. Change is always hard, but the hardest things in life sometimes become our greatest achievements. Move back to Aspen, and find your paintbrush."

He was right. I was the only one responsible for my life now, and if I wanted things to be different, then it was up to me to make it happen. After we got dressed, he lifted my chin, looked into my eyes, and said, "Life is short, Hope. Do what makes you happy."

For too long, I had been stuck, submerged in a quicksand of grief. Somewhere along the way, I had forgotten who I was and what I had once wanted out of life. A long time ago, I wanted to be an artist. I wanted to live in Aspen. I wanted Christopher back, too, but that wasn't part of the equation. Seeing Richard was a wake-up call. There was a light out there. It might be lurking far away at the end of a deep tunnel, but it was there. I was sure of it. I just had to figure out a way to find it.

Even though we promised to stay in touch, I wasn't sure if I would ever see him again. I left the Hamptons a different woman. Erika, Marcy, and of course, Richard, helped me recharge my batteries, and guided me onto a new trajectory.

* * *

During the bus ride back to Boston, I called Tracy. "Do you have a sec?" I asked when she picked up the phone.

"Yeah, what's up?"

"I had the craziest weekend, which I'll tell you about later. But first I need you to do something for me."

"I'm yours. What can I do?"

"Find me a place to live. I'm moving back to Aspen."

She screamed so loud I thought she was going to pop my eardrum.

Telling Tracy was the easy part. Next I would have to break the news to the kids, but since they were fast asleep when I got home, it would have to wait until the morning. Bobby would be going into first grade, and Megan would be going into fourth grade. I realized that uprooting them wouldn't be easy, but they were still young enough to start over—and this was something I needed to do.

My parents' response was nothing like Tracy's.

"Oh, my stars, Hope," my mom cried out. "Moving to Aspen seems like a ridiculous idea."

I should have expected that from my mother. I looked at my dad, praying he would say something more encouraging. "Honey, I understand your desire to leave Concord, but don't you think you're making a rash decision?" he asked.

Their reactions felt like they were lighting a match under my belly, starting a fire that was working its way up through my body. I gave them a stern expression and said, "I've already made my decision. I'm calling a realtor tomorrow and putting the house on the market."

My mother was shaking her head. "Running away is not going to solve your problems," she said.

"Running away? From my problems?" My voice had a wicked undertone. "How the hell could you understand? Do you know what it's like to drive down Main Street every fucking day? Do you know what it's like to have to relive the accident all the time? I'm suffocating here. I'm suffocating in this life. I can't do it anymore."

"I'm sorry," she said in a soft voice. Her eyes filled with tears. "Your dad and I just want to help you, but Aspen seems so far away."

"Then support me. Please. Support me."

She looked down. "Okay, honey."

"We support you, Hope," my father said.

They said what I wanted to hear, but they didn't mean it. And I didn't care. Nothing they could have said was going to change my mind.

The following morning, when the kids woke up, I took them out to Dunkin' Donuts for a special treat. When we were settled in a booth, eating our doughnuts, I told them I had something important that I needed to discuss with them.

Bobby chimed in, "Are we going to get a puppy?"

"No, sweetheart."

He lowered his head and pouted.

"Well, maybe someday, but not right now." I wiped my sticky hands with a napkin. "I've made a decision that I think is going to be great for all of us." Raising my voice in excitement, I said, "We're going to move to Aspen."

Megan put her half-eaten, pink frosted doughnut on the table. "You mean like forever?"

"Well, honey, nothing is forever, but let's try to think of this as an adventure. You guys will go to a new school and make lots of new friends."

Her eyes were filling up with tears. "But I don't want to make new friends. All my friends live here."

"Will we be able to go skiing every day?" Bobby asked.

"Not every day, but certainly every weekend during the ski season."

Bobby's face lit up, while Megan's mouth curved downward. I rambled on about how much fun it would be living there, desperately trying to convince Megan that our life would be much better, but she tuned me out. At that point, all I could do was pray that she would come around.

* * *

I spent the next few weeks getting the house ready for potential buyers. My real estate agent already had a family who might be interested. Since our house was in one of the better elementary school districts, she promised it would sell quickly. She was right. Two days after we listed it, a bidding war ensued, and the house sold for over the asking price.

My in-laws took the news about our moving better than my parents. Donna brought Winnie over to the house every day for a week, and the two of them helped me pack. One afternoon, while Winnie was boxing up the kitchen, Donna and I stood in the dining room, pulling my fine china from the cabinet and carefully wrapping each piece before placing it in boxes.

"I remember when you and Christopher registered for these plates at Tiffany's," she said as she cut a large piece of bubble wrap.

"Me too." I smiled at the memory. "He was more into picking this stuff out than I was."

"It was cute," she said. "Especially coming from someone who hated shopping." Donna's bottom lip trembled slightly. "Truth is, it wasn't really about the dishes. He was just excited about starting his life with you."

Tears burned my eyes. "Thank you."

"Hope, as sad as I am that you and the kids are leaving, I understand. I know that Aspen has a special place in your heart, and it's where you and Christopher fell in love. My only wish is for you and the children to be happy."

I wanted to tell her how much I appreciated what she was saying, but I was afraid if I let the words come out, the lump in my throat would rise too, and I didn't want to cry. Instead, I placed the platter on the dining room table, and gave her a warm embrace.

* * *

By the end of July, we were packed and ready to leave. I rented a U-Haul, and had it hitched to the back of my Chevrolet Tahoe. My plan was to drive with the kids to Ohio and drop them off at my parents' house. From there, I would make the trek all the way to Aspen, like a pioneer on a westward journey. I wanted to get settled before my parents brought the kids to Aspen, so I could give them a sense of stability to help with the transition.

After throwing the last box into the car, I told the kids to run back into the house to use the bathroom. While I waited outside, I took one last look at the home I had shared with my husband, the home where we had started our family, the home where I had lived when my life fell apart. In my heart, I knew I was doing the right thing. There were too many memories in Concord, and unfortunately, the painful ones outweighed the good ones.

"Hope!" Marcy was screaming as she ran down the street.

"Marcy, I wasn't going to leave without hugging you goodbye," I told her when she met up with me on the driveway.

Frowning, she said, "I promise I won't lose it right now."

"Let's not make this any harder. We can still talk every day, and think of it this way: You just scored a free vacation home in Aspen. My home is your home."

"Thank you, but I'm still going to miss you so much."

I reached out to hug her. "I'm going to miss you, too." Holding my best friend securely made my heart sing a sweet lullaby.

"Oh, I almost forgot." She dug her hand inside her pocket and then pulled out a white jewelry box. "Here, I got you a small going-away present." She smirked mischievously when she handed it to me.

"Marcy, you didn't have to get me anything."

"Just open it. It's a funny gift."

Inside the box was a bag of marijuana, a pipe, a lighter, and twenty-five pills of Xanax and Valium.

"Are you kidding me?" I asked, laughing. "Why do you have all these pills?"

"I stole them from my grandmother's medicine cabinet before she went into a nursing home. Think of this as your emergency kit—to be used in times of desperation."

"Mommy, are we going now?" Bobby asked, running toward the car. Megan trailed behind him. She was staring at the ground and her gait was slow. I quickly threw the box into the glove compartment before the kids could see it.

"Yep, this is it. We're off. Give Marcy a hug goodbye, and then hop into the car."

As soon as the kids were settled in their seats, I gave Marcy one last embrace. "Seriously, Hope, how the hell are you going to drive with that big U-Haul attached?" Marcy asked when I got into the driver's seat.

"Just watch the expert," I said boastfully as I turned the car on.

She stood there, hiding her sad face behind an awkward smile, while I backed out of the driveway.

Once I was on the road, there was a part of me that wanted to look back at Marcy—and at my house—but it hurt too much. I could only look forward.

15

THE FIRST FEW HOURS OF the ten-hour ride to Ohio were seamless. I hadn't heard a peep from the kids. They were binge-watching movies in the backseat while they munched on the healthy snacks that I had packed—sliced apples, carrots, grapes, and cheese sticks.

"It's over," Bobby called out.

I handed the box of movies over the backseat. Megan grabbed it from my hand.

"It's my turn to choose the next movie," she said, flipping through the DVDs.

"No, I don't want to watch Cinderella," Bobby whined, as he glanced at the picture on the cover of *Cinderella*, showing the princess dressed in a poufy blue ball gown.

"Too bad. It's my choice," Megan said, putting the movie into the disk player. As soon as it started, the kids were quiet again for a little while.

"Mommy, guess what?" Bobby asked in a loud voice.

"What, honey?"

"My friend Carson's mommy is getting married soon. He's getting a new daddy. Can we get a new daddy too?" His voice squealed with excitement.

I wasn't sure how to respond. Getting remarried wasn't something I had ever discussed with the kids. And since I wasn't even dating, I never imagined it was something they had thought about.

"You're so dumb, Bobby. What do you think Mom's going to do, buy a dad from Target?" Megan asked in a snotty tone.

"Megan," I reprimanded. "You're not being nice."

"So-rr-y," she said. "But just so you know, Bobby, Carson is getting a *step*father."

"You mean like Cinderella?" he asked. "Her stepmom wasn't nice."

I had to intervene before this conversation took a turn for the worse. "For now, neither of you need to worry about something like that, and even if I do meet someone, I would only be with him if you both like him." To change the subject, I pulled out my emergency treats and asked, "Here, do you guys want these?"

"Yay! Gummy bears," Bobby cheered.

"I hate gummy bears," Megan complained.

I couldn't win with her. Taking a deep breath, I tried one more time with lollipops. It worked. They both shoved the candy into their mouths like pacifiers.

The kids were exhausted by the time we arrived at my parents' house in the late evening. My mom answered the door wearing her pink terry cloth robe and the same white satin slippers she had owned since I was a little girl.

"Oh, my. I can't believe you kids are here already. I wasn't expecting you for at least another hour. How was the drive?" she asked, leaning in to hug Bobby and Megan. "Are you hungry? I made a tuna casserole and some deviled eggs."

Of course she made deviled eggs.

After they both nodded, she said, "Grandpa fell asleep on his recliner in the den. Why don't you go in there and wake him up with a kiss while I get the food ready?"

When the kids ran into the other room, my mother gave me a concerned look. "Honey, you look so tired. What time are you planning to leave tomorrow morning?"

"Early. Probably around 6:00 a.m."

Tilting her head, she said, "Why don't you stay for a few days, or at least sleep in tomorrow before getting into your car?"

"I'll be fine," I told her.

"Are you sure, dear?"

"How many times do I have to tell you? I'm fine."

"Alrighty, then. I packed you an assortment of deviled eggs for the road. I made a special batch with spinach and Spam that are going to just tickle your taste buds."

Hearing the word *Spam* made my insides shudder. *Gross.*

"I'll leave you a note, so you don't forget to grab them from the refrigerator in the morning."

I rolled my eyes and walked into the den to greet my father.

The kids were sitting on his lap. Megan had one arm around my father's neck, snarling at Bobby while he was talking.

"My mommy said if we get a new stepfather he won't be like the mean stepmom from Cinderella," Bobby was saying.

Hearing this made my heart sink. I needed to have a talk with Bobby, but I wasn't sure what to say. Was he craving a stepfather because he wanted someone to come along and save our family? Maybe once we were settled in Aspen, I could find an older guy to babysit him and take him to the park to play sports. Aspen was filled with ski instructors and servers looking for odd jobs to supplement their income.

"Bobby, you're so stupid," Megan said.

I rushed toward Megan to distract her from starting another fight.

"Okay, you two, why don't you go check on Grandma and see if the food is ready?"

They hopped off my father's lap and scurried toward the kitchen.

"Hey, Dad," I said as I leaned over his chair to kiss him. I noticed he had a more pronounced double chin. He must have put on some weight since the last time I had seen him. I wished he would start exercising and take better care of his body.

"My baby girl, it's so good to see you."

Even as an adult, I would always be his little girl. Sadly, my kids would never again hear such loving sentiments from their father.

My father got up from the chair, and we headed into the kitchen. After stuffing our bellies with my mom's comfort food, the kids and I said goodnight to my parents and went upstairs. I had promised them we could cuddle in bed for a little while, but Bobby passed out as soon as his head hit the pillow.

"Mommy, can I ask you something?" Megan whispered.

"Sure, sweetheart."

"Are you going to get remarried?"

"Oh, sweetie," I said, stroking her back while she rested her head on my chest. "I don't know. It's possible...I suppose. Maybe one day I'll meet someone and decide to get married again. But I can assure you, nobody will ever replace your father. You and Bobby will always come first in my life."

"I don't want you to leave us tomorrow." The angry little bee, who had been stinging me for weeks, had been replaced with a voice filled with honey. "Can't I go with you?"

"I would love to take you, but I have a long, boring car ride ahead of me. You'll have more fun hanging out with your grandparents than driving with me for two days. The time will go by quickly, and before you know it, you'll be on a plane to Aspen."

Megan inched her body closer to mine. "I'm going to miss you, Mommy."

"I'm going to miss you too. You can call me every day until I see you. Now, try to get some sleep."

Wrapping my arms around her, I held on until she drifted off. As if losing their father wasn't hard enough, I was beginning to feel guilty about my decision to uproot the kids from the only life they had ever known—but it was too late to go back.

The following morning, I got on the road bright and early, stopping at Starbucks for a Venti Frappuccino before hitting the highway. From a distance, the glinting sun grew larger, peeking its bright head over the horizon. The forecast was calling for an oppressive heat wave to hit the Midwest, but the cool breeze of the air conditioner blowing on my face would keep my body well-regulated. I had a twenty-hour drive ahead of me, and I was determined to make it more than halfway before nightfall. I was not thrilled about spending the night at a cheap roadside motel, but it would break up the trip, and with a couple of hours of sleep, I would have enough energy for the rest of the drive to Aspen.

Driving along the endless highway was monotonous. Listening to the radio helped take my mind off my boredom and kept me from thinking too much. I was afraid my thoughts would make me second-guess my decision. Farther along, the skies had darkened, preparing to cool down the sweltering atmosphere. A pitter-patter of rain fell onto my windshield, but the rain only lasted about an hour, eventually giving way to a hint of sunshine breaking through the clouds. I opened the windows, welcoming the fresh air that blew through the car and ravaged my hair like an undomesticated animal.

The hours flew by as I drove, occasionally stopping for gas and snacks. Thirty miles outside of Iowa, I was considering pushing on to Nebraska when I noticed the tire warning light was on. Pulling off the highway, I drove into a parking lot in front of a convenience store and got out of the car to check the tires. *Shit.* The back tire on the driver's side was flat. I called roadside assistance and was told that someone would arrive within fifteen minutes.

In the meantime, I called my mom's cell phone to check on the kids.

"Hi, honey. How's it going?" my mom asked when she answered the phone.

Not wanting to worry her, I didn't mention the flat tire. "It's going well. I'm making great time. What are you guys up to?"

"Oh, everything is just wonderful." Loud giggles and screeching voices reverberated through the phone. "We're at Funtime Amusement Center right now."

"Do the kids want to talk?"

"I'm sure they do, but they're running around in the dodgeball cage."

"All right, please give them kisses for me." It was too difficult to hear her over the background noise. "I'll call back later."

"Okay. Bye, honey."

A few minutes later, roadside assistance arrived. A heavyset man with a handlebar mustache and long sideburns jumped out of his tow truck.

"Hello, ma'am. Is this your vehicle?"

My eyes darted in the direction of his hairy belly, which was popping out over his jeans.

"Wow, you arrived fast."

"You got a flat?" he asked, glancing at the tire.

"Yep. Will it take long to fix?"

"No, ma'am. I should have it fixed in a jiffy, but I'll need to unlatch the U-Haul in order to change the tire. It ain't a big deal, though."

"Can I get you anything to eat or drink?" I asked, before turning to enter the convenience store.

"No, thanks. This is my last stop of the day. After I leave you, I'm picking up my lady and taking her out for some smoked pork loin. I'm actually running a bit late, and my lady don't like when I'm late, so I'm just gonna get right to it."

Since I was already on a bad eating binge, I grabbed a pack of Skittles, a bag of Doritos, and a Red Bull for an added burst of energy to get me through the next few hours of the trip. After paying, I ran into the bathroom and almost did a double take when I checked my appearance in the mirror. My hair was a wild, greasy mess; my skin looked pasty; and my eyes were bloodshot. I washed my hands with the pink liquid soap from the dispenser, which might as well have been dish detergent, and splashed some cold water on my face. The sink water got into my hair, making it look extra oily, further adding to my sickly complexion. It was a good thing I didn't know anyone in Iowa.

"You're all set, ma'am," the mechanic called out as I walked back to my car.

"I'm impressed. You really did change the tire in record timing."

He handed me a clipboard and pointed to where I needed to sign. I scribbled my name, thanked him, and jumped into the car, elated to be back on the road.

While I drove, I opened the Red Bull and guzzled the entire cough-medicine-tasting beverage while munching on chips. The caffeine went straight into my bloodstream, pumping my heart so fast, I thought it was going to pop out of my chest.

Singing along with the radio, I continued on the highway, relieved that the tire incident had taken less than an hour. At the rate I was going, I would definitely make it to Nebraska in no time. Turning up the music, I tapped on the steering wheel to the beat and bounced my head, enjoying the ride and the excitement of getting closer to my destination.

Suddenly, as if struck by lightning, the piercing sound of sirens went off, breaking my euphoric state. Behind me, flashing red and blue lights approached as a police car made its way toward me.

What the hell did I do? I didn't think I was speeding.

Pulling off to the side of the road, I waited for the officer to get out of his car. The sight of the giant man with his dark five-o'clock shadow, dressed in his navy blue uniform, was making the Skittles rise from my belly.

"Hello, Officer," I said in a timid voice. "Was I speeding?"

"No," he said in a stern, business-like tone. "Your brake light isn't working on your U-Haul. I need to see your license and registration." He looked at me with squinted, beady brown eyes.

"I'm so sorry, Officer. I just had a flat tire changed. Maybe the mechanic forgot to plug in a wire when he reconnected the trailer."

"I still need to see your license, registration, and insurance. You're endangering the other vehicles on the road."

I wanted to tell him that he didn't need to be such an asshole, but, of course, I kept my mouth shut. I reached over to the passenger side and pulled the latch on the glove compartment. As soon as it opened, the jewelry box that Marcy had given me fell out, spilling the contents—the joints and pills—all over the seat. I froze. My body started to tremble. I turned to face the cop.

His forehead was crinkled.

In a shaky voice, I said, "That's not mine."

"Yeah, lady. I've heard that one before. You sure as hell look like you've been enjoying those. Now get out of the car."

I reached over to unbuckle my seatbelt, but my hands were shaking violently. Finally, it released, and I slowly stepped out of the car, holding onto the door for extra support. I was afraid if I let go I would tumble to the ground.

"Now why don't you make my life easier and tell me where you're hiding the rest of the drugs in that great big U-Haul of yours?"

My breathing was erratic, and my bottom lip was quivering. Bursting into uncontrollable sobs, I pleaded with him. "Please,

Officer. I swear, I don't have anything in there. Please believe me. I'm telling the truth."

"I guess you just don't want to cooperate. You'd rather do this the hard way. All right—now, let's go."

I couldn't feel myself move. My legs were heavy, like tree stumps rooted in the ground. The earth was spinning before me. The officer told me he needed to perform a sobriety test. First, he commanded that I walk in a straight line. Then I lifted my hands over my head and touched my nose with my index finger. Despite my feeble and weakened limbs, I performed the test with perfection. He then took a small flashlight and looked into my reddened eyes. I bit my tongue to keep myself from screaming in his face that the only drug I had in me was caffeine—*you schmuck!*

"Sir, I swear I'm not part of any drug-smuggling operation, and someone gave me that box."

"I'm not interested in your excuses."

He placed my hands behind my back and handcuffed me. Then he walked me to his car. The lights on the roof were still flashing, and when he opened the back door, I could hear voices coming from the radio dispatch. Bending my lumbering body, I took a seat behind the driver's side. Tears were plunging down my face. He called in to the station, saying something about a drug dealer crossing state lines. Hearing the words *drug dealer* made me want to hurl all over the leather seats. The handcuffs were pinching me from behind, while I was screaming in my head, *Please save me, Christopher. Please, help me. Please, please, please...*

16

THE OFFICER DROVE ME DIRECTLY to the police station. No words were exchanged between us. I wanted to argue with him that I wasn't a drug smuggler, but I knew my words would be futile. This guy was convinced that I was involved in an organized crime ring. My hands started to tingle behind my back, and the indentation from the handcuffs was causing my wrists to go numb. I kept telling myself that this was a big misunderstanding and that everything would work out, but my body wasn't responding to my words. The churning inside me was moving through each individual cell like a tornado.

Upon arriving at the station, the cop escorted me to another police officer, who had a shiny bald noggin and was wearing clear, round eyeglasses. He performed the same sobriety test as the arresting officer had given me, and once again, I passed. Next, he asked me to take a seat in front of his desk.

"I need to ask you a series of routine questions," he said.

I nodded my head, unable to speak as the tears continued to plunge down my cheeks.

"Why don't you take a deep breath and relax before we begin?"

I made a feeble attempt to inhale and exhale, and then stared at his short, stubby fingers, while they pounded the computer keyboard as he recorded my responses. He took down my name, birthday, and social security number. With each answer, I was becoming a little less frazzled, until he asked, "Marital status?" This question forced the dam to collapse again, and I sobbed hysterically.

"M-m-m-my husband died. I'm a widow," I told him in a barely audible whisper.

After he completed his questioning, he said, "You're free to make a call."

A phone call? Who the fuck was I going to call? The only person I wanted to call was Christopher. He would know how to get me out of this mess. He would help me stay calm, tell me what to do—if only the dead could talk.

When the officer noticed the pools of water filling up my eyes, he picked up a card on the desk, handed it to me, and said in a placating tone, "Here, try this guy. He'll be able to help."

I took the card in my shaky hand, studying the black and white image of a jail cell. On the back was information for a bail bondsman. I dialed the number. After a few rings, a man with a raspy voice answered. The words spilled out as I explained my situation. He apologized and said he couldn't get there until the morning.

"That's not going to work!" I screamed into the phone.

"There's nothing I can do for you right now," he replied.

When I hung up, the officer took my belongings and escorted me down a white brick hallway toward the holding cell. The only sounds I could hear, along with the loud thumping in my chest, were my sneakers squeaking against the cement floor. A vile odor penetrated my nose when he opened the door, and I couldn't take my eyes off the woman with straggly hair slumped in the corner. Her head was cocked to one side, her eyes were glazed over, and a stream of drool dripped from the corner of her mouth.

"Is she okay?" I asked.

"She's strung out on drugs, but don't worry, she's harmless."

The officer left me there, and I curled my body in the corner opposite the woman, unable to move. I tried not to stare at the drug addict, instead focusing my attention on the large, black cockroach crawling around on the concrete slab below me. If hell existed, I was in it. The car accident was the worst moment of my life, but this nightmare was coming in at a close second. If only I had the Xanax now, anything to numb the fear that was swallowing me whole. I squeezed my eyelids shut, and tears slipped down my cheeks, until finally, a dark, heavy sleep fell over me.

When I awoke, a sharp pain rippled through the side of my neck from sleeping for hours with my head in a lopsided position. I glanced at the woman in the corner of the cell. Black makeup was smudged down her ghostly complexion. Her worn-out skin read like a sad story, one that carried more demons than I would ever understand. She looked like a stray cat in desperate need of human affection.

Somehow, sleeping had helped quiet my erratic mind, and it was in the stillness that I could hear something I had never paid attention to before. I heard love from a distance. It was channeled through my heart, flowing into me from my children. And it was flowing into me from Christopher, too. If I listened closely, I could hear him signaling to me that everything was going to be okay.

Moments later, the door to my cell opened.

"Mrs. Whitmore, you're free to go," a lanky female officer with a pixie haircut said to me. "We didn't find anything in your U-Haul, and they're not charging you with possession of weed."

She walked me to the front of the station, handed me my belongings, and told me that my car was parked in the rear. With my head down, I bolted out of there. If my car could talk, it would've been crying too. When I opened the back of the U-Haul, I seethed. Those fuckers had ripped my boxes apart. All my material possessions that I had accumulated from my marriage were ransacked, pillaged by barbarians. When I sat back in the driver's seat, I barely had any fuel left in me. I was completely drained, sucked dry. Yet, my eyes were wired, and although my body craved sleep, I had to get away from there as fast as I could.

The crescent moon hovered in the blackened sky overhead, and a few stars glimmered above. I kept my eyes focused on the dimly lit highway of Interstate 80, and within minutes I spotted the welcome sign for Nebraska...the good life. Somehow, I got a second wind and drove through the night, stopping only once for gas. Just as the sun's orange glow began to emerge from beyond the horizon and the smallest bit of light took away the darkness, I sped past the cheery sign that invited me into colorful Colorado. I knew more than ever that I would never look back.

* * *

As soon as I caught sight of Mount Sopris, one of the largest peaks in Colorado, my pulse quickened, signaling that I was close to my new home. Although I was functioning on no sleep, and my body felt like it had just come back from war, the sight of the astounding beauty breathed new life into me, dissolving the stress and tension that hours ago had torn through me like an exploding bomb. Brilliant sunlight reflected off the apex of the mountain ranges, kissing the heavenly sky.

I was beaming inside because I had finally fulfilled my promise to one day return to Aspen. Driving through town, I admired the Victorian architecture on the way to Tracy's townhouse, located three blocks from Aspen Mountain. I parked my car along the street and then walked up the wide stone steps to a sleek front door made of stainless steel and glass. Her successful realtor career was booming, affording her an overpriced, luxurious townhome. This was a far cry from the dated seventies-style residence we had once shared together. I rang the bell, and a moment later she answered the door, looking fashionable in jeans, a white tank top, and a long funky necklace with a small ivory horn dangling from the chain.

"You look like shit," she said, giving me the once-over. We gave each other a long hug. "But I'm happy to see you, even though you also smell like you rolled in a pile of shit. What the fuck happened to you?"

I followed her into the house. "Let's just say, I survived a trip from hell, but now that I'm here, it's all good."

"I'm sure the Aspen sun, fresh mountain air, and a hot shower will fix you right up."

I glanced around her home, taking in the high ceilings and well-appointed living room decorated in cool earth tones, which opened to an ultra-contemporary kitchen that she probably never used other than for eating take-out food.

"This place is amazing."

"Thank you. Now, why don't you fill me in on your adventure?"

I took a seat on the black leather barstool at the kitchen counter and told her my story, while she poured us each a glass of wine.

When I finished spewing all the details, she said, "That's insane!"

I covered my mouth to hide a wide yawn. The wine had pushed my exhaustion over the edge.

"Why don't you take a shower and then get into bed? I'll show you the house tomorrow morning."

I thanked her, and then, using the last of my energy, made my way into the guest room. Following a much-needed shower, I called my mom to check on the kids, and then I crawled into bed and slept for twelve straight hours.

I woke up feeling like a new person, fresh and reenergized. After I got dressed, Tracy and I walked over to Poppycock's for breakfast. The hostess sat us at a table outside. Right away, we ordered coffee and their famous oatmeal pancakes.

"See that woman over there?" Tracy said, pointing to a woman with frosted blonde hair walking into a store across the street. Her face looked like it suffered from too much plastic surgery and an overdose of Botox. "She's an heiress to a Texas oil company, and I just sold her a twenty-five million-dollar house on Red Mountain."

"Holy shit. That's incredible. You're killing it in this town." I took a sip of my coffee. "I'm so proud of you."

The server placed our pancakes in front of us. "Thank you, but enough about me. You never told me what happened when you saw Richard."

"Oh yeah," I said, grinning as I picked up the syrup and poured it all over my pancakes.

After I explained the sequence of events from my trip to the Hamptons, and of course, sharing the details about sleeping with Richard, she said, in a loud voice, "Finally, Hope! I was afraid your pussy was going to wilt away after Christopher died."

I could always count on her for caring about my sex life.

"Next order of business," she said, "is Megan still bumming about the move?"

"Well, let's just say my ten-year-old girl has been acting like she's been on the rag for a month, even though she's not even close to getting her period. So, yeah, I'd say she's still bumming."

"Aspen is a welcoming community. I'm sure she'll adjust as soon as school starts."

I signaled to the server to bring our check.

"And what about you?" she asked.

I gave her a questioning look.

"Are you going to start painting again?"

I shrugged my shoulders. "I will...one of these days. But my first priority is getting the kids settled." I handed my credit card to the server, and when Tracy reached for her wallet, I said, "Don't even think about it. Breakfast is on me. It's the least I can do." Finishing the last sip of my coffee, I added, "If it wasn't for you, there's no way I'd be able to survive this move."

* * *

After we left the restaurant, we walked back to Tracy's house, climbed into her silver Mercedes SUV, and drove to see the house that she was convinced I would love. I wasn't sure what to think when we pulled up the steep driveway to a small house perched on a hill. It was more expensive than my house in Concord, yet it was half the size. The structure of the home had an odd shape. Nothing was symmetrical, and the brown wood paneling looked like it had taken a nasty beating from the weather.

"This is it," she said, shutting off the car's engine. "I know it's not as contemporary as you would have liked, but the views from the master bedroom and the deck outside the living room are spectacular. The pictures I e-mailed you don't do it justice."

We walked up the concrete steps to the front door.

"The owner of the home was transferred to London, and he's pretty desperate for the cash, so I think if you want it, I can get the price down quite a bit."

Nasty thoughts of regret started to creep back into my brain. I could not believe I had traded my gorgeous home for this. But once we stepped inside, my eyes were immediately drawn to the wall of windows that showed off the stretch of treetops, mountain ranges, and the town of Aspen.

"Wow, the views are incredible."

"I knew you'd love it," she said.

But then I turned my head toward the taxidermy that adorned the walls—deer, moose, and elk showing off their sharp horns were staring at me.

As if she was reading my mind, Tracy said, "Don't focus on the strange knick-knacks. Just look around and try to visualize the space with a simple, clean-lined decor. I'm sure your own artwork will dramatically enhance the home."

She was right. Without the heavy red oriental carpets, floral upholstered couches, and collections of bronze horse sculptures all over the bookcases surrounding the stone fireplace, it would look entirely different.

We toured the rest of the home, and although the kitchen and bathrooms looked like they had not been updated since 1985, the interior had been well-preserved and was in immaculate condition. But it was the bird's-eye view of Aspen Mountain that sold me. There was a large wooden deck off the living room with a hot tub off to the side, a small fire pit surrounded by three chairs, a new barbecue grill, and an outdoor dining table. I could imagine myself and the kids sitting outside, enjoying the serenity of the views.

"I'll take it," I told her.

17

"COME IN," I YELLED AS I made my way through an obstacle course of boxes that were scattered all over the living room. Before I reached the front door, Tracy walked in holding a large basket filled with champagne and gourmet snacks in one hand and a shopping bag in her other hand.

"Here," she said, handing me the basket. "A housewarming gift."

"Thank you. This is awesome."

"I wanted to stop by earlier, but I was busy at work. I feel bad I didn't get to see your parents."

"Don't worry about it. They were flying out of Denver, so they had to leave early this morning."

"Where are the kids?" she asked.

"They're in their rooms. Let me get them."

I called the kids, and then Tracy and I walked into the kitchen. Unwrapping my goodies, I pulled out the champagne and said, "I think we need to open this and make a toast."

"Bobby," Tracy said when he entered the kitchen, "I can't believe how big you've gotten. Get over here and give me a hug."

He ran into her arms and squeezed her tightly.

"Here, I brought you a little something." She removed a present from her shopping bag and handed it to him

He ripped off the paper and gave her a big smile when he saw the new Lego set. "Thank you so much."

"You're welcome." Tracy looked at me and said, "Hope, he's the spitting image of Christopher."

"I know," I said as Bobby left the room to play with his toy.

A moment later, Megan walked into the kitchen. "Hi," she said in her sweet voice, making her way toward Tracy.

"Megan, you're getting more and more beautiful every time I see you."

Megan blushed at the compliment.

"Here, honey, this is for you," Tracy said.

"Thank you," Megan said, taking the gift.

"How do you like your new house?" Tracy asked, while Megan opened her present.

She shrugged. "I like my old house better. My old bedroom was pink and had pretty curtains on the windows. This room is an ugly brown color."

When the wrapping paper came off, Megan forced a smile. "Thanks for the Polly Pockets."

"You're welcome," Tracy said. "I bet once your mom paints your room and finds pretty curtains, you'll like it better. And you certainly can't compare the views in this house to your old house."

"Paint isn't going to make it better here. And besides, who cares about a stupid view?"

Megan walked over to the trash compactor and struggled to pull open the dated appliance. It was on my list of things that needed to be fixed. I walked over to help her.

"Nothing even works in this stupid house," she said, throwing away her garbage before she stormed out of the kitchen.

"Let's go outside and drink this," I told Tracy. Since my glasses were still packed away, I grabbed two red solo cups and the bottle of champagne and led Tracy out to the deck.

We sat around the wooden dining table, which the previous owners had left behind, and I poured us each a cup of champagne. At some point, I was going to refinish the outdoor furniture, but with all that I had to do in the house, it was not a high priority. "Sorry about Megan's attitude in there."

"No need to apologize. She's a kid. It's going to take time for her to adjust. Let's make a toast to your new house."

We pushed our plastic cups together and then took sips.

"Bobby seems happy," Tracy said.

"I know. He's been great, especially compared to his sister. But even though he hasn't said anything, I feel kind of bad that he doesn't have a backyard like we had in Concord, or even a swing set."

"Come on, Hope. He's going to grow out of that silly swing set soon. And just wait until he figures out that instead of a flat piece of grass, he's got that." She pointed to Aspen Mountain. "Some of my friends' kids don't even like to go away during winter vacation because they don't want to miss out on ski days." She took a sip of her drink. "Why don't you take a break from unpacking tomorrow and ride the gondola up there for lunch with the kids? It's bustling with energy in the summer months with live music and fun activities."

Taking another gulp of my bubbly drink, I stared out at the rugged mountains, illuminated by the brilliant sun, which was surrounded by a few wispy clouds floating in the azure sky. The dramatic scenery was almost surreal, yet my negative thoughts, questioning my decision to move here, began to take hold, trying to knock me off the perch.

* * *

I enrolled the kids in a small private school in town. Donna and Bill had graciously offered to pay the tuition. With only about fifteen to twenty students per grade, the children and their parents welcomed new families, which helped make our transition a lot easier. I made a point of picking up the kids from school each day, rather than sending them home on the bus, so I could meet the friendly faculty, students, and parents.

One afternoon, while I was waiting for the kids to come out of school, I found myself standing next to a woman with long blonde wavy hair that cascaded over her slender shoulders. She was dressed in a black Lululemon outfit and hiking boots. Gold aviator sunglasses rested on her high cheekbones. She looked like she had stepped off the cover of the glossy magazine *Aspen Peak*.

"Hi," she said, catching me staring at her. "Are you Bobby's mom?"

I adjusted my baseball cap to distract myself from staring at her. "Yes, do you have a child in his class?"

"My son Jack is in his class. I heard our boys are inseparable."

"Bobby talks about Jack all the time."

"I'm Dani, by the way. Did you guys just move here?"

"I'm Hope." I reached out to shake her hand. "We moved here about a month ago. What about you?" I always enjoyed hearing people's stories of how they ended up here. "Have you lived in town for a while?"

"We moved here about two years ago from New York City. My husband and I were tired of the rat race. We haven't looked back for a minute—Aspen is a wonderful community. Where did you move from?"

We both looked toward a pack of kids as they poured out of the classrooms. Some of the children raced toward their parents, while others made their way toward the buses.

"Massachusetts. I lived here after college, but left as soon as I got engaged. My husband and I always dreamed of coming back one day."

"Does your husband work in town?" she asked.

I had met many people over the past few weeks, but this was the first time someone had asked me about Christopher. The words fell out of my mouth. “No, my husband passed away,” I told her, looking down at the ground.

“Oh, I’m so sorry,” she said, touching my arm. “Is it just you and Bobby?”

“No, I have a daughter. She’s in fourth grade.”

“I can’t even imagine what that must have been like for you. My brother and I lost our father at a young age, so I can certainly relate to your children’s pain.”

It was in that moment that I felt a strong connection with her. I wanted to continue talking to her and ask questions about her grief, but the conversation ended abruptly when Bobby and Jack bolted toward us. Loud giggles spilled out of their mouths.

“Hi, honey, how was your day?” I asked Bobby, grabbing his Lightning McQueen lunchbox from his hand.

“Good. Can I have a playdate with Jack today?”

Jack looked nothing like his mother. He had big brown eyes, and his short brown hair was spiked in the front. “Please,” he pleaded with his mom. “Can Bobby come over?”

“It’s fine with me, if it’s okay with Bobby’s mom,” Dani said, looking at me.

“Sure,” I responded.

Dani and I exchanged cell phone numbers as the boys sprinted off together toward her car. A moment later, Megan came out of class, chatting with a cute girl with two long braids wearing a plaid skirt. As soon as Megan noticed I was standing there, she said goodbye to her friend and headed in my direction. A warm, relaxed sensation came over me as I watched her, happy to see that both my kids were making friends.

* * *

On the drive home, Megan rambled on about her day, sharing every detail, from what she ate for lunch to whom she hung with at recess and which teachers she liked best.

primarily made up of stay-at-home moms, Aspen fathers had a stronger presence during the day, shuffling kids around and volunteering at school.

"Sorry," I told him before getting into my car.

Eventually, I would have to get used to seeing so many dads everywhere and find a way to tame my green-eyed monster. On the drive back to the house, I did my best to stop feeling sorry for myself and be grateful that my kids were making friends and doing well. But unfortunately, no matter how hard I tried to wipe away the sadness, the stain on my heart would always be there to remind me of what my children were missing.

18

A VIBRANT ENERGY REVERBERATED throughout Aspen during the Christmas season. Evergreen trees, Aspen trees, and bushes covered in white were brought to life with twinkling lights. Rooftops, balconies, and lampposts were entwined with lit-up garlands and red bows, along with dressed-up wreaths hanging on doorposts. The white carpet of snow on the mountains and streets added an extra gleam to the sparkling town. Packed with visitors, the ski mountains were crawling with skiers and snowboarders. From a distance, they looked like ants scurrying on an anthill.

After more than ten years of yearning to get back to Aspen, I was finally there. I should have been happy. My kids were settled. We had friends. And yet I was still lonely, still desperately missing my husband. Having already survived our first holiday without Christopher, I had expected our second one to be easier. But it wasn't, most likely because we had celebrated our last Christmas vacation together in Aspen.

Instead of swimming against the current, I decided the best way to flow upstream was to force myself to get into the holiday spirit by decorating the house, so I searched the garage for my box of Christmas decor. Piled up against the back wall were three large stacks of boxes, filled with crap that I probably should have discarded when we moved. One by one, I pulled them down, reading each label before grabbing another, until I eventually located the word "XMAS" written on a box top in black Sharpie. I picked up the box, and underneath it the label "ART SUPPLIES" jumped out at me, almost as if it were trying to get my attention. I stood for a moment, staring at it and contemplating whether I should open it, but then the phone rang, and I ran back into the house to answer it, still holding the Christmas box.

"Hi, Hope," Bethany said when I picked up the phone.

"Hey." Resting the phone between my shoulder and ear, I opened the box.

"Have you spoken to Aunt Myrna?"

"Shit, now that you mention it, we've been playing phone tag. I think I owe her a call." Grabbing an ornament, I unraveled the bubble wrap. "Why? What's up?"

"Aunt Myrna has a boyfriend. She met him on a dating site."

I held the delicate glass-blown ornament in my hand and studied it. The ornament was adorned with gold and silver glitter. "That's great," I said casually, wanting to get off the phone so I could finish unpacking the box.

"Hope, I think they're going to get engaged."

The ornament fell out of my hand, thankfully landing on the soft carpet. "What? How long have they been dating?"

"Not even a month. She's crazy in love with this guy."

"Have you met him?" I asked, still in shock.

"Not yet, but word around town is that she's never been this happy."

"Bullshit. She was happy with Uncle Ralph."

"Of course she was. She loved Uncle Ralph, but she found love again." She waited for me to say something, but I didn't. I was confused. I didn't want my aunt to be alone, just as much as I didn't want to spend the rest of my life alone, but in a way, I also felt like she was betraying my uncle.

"I think you should consider putting yourself out there too," Bethany said. "Maybe sign up for an online dating site."

I was so tired of this conversation. She brought it up every time we spoke. "Whatever, Bethany. Not everyone needs to find a man to be happy."

"Hope, don't put words in my mouth. I just think you should at least try to meet someone."

"Why? Why do I have to meet someone? I'm perfectly happy without a man in my life," I snapped back at her.

"I'm only trying to help."

"I know. I'm sorry. I just don't want to have this discussion anymore."

* * *

Christmas was better than expected. Pouring my heart into decorating the house had been the best medicine, helping to revitalize me. Donna and Bill came for a short visit to celebrate the holiday with us, and having them around was a nice distraction. Instead of cooking, we ate our meals out and spent most of our time with them at their hotel, which made it feel like we were on vacation too. Donna and Bill skied with us during the day, and Megan and Bobby loved showing off their new skills. Following a full day on the slopes, the kids swam in the heated hotel pool while my in-laws and I enjoyed après-ski drinks surrounded by fancy tourists dripping in diamonds and fur. With all the festivities around me and the daily trips to the slopes' skiing powder, I caught the buzz, and it managed to stay with me for the next two months.

* * *

As March approached, the anniversary of Christopher's death was around the corner. Like clockwork, the dark cloud came back, robbing me of my euphoria. After dropping the kids at school each day, I drove home immediately and crawled back in bed. Even though the slopes were filled with powdery fresh snow, I could not bring myself to get out on the mountain.

On the evening of the dreadful day, I took the kids out to Boogie's Diner for dinner. Driving around the block three times, I searched for an open parking space.

"Mom, there's a spot right there. You just missed it," Megan pointed out.

I drove around the block again. "Mom, what's wrong with you? You just passed another spot," Megan said in a condescending voice.

I tried to snap out of my funk and focus. Eventually, I pulled into a parking space about three blocks from the restaurant. Large snowflakes blew in an almost horizontal direction in our faces as we walked.

"I'm freezing," Bobby whined.

"Bobby, why don't you have your jacket on?" I scolded him.

"I forgot to grab it," he said through trembling lips.

"Mom, what's wrong with you? You haven't been paying attention to anything." My body was too numb to respond, so I didn't say anything until we arrived at the restaurant.

The bright fluorescent lights of the ground-level retail shop called Boogie's was overbearing in contrast to the blackened skies outside. We made our way past the overflowing racks of jeans and flannel shirts and upstairs to the 1950s retro-style diner. The hostess sat us in a red leather booth in the far corner, away from the lively patrons at the center of the restaurant.

Bobby and I opened our menus, but Megan wouldn't touch hers. Her arms were crossed, and she was staring at the exit sign. It seemed as though my bad mood was contagious, and Megan had caught the bug.

"What are you guys in the mood for?" I asked, changing my voice to sound chipper.

"I'm getting grilled cheese," Bobby said.

"Megan, you love the mac and cheese here," I said, but she kept her lips sealed and wouldn't speak. I hated myself for ruining the night by spreading my bad mood on the kids. "All right, guys, I'm sorry I've been so nasty. This time of year is hard for me. I just miss your dad."

"I miss him, too," Bobby said.

I glanced at Megan. Her head was still turned away from us.

"Can we start over and try to have a fun dinner?" I asked. "Megan, please?"

Finally, she burst out, "I miss Dad all the time. I hate that all my friends have dads except for me. I hate that my friends have nice dads who do things with them. I hate that he can't go to my dance recitals. I hate that he's not here and he's never going to be here, ever...ever again."

I grabbed Megan's hand. "I know, baby." Tears welled up in my eyes. "I know."

The server approached us, ready to take our order, but I signaled that we needed a few more minutes.

"It's not fair," Megan said. Her head was low.

"You're right. It's not. And some days it hurts more than others." I squeezed her hand. I needed to find a way to turn this night around. "Hey, did I ever tell you guys about your dad's favorite practical joke? The one with the fake booger?"

Bobby nearly jumped out of his seat when he heard the word *booger*. "No, tell us," he sang out.

"Well, years ago, when your dad and I were living in Aspen, I got a phone call from Grandma Audrey telling me that my Uncle Ralph had died."

"Who was Uncle Ralph?" Bobby wanted to know.

"He was married to Aunt Myrna," Megan told him in a sassy tone.

"Anyway," I continued before a fight ensued, "I was so sad when I found out. To cheer me up, your dad suggested that we celebrate Uncle Ralph by going out and ordering his favorite dessert, which happened to be mint chocolate chip ice cream." Megan and Bobby's eyes were glued to me. "When we got to the ice cream store, Dad bet me that I would laugh when he placed the order. Of course, I was in no mood to laugh. He turned his back to me, so I couldn't see what he was doing. He put a long, slimy, fake booger in one nostril, and then he walked up to the clerk with a straight face and asked for a double scoop of mint chocolate chip ice cream."

"Were you laughing?" Bobby asked.

"So hard, I almost peed in my pants."

A smile spread across Megan's face. "Was the person taking the order laughing?" she asked.

"Yeah, she was. But the best part was that Daddy kept a serious face the entire time."

"I like that story," Bobby said. "Can you tell us another funny one?"

"Sure, but let's order dinner first." I signaled to the server that we were ready to order. While we waited for our food to arrive, I told them about the time I had left Christopher home alone with Megan when she was a newborn, and he couldn't figure out how to get her dressed, so he left her wrapped in a towel. Each time I finished one story, the kids begged for another. Sharing happy memories was the perfect remedy for our sadness.

When we finished eating our meals, the server picked up our dirty dishes. "Can I interest you guys in dessert tonight? We have some delicious homemade pies."

The kids gave me pleading looks. "Sure, what do you have?" I asked.

After she listed the desserts, Bobby screamed out, "I want the banana cream pie. That's my favorite." His expression, his upturned dimples, the same small face as his father's, and the chosen dessert caused me to burst into a fit of weeps.

The young waitress looked at me like I had two heads. "Are you okay?"

"Mom, what's wrong?" Megan asked.

"That was Dad's favorite dessert." I picked up my napkin, wiped my tear-stained cheeks, and told the waitress, "We'll take a piece to share."

"I'll be right back with your pie," the waitress said, clearly uncomfortable with my behavior.

Bobby slid closer to me and gave me a hug. This time, Megan grabbed my hand from across the table.

"I love you guys. And your dad loved you a lot, too," I told them.

Before I had a chance to lose it again, the waitress came over with a slice of pie, overflowing with billowy clouds of whipped cream. "Please enjoy. It's on the house," she said.

Thanking her, we picked up our forks and dove into the sinfully rich, creamy banana filling nestled in a thick graham cracker crust.

* * *

The following morning, I got a text message from Tracy: *Where the hell have you been? Are you alive? You haven't responded to any of my calls or text messages. Please text me and let me know that you're okay.*

I finally called Tracy back while I was folding a pile of laundry. "Sorry I've been out of commission," I said when she picked up the phone. "It's a shitty time of year for me. The memory of losing Christopher hits me like a tidal wave, and I have trouble dealing with my emotions."

"Hope, I'm so sorry. It must suck," Tracy said.

"I'll be fine. It's almost like an extended case of PMS that hits before the anniversary of the accident. By next week, I'll be okay again."

"The Spazmatics are playing at Belly Up next Thursday. How about I get us tickets? It will be so much fun."

"I don't know if I'm up for a night out."

"I'm not taking no for an answer. Get a sitter. I promise it'll be a great night," she insisted.

19

2012

"I PROMISE MEGAN AND BOBBY will love Natalie," Dani told me over the phone, while I was getting dressed.

Since the day I had met Dani at school pickup back in September, she and I had become close friends. Dani was my go-to mom for all child-related questions, so, of course, when I needed a babysitter, she was the first person I called.

"Would you stop worrying? Your kids will be fine. Bobby has been to my house a million times when Natalie has watched my kids. You're going to have an amazing time tonight at Belly Up. The Spazmatics are one of the best eighties cover bands out there."

"All right. I know I'm acting a little over the top," I said.

"I have a great Madonna outfit you're welcome to borrow. It's fun to dress up in an eighties costume for the show."

"Thanks, but I'm not in the mood to wear some crazy outfit."

"Okay. Have fun, and call me tomorrow," she said before hanging up.

Since moving to Aspen, I hadn't had a night out without my kids. I was looking forward to having a few drinks and enjoying some live music. Earlier in the day I had purchased a new outfit from Pitkin County Dry Goods, a trendy clothing store in Aspen. I ripped the tags off my dark skinny jeans and off-the-shoulder gray cotton sweater and then threw on my stylish ensemble, finishing the look with short black motorcycle boots. I added a coat of bright red lipstick and then glanced at myself in the full-length mirror before heading downstairs, feeling good about my appearance.

When I walked into the kitchen to say goodbye to the kids, Megan looked at me and said, "Mommy, you look pretty," between bites of macaroni and cheese.

Even though I was only wearing jeans, I couldn't remember the last time the kids had seen me in anything other than workout clothes with my hair in a messy ponytail.

A few minutes later, the doorbell rang, and Bobby ran to answer it.

"Hi, Natalie," he said when she stepped inside. "Want to play Monopoly?"

"Only if your sister plays too," she said, winking at Megan as she walked into the kitchen.

Megan smiled and nodded her head.

Relieved that the kids seemed comfortable with the sitter, I kissed them goodbye and hopped on the Dial-A-Ride bus to town. The bus dropped me off at Ruby Park, about a block away from Belly Up. It was a mild winter night, so I left my coat unzipped and made my way to the music venue.

"Hope, over here!" Tracy yelled, waving her hand. She had just come from a dinner meeting with a client, so she was dressed more conservatively than usual in a blazer and jeans. "Wow, you're looking good tonight," she said. "And I'm loving your sexy red lips."

"Is it too much?" I asked, suddenly self-conscious about wearing such a bright color.

"Stop it. You look great. Come on, let's go to the bar and grab a drink."

I followed her down the steps. Since we had arrived a little early, the line wasn't long. She handed our tickets to the doorman and bee-lined to the bar in the back corner, closest to the bathroom. I stepped in front of her and insisted on ordering the first round of cocktails.

While I waited for the bartender to hand me the drinks, I looked around the intimate music venue. Framed photos of famous musicians adorned the walls. If I closed my eyes, I could see myself back in the same spot in my early twenties with my future husband. Back then, Belly Up was called The Double Diamond, and I had been drinking beers and listening to the Spin Doctors, holding Christopher's hand as we swayed to the music. We had been carefree, with no responsibilities—just each other and a world of endless possibilities before us. What I would give to go back in time, even for a single night, and spend it with the only man I had ever loved. The memory was like hot lava simmering through my mind, waiting to erupt. Maybe coming out tonight was a bad idea.

The bartender handed us our tequilas on the rocks, snapping me out of my trance.

"Cheers," Tracy said, clinking my glass. "To a fun night."

I gave her a partial, closed-mouth grin, which, of course, she called me out on. "Hope, what's wrong?"

"I don't know. I guess being here reminds me of Christopher."

"Yeah—so that's a good thing. The Christopher I knew would want you to loosen up and have fun." She took off her blazer; underneath she was wearing a low-cut lacy top that revealed too much cleavage. Her breasts were like a magnet, drawing every man's eyes toward them. "Now would you drink up? And let's party."

Wrapping my lips around the thin cocktail straw, I took a huge sip of my drink. The strong, astringent taste caused the muscles in my face to tighten. I squeezed the juice from the lime into my glass and took another gulp. *Better*, I thought.

Tracy grabbed my hand. "They're coming on in a few minutes. Let's move closer to the stage."

I followed behind her, checking out the different characters standing around, many of whom were dressed in eighties costumes. A young woman wearing a short neon pink tulle skirt with a half shirt and a big bow on top of her fiery red hair accidentally elbowed me in the head, while we were walking toward the steps. I was tempted to tell Cyndi Lauper to watch it, but I bit my tongue and took another sip of my tequila instead. We pushed our way toward the middle, giving us a perfect center-stage view. A guy with ruffled sandy blond hair wearing a Yankees hat backward looked at us.

"Hey, David," Tracy said, reaching toward his cheek to kiss him hello. He wrapped his bulging muscular arms around her body in an embrace.

"Hope, this is my good friend David," she said.

Tracy's friends ranged from twenty-five-year-olds to ninety-year-olds. This guy fell into the category of young and hot.

I pushed my hair behind my ears. "You look familiar."

"Aren't you Megan's mom?"

"Yeah," I said, still trying to figure out how I knew him.

"I'm her gym teacher."

"Oh, right. I've seen you around school." Up close, I could see why all the girls had crushes on him.

"She's a great girl," he said.

I smiled at the compliment.

"I'm going to get a drink. What can I get you?" he asked both of us.

"Two tequilas on the rocks with limes," Tracy told him. "Thanks, hon," she called out as he walked away. Laughing, she turned to me, and said, "You can stop drooling now, Hope."

"I wasn't drooling, and besides, he's Megan's teacher, so he's totally off limits."

"As if that even matters," she said, rolling her eyes. "I saw the way you were checking each other out."

Suddenly, the house lights dimmed and the spotlights turned on, adding a fluorescent purple glow to the stage. Bubbling with energy, four men dressed in nerd costumes, donning an outrageous array of clothes—a combination of thick-rimmed glasses, suspenders, knee socks, tennis shorts, floods pants, and ill-fitting neckties—jumped onto the stage. The crowd went wild cheering for them. Right away, they started playing "I Love Rock 'n' Roll." The upbeat music penetrated my body as I rocked back and forth to the tunes.

I felt a tap on my shoulder and turned around to find David standing behind me. He handed me my drink. I mouthed thank you, took a large sip, and continued to dance. By the time the band started the next song, "Video Killed the Radio Star," I had almost finished my second drink. The loud, feel-good music and the alcohol surged through my insides, taking me back to my childhood, growing up in the eighties, and listening to these songs throughout my formative years.

Tracy put a red gummy bear in my hand and whispered in my ear, "It's a marijuana edible. Try it."

Without hesitation, I put the sweet and tangy candy in my mouth, enjoying the small morsel and remembering that I had forgotten to eat dinner.

One after the other, the band played my favorite eighties songs. I danced. I sang. I jumped up and down to the beat. Sweat dripped off my forehead. My heart raced wildly. And then, slowly, the room started to spin. I could feel the earth moving around its axis. Crowds of people were rubbing against me and whirling around me. And I was whirling around them. Focusing on the music, I tried to block out the dizziness.

A large hand wrapped around my waist, pushing my hips to the sway of the song, "Jessie's Girl." When I looked back, David gave me a salacious grin. I leaned closer into him and could feel his sweet, warm beer breath against the back of my neck. Goosebumps prickled my skin, as he lightly kissed my earlobe. The large, hard bulge in his jeans was pressing into me. I pushed my ass into his crotch, and we started grinding like animals. In the heat of the moment, I didn't care who he was. I only cared that I wanted him like he was my prey. When I turned to face him, he opened his mouth wide, shoving his tongue inside my mouth. Our bodies were entwined, and we were dry humping each other in the middle of the dance floor. But the harder we moved, the dizzier I got, almost like I was on a high-speed Ferris wheel.

"Get a room," someone called out.

The music was echoing like waves, swooshing inside my brain. Pulling away from David's embrace, I looked at him. *Shit. Who is this guy?* I couldn't recall what he had said his name was. *Did he even tell me his name?* I said something incoherent about needing to get home, and then I tapped Tracy on the shoulder and told her I would call her in the morning.

An acidic bile was sloshing around at the bottom of my belly. Pushing past hordes of people, I ran outside as fast as I could. The crisp air helped settle my stomach, but my eyes were having trouble focusing on where I was. Somebody helped me into a cab. Slurring my words, I managed to give my address to the driver, and then I opened the windows and squeezed my hands together, so I could concentrate on not barfing all over the backseat of the car. The windy, uphill ride was causing a pool of sweat to drip off my forehead. The last thing I remembered was the driver pulling up the hill to my house.

I woke up splayed out on top of my bed, still wearing my jeans, sweater, and boots. The time on my cell phone read 3:00 a.m. My mouth tasted like cotton balls, and my head felt like a drummer was beating it from the inside. I went into the bathroom, cupped my hands, and guzzled the sink water with desperate urgency. A nervous pit started to creep through me as I tried to remember what had happened earlier that night, but most of it was a blur. I got back into bed, squeezed my eyes shut, and tried to fall back to sleep.

The alarm startled me out of a deep slumber. I was about to hit the snooze button when I remembered it was Friday morning and I had to get the kids ready for school. Flashes of the night were haunting me. Dirty dancing with David—the gym teacher. The kiss. The spinning room.

I forced myself to get out of bed. Through the window, I could see large snowflakes piling up, blanketing the mountains with layers of pristine white powder. As much as I wanted to spend the day in bed and sleep off my hangover, I knew it would only make me depressed about my behavior the previous night. I needed to get outside and ski a few runs. After all, it was a powder day, and I had already missed some great snow days during the weeks leading up to the anniversary of Christopher's death. Decision made: I was going to ski off my hangover, and the invigorating air would make me feel better.

As soon as I dropped the kids off at school, I drove over to Peaches Corner Café. My empty stomach was screaming for fuel—anything to absorb the tequila and give me some energy before I got on the mountain. I put on my dark sunglasses and a slouchy knit hat to cover my greasy hair. On my way into the light-filled restaurant, I grabbed a copy of *The Aspen Times*, walked to the counter, and ordered my favorite breakfast, the Farm Table: a sunny-side up egg over sautéed spinach, mushrooms, and goat cheese on olive bread. I also ordered a chocolate-filled croissant to nibble on while I waited for my meal and a large coffee. After I paid, I grabbed my pastry and hot brew, took a seat facing the window overlooking the sidewalk, and buried my head in the newspaper to hide from seeing anyone I might know. Images of the night before were haunting me. I never should have mixed the alcohol and the edible on an empty stomach.

Within a few minutes, the server put the piping hot plate of food in front of me. "Wasn't last night great?" he asked.

I had never seen this man before in my life. I flashed him a bewildered look.

"The Spazmatics," he said.

"Oh, yeah. It was fun."

"David is my roommate. He was super bummed that you ran out without saying goodbye."

Heat rose through my face. "I wasn't feeling well."

"It happens to the best of us," he said before walking away.

I hated myself in that moment, but the hunger pang tugging at my belly, along with the smell of the food, was begging me to eat. I doused Cholula hot sauce all over the meal and cut into the egg, letting the yolk ooze over the plate, saturating the cheese and vegetables. Inhaling the tasty food, I ate every morsel. After I finished the last sip of my coffee, with my belly feeling full, I walked outside into the fresh, snow-filled air, and made my way toward the mountain.

Happy to see that a line hadn't formed in front of the gondola yet, I took a seat on an empty bench and quickly buckled my ski boots. When I stood up and grabbed my skis from the ski rack, a small rumble of pain pierced through my abdomen, making me feel like I should head to the bathroom. But I was too anxious. The sky was dumping white flour. I had to get up there before the other skiers. Visions of myself floating through the light and creamy snow made me giddy. In that moment, the urge to ski was greater than the urge to relieve myself.

Running toward the gondola, I hopped into an empty car, praying that I could ride solo. Just as the door was about to close, a man wearing a one-piece ski outfit jumped in and sat across from me. Annoyed that he had poached my ride, I could feel my blood pressure rising. I wasn't in the mood for idle conversation. He smiled at me, showing off his large white teeth that glowed against his bronze-colored skin and scruffy dark facial hair. He looked like a stereotypical ski bum in his late forties, who had moved here after college and never left. Guys like this tried too hard to maintain their youth, particularly by wearing ski clothes intended for young twenty-year-old rippers.

Turning away from him, I looked out the window, trying to decide where I would take my first run of the day. The gondola ride felt like it was moving at a snail's pace. Midway up the mountain, the cramping in my stomach started tightening again, steadily increasing in intensity and causing tiny beads of sweat to form along my hairline underneath my helmet. The pain was shooting inside of me like it was slicing my belly open. *I'm such an idiot. Why didn't I just go to the bathroom before I got on the gondola?* I bent over slightly to push back the achy feeling. It didn't help. A gas bubble was growing larger by the second, making its way down toward my asshole. I squeezed my sphincter as hard as I could to keep it from coming out, but the force was so great that I had no control. The volcano erupted. A loud, wet fart shot out of my butt. It was more than flatulence—it was a shart, a fart and shit combination. The smell hung in the air like a black cloud. My face turned beet red. I wanted to jump out of the gondola. My poison was sucking all the oxygen out of the tiny space. I wanted to open the window, but I was afraid to move. Instead, I grabbed my phone and pretended to stare at it, ignoring the hot, wet feeling in my underwear.

As soon as the gondola door opened, I pulled my skis off the rack and sprinted to the bathroom in the Sundeck. Once inside the stall, I ripped off my ski pants and long underwear and saw a large shit stain on my panties. When I sat down on the toilet, explosive diarrhea came blasting out of me. The violent pain in my stomach was masking the mortal embarrassment I had just experienced in front of the guy on the gondola. When I finally felt better, I took my lacy underwear off, threw it in the garbage, and realized that today was not my day. I needed to get the hell off the mountain and go home.

After clipping my boots into my bindings, I made my way down the mountain, carving wide ski turns through the heavy layers of waist-deep snow. Tears streamed down my face and wet snot dripped out of my nose. Why couldn't I get my life together? Living in Aspen was supposed to be better, a chance to start over and get my life on the right track, but I was a disaster. Static filled my mind. I screamed over and over in my head: *Please, Christopher. I can't do this anymore.*

Once I made it back to the safety of my home, I decided I was done for a while. No more going out. No more leaving the house, except for dealing with the kids. I was going to punish myself and stay in lockdown until I figured out how to make everything work again.

Later in the day, Tracy called to check on me. "You okay?" she asked.

"No, I feel like shit." *No pun intended,* I thought to myself.

"You and David seemed pretty into each other."

"That was a mistake. A big mistake. I was drunk and stupid. Megan would kill me if she found out I was with one of her teachers. I think I need to take a break from man hunting."

"A break? A break from what? You haven't even been on a proper date since Christopher died." Her voice was agitated.

"I'm just not ready. Why is everyone trying to force me to go out on a date?"

"Bullshit, you're not ready. You're like a dog in heat. I saw the way you were all over David last night."

"Did you have to remind me?"

"Yes, now stop feeling sorry for yourself all the time and sign up for an online dating service. And if you don't do it, then I'll do it for you. And if I have to drag you out on a date, then that's what I'll do."

I thought about Aunt Myrna and how she had fallen in love with someone she had met online. "Fine. I'll think about it," I said.

I could hear her grunting through the phone.

20

IT TOOK MONTHS AFTER THE conversation with Tracy before I finally decided to take her advice and sign up for an online dating service. To pump myself up I poured a glass of wine, listened to Beyoncé's "Single Ladies," and perused two websites, LoveConnection.com and FindYourLover.com. Filling out basic information about myself was easy, but when I was asked to write a descriptive profile, I froze. How would I sell myself? A middle-aged, washed-up widow raising two young kids on her own didn't sound appealing. Each time I tried to type something, I couldn't get any words out.

I thought more wine would help, so I grabbed the bottle from the refrigerator and poured myself another glass. I hit repeat on Beyoncé's song, turned up the volume, and danced around the kitchen, singing the lyrics between sips of wine. Eventually I forced myself to stop procrastinating and sat down in front of the computer, racking my brain to come up with a good description of myself.

I'm sick of being alone. It sucks. Thirty-seven-year-old widow seeking a hot, sexy, great-in-bed, forty-year-old guy to save me from my wilting vagina and help me raise my kids. They need a father figure, especially my boy.

Maybe that was a little too blunt.

Sad, pathetic, thirty-seven-year-old widow desperately searching for a man to save her and put some loving back into her life.

No, I couldn't use that either.

Finally, the best I could come up with was:

It's the simple things in life that turn me on—the first ski tracks on a powder day, when my kids say, "I love you," a glass of fine red wine paired with gourmet cheese, traveling, art, when I'm outside in nature, laughing, and spending time with people I care about. I don't do yoga or surf, and I'm not a great cook. I'm deep, intuitive, and often find myself stuck in embarrassing situations, but at least I can make fun of myself. I like dogs, but I don't have one. I have a twelve-year-old daughter and a nine-year-old son, both of whom were brought into this world with the love of my life, who tragically passed away. I'm finally ready to get out there, have fun, and embrace life with a partner.

It was honest and real. After posting my profile, I spent hours scouring the site for potential guys. Scrolling up and down, I clicked a heart next to about fifteen guys to indicate my favorites. Later, I would decide if I wanted to go back and contact them. My criteria were a man in the Aspen area, between the ages of thirty-five and fifty, decent-looking, preferably never been married, and who made a comfortable living.

I read profile after profile of different men. In the back of my mind, I couldn't help but wonder if I might end up dating the next Ted Bundy. I kept telling myself to shut down the computer and go to bed, but I couldn't stop looking, studying, and analyzing the pictures. Names like "MountainLover," "HornyforLove," or "PromiseIWon'tKillYou" were intriguing and horrifying. I had to keep reminding myself as I picked apart each person that someone good must be out there. I just had to be patient. After a few hours perusing the dating sites, my eyes started to burn from exhaustion, and eventually, I logged off and went to sleep.

I woke up the next day to ten messages in my inbox from different guys. The first message was from a fifty-five-year-old man, who had written a poem: "Roses are red, violets are blue, I really, really want to go on a date with you." Not good. I deleted him immediately.

The next guy had written a sweet message saying that I had a beautiful smile in my photo. His profile didn't exactly match what I had in mind for a potential date—he wasn't athletic, and he spent most of his free time reading adult comic books and watching reruns of *Star Trek*. There was, however, a softness in his face that made me feel sad for him. He seemed lonely, but unfortunately, he wasn't my type, so I moved on to the next message.

One guy seemed promising. He called himself MountainSporty512. A graduate of Princeton, he lived in Aspen, was divorced with no kids, and he worked as a local architect. He had sandy-blond hair, large hazel eyes, and was six-foot-two. Perfect. We had a series of good e-mail conversations, until MountainSporty512 revealed his last name and I asked Tracy if she knew him.

"Bruce Hanover! Stay away from that guy. Not only is he a womanizer, but he also has a cocaine addiction," she warned me.

He had seemed too good to be true. Living in a small town made dating challenging, especially since our pool of men was somewhat limited. On the other hand, I was grateful that Tracy knew him, and at least I didn't have to waste my time with Don Juan of Aspen.

The next guy, John Randolph, had recently moved to town from Kansas, so Tracy didn't know anything about him. After about a week of chatting on the phone, we made plans to meet one evening at Kenichi, a popular Japanese restaurant.

* * *

"Hey, what's up?" Tracy asked when she picked up the phone.

"Where would you suggest I go for a bikini wax?" If this dating thing was going to start, it was time I cleaned up down under.

"Definitely make an appointment with Elena at Lips Wax Salon."

"Thanks. Can you text me the number?"

"Sure. I would suggest a Brazilian. Bush is out, and if you plan on hooking up, you're going to want a smooth vajayjay."

"Really? Christopher liked my dark pubes. Do you honestly think I need to go to such an extreme?"

"Yes, Hope. Would I steer you wrong? Wax that beast off!"

After I hung up, I waited a few minutes to process the idea of no hair down there, before I could muster the energy to make the call. It seemed crazy to wax it all off.

My phone beeped, indicating that I had a text message from Tracy. She had sent me the contact information for the waxing place and had also written, *Don't be a pussy, get a Brazilian -:).*

I laughed out loud and made the appointment for the following day.

* * *

"Can I help you?" a bleached blonde woman sitting behind the reception desk asked when I walked into the salon.

I gave her my name. "I have an appointment for a bikini wax," I said.

"Elena is running a few minutes behind schedule. Why don't you take a seat? She'll be out soon."

Before sitting on one of the wooden chairs near the window, I realized it would be a good idea to use the bathroom before getting waxed.

When I sat down on the toilet to pee, I noticed drops of blood coming out. *Oh no, why now?* The timing couldn't have been worse. I pulled a tampon from my bag, unsure how I was going to deal with this situation. I couldn't possibly get a wax with a string hanging out of me. I would just have to tell the receptionist that I needed to reschedule.

A woman dressed in a white lab coat with jet-black hair, the same color as her thick eyeliner and matching dark lipstick, was standing outside the door waiting for me when I stepped out of the bathroom.

"I'm Elena," she said in a heavy eastern European accent. "It is good to meet you."

Up close, I could see her nose ring. My hands were still wet from not properly drying them off. I wiped them on my jeans and then reached out to shake her hand.

"I think I need to reschedu—" I tried getting the words out, but she didn't hear me.

"Follow me," she said, leading me to a tiny, white-walled room. She walked over to a pot of hot wax on the counter and stirred it.

"Take off your underwear and hop on table," she instructed.

Unable to move, I stood like a statue and stared at her while she pulled wooden sticks from the cabinet above her head.

"You okay?" she asked.

"Well, actually, not really. This is so embarrassing, but I think I need to reschedule this appointment. It's that time of the month."

"What time? What do you mean?" she asked, scrunching her eyebrows.

"I'm menstruating," I said in a louder voice, as a rush of warmth rose through my cheeks.

"Oh, you have period. No worry, I've seen it all. I am master at cleaning lady parts. Now, don't be shy, get undressed, and get on table," she commanded while she put on disposable gloves.

I imagined that she had seen and smelled it all—private parts of many different shapes and sizes. I took off my pants and underwear, ignoring the string that dangled between my legs, and I lay down on top of the wax paper covering the table.

Elena sprinkled baby powder all over my bush and then immediately got to work, painting section by section with hot, purple wax. I squeezed my hands together each time she ripped off the dried wax, pulling my dark pubic hair out from its follicles under my skin. She talked to me the entire time, trying to distract me from the pain. Unfortunately, it didn't help. It fucking hurt like hell.

"Very good," she said, admiring her work. "Now let's clean hairy ass. Turn over. Get on all fours."

It was crazy. I couldn't believe I had agreed to it. Like a dog, I turned around and stuck my butt in the air, imagining what would happen if I farted.

When she finished, I flipped over and looked at my hairless vagina, which now resembled a prepubescent little girl's—just like Megan's.

"You look not happy," Elena said.

"No, I just...it just looks so different. I'm not used to it."

"Why don't we vajazzle to give it dressed-up look?"

"What's that?" I asked, dumbfounded.

"It's temporary crystal rhinestone tattoo. I paste right above pelvic bone. I have many different designs to choose from," she said, pulling out a few sheets of various shaped patterns to show me. "It not hurt, and in few weeks stones fall off."

"All right, why not?" I said, looking at the different patterns. "I'll take the butterfly design."

"Good choice. You'll have prettiest snatch in town."

When she finished sticking it over my privates, I peeked at it and chuckled softly. If only Christopher could see me now.

* * *

Every time I looked at my unrecognizable and decorated vagina, a large grin spread across my face. It almost felt like the butterfly was flapping its wings when I got dressed for my date. Feeling comfortable and confident in my skinny jeans, a royal blue chiffon blouse, and high-heeled shoes, I said goodbye to the kids and then hopped on the bus to town. Before entering the large wooden doors to Kenichi, I slathered on another coat of lip gloss. Upbeat pop music was playing in the background of the ambient-lit, modern Asian restaurant. I grabbed an empty seat at the long wooden bar near the entrance.

The young bartender had overgrown, messy blond hair that brushed over his forehead in a relaxed style. "What can I get for you tonight?" he asked in a deep, raspy voice.

"I'll take a glass of the Cakebread Chardonnay."

"Good choice."

When he turned his tall, muscular body around, I gaped at his hard buttocks and imagined myself taking a bite out of it.

Each time the door to the restaurant opened, I looked up to see if it was my date. All I had to go by was his profile picture. I knew he was about five-eleven (less than my desired height requirement), fifty years old, and had short dark hair.

The bartender put the wineglass down in front of me. "Here you go."

"Thank you," I said, looking into his captivating blue eyes.

"Do you want to order any food?"

I took a sip of the cold, crisp wine. "No, thank you. I'm meeting someone for dinner." Flipping my hair back in a feeble attempt to act sexy, I asked, "So what are your favorite rolls on the menu?"

"I'm a huge fan of the Blake roll. It's tempura shrimp with cucumber and avocado topped with spicy tuna and eel sauce."

"Mmm, that sounds good."

"Do you live in town?" he asked.

I watched his large hands stacking bar glasses on the shelf, wondering what his hands would think of my crystal tattoo. "Yeah, I moved here about a year ago from Massachusetts."

"Dude, no way. I'm from New Hampshire. I moved here three years ago after graduating from college."

Calling a woman *dude* was not sexy, yet he had graduated from college, so at least he had a little ambition.

"My name is Jason. It's a pleasure to meet you."

Why was I analyzing his vernacular? His sex appeal far outweighed his intelligence.

"I'm Hope."

A man sitting on the other side of the bar was signaling for Jason to go over there. "Excuse me, Hope, I need to take an order."

Jason reminded me of Christopher when I had first met him. He was young, handsome, and moved behind the bar with a relaxed confidence. Any minute my date would be walking through the door, but I was no longer looking forward to meeting him. I wanted to continue talking to Jason. I finished my wine and was about to order another one when I felt a tap on my shoulder.

* * *

Standing behind me was a man with a large forehead and a thick head of dark hair sprinkled with gray strands. He was wearing a white button-down shirt and jeans.

"Hope?" he asked in a quiet, unsure voice.

"John?"

"Your picture doesn't do you justice. You're much prettier in person."

I blushed slightly. "Thank you," I said, noticing the deep creases in his forehead. I thought he looked better in his picture than he did in person.

A woman holding two menus approached us. "Do you want to take care of your bar bill now, or should I have it transferred to your table?" the hostess asked.

"Have it transferred to our table, please," John said to her.

Waving my hand, I tried to get Jason's attention so I could say goodbye, but he was busy pouring drinks and didn't see me. We followed the hostess over to a cozy booth in the corner of the restaurant. Before taking a seat, I noticed a familiar-looking guy sitting at the sushi bar. He was wearing a white T-shirt with a marijuana leaf on it. Just as I was trying to figure out how I knew him, he spotted me staring at him, gave me a wide grin that revealed his gleaming white teeth, and winked at me. My pulse shot to the moon when I realized he was the guy from the gondola. As soon as I took my seat, I turned away from him.

"Should we order a bottle of wine?" John asked, displaying a warm smile.

"Yes," I said too quickly, my face still ablaze. "I mean, sure, if you want. I was drinking Cakebread Chardonnay. It's delicious, if you like white."

"Sounds great." His nose twitched when he signaled to the server.

Minutes later, our wine was poured, and we let the conversation flow naturally while we sipped our cold beverages. The more I drank, the more John was growing on me.

"What do you like to eat?" John asked as we both scanned our menus.

"I eat everything," I told him.

"How about I order a bunch of sushi rolls as starters and we can share?"

"Perfect. I hear the Blake roll is delicious." I took a deep breath, relieved that I didn't have to make the decision about what to order.

"Have you always lived in Kansas?" I asked after the server took our order.

"Born and raised in the Sunflower State." He made that same strange twitching movement again with his nose. I wondered if he was aware of it. "Moving to Aspen full time was a major transition for me. After I caught my wife cheating on me, I had to get out of there."

I wasn't sure how to respond to that, even though I was kind of curious as to what had happened and how he had caught her.

"How did you end up in Aspen?" he asked.

I gave him a brief synopsis of my life, explaining that Aspen had always been like a magnet, pulling me back. We continued to share our life stories with one another until the server brought us a large wooden boat filled with a colorful array of artfully arranged sushi rolls. I picked up my chopsticks and grabbed a plump roll, popped it into my mouth, and ungracefully filled both my cheeks—most likely resembling a chipmunk.

"Which one did you try?" John asked.

I couldn't speak, because the roll was taking over my mouth. Turning my head in the opposite direction, I chewed as fast as I could, but it was taking forever to swallow. At the exact moment that I glanced toward the sushi bar, feeling like Miss Piggy, the guy from the gondola stood up to leave. When our eyes met, he smirked at me before heading toward the exit. Slouching low into my seat, I took a sip of wine to wash down the remaining rice and seaweed and to cool off the blaze in my face.

"I think that was the Blake roll, but I'm not sure," I said. "Whatever it was, it was messy but tasty."

I watched John stab a roll with a fork, put it on his plate, and cut it up into small pieces. I had never seen anyone eat sushi like that before. It was odd, and it seemed rather unsophisticated.

John told me about his custom corrugated box company, which he had sold. While he spoke, he continued to make involuntary movements with his nose.

"I got lucky. I managed to make more money from the sale than I would have expected. It was enough that I don't have to work anymore," he said. A guy with money was a bonus.

I told him about Bobby and Megan, and then I asked, "Do you have kids?"

His eyes lit up. "I have a son." The nose twitched. "His name is Peter, and he's a sophomore at Washington University in St. Louis. He's my pride and joy. We used to travel to Aspen twice a year to ski together." Another bonus—he had a great relationship with his son. "My ex-wife had no interest in joining us. She was probably too busy in bed with our accountant, who is now my ex-best friend."

I could detect a hint of tears filling his eyes when he mentioned his ex-wife. Although I couldn't relate to having had a spouse cheat on me, we seemed to both suffer from broken hearts.

"Tell me about your artwork," he asked with genuine interest. I started to count the number of times he was making those subtle, involuntary movements with his nose.

"There's not much to tell. I used to paint, but I haven't picked up a paintbrush in years."

"Well, what's stopping you?" John asked, tilting his head to one side, smiling, and twitching his nose again. I was taking a mental inventory of what I liked and didn't like about him. The fact that he seemed like a great father and a good provider was taking precedence over the things I wasn't too fond of.

"I don't know. It's hard to find time. My kids keep me busy."

"I'm sure when you're ready, you'll begin again."

When he smiled, I noticed a piece of seaweed between his two front teeth. I took another sip of my wine to distract myself from focusing on it.

At the end of the meal, he handed the server his credit card.

"Thank you for dinner. I had a nice time," I said. Glancing at my watch, I realized I had to hurry. "I'm so sorry to run out of here, but I have to catch the next Dial-A-Ride bus."

"My car is outside. Let me give you a ride."

"Are you sure? It's not a big deal to get on the bus."

"I insist," he said.

Before exiting the restaurant, I looked back at the bar. When Jason and I made eye contact, he gave me a wide grin that sent an electric current through the air, making me wish I was leaving with him. *Shit, Hope. What are you doing*? I scolded myself. Jason could only be a boy toy. John was wholesome, kind, chivalrous, and would be an ideal provider for me and the kids.

He walked over to the passenger side of his black Audi Q7 and opened the door for me. In the dark car, John's profile wasn't bad. I could picture him being gentle and attentive in bed. He was like a fine wine; his age could actually make him tastier. I decided that I should get to know him a little better.

"Do you want to come in?" I asked when he pulled into my driveway.

He flashed me an excited grin. "I'd love to," he said eagerly.

He waited in the car while I paid the babysitter and checked to make sure the kids were sleeping. Then I opened the garage and let him inside.

"What can I get you to drink?" I asked as he followed me into the kitchen.

"What do you have?"

"How about a vodka on the rocks?"

"Sounds good."

Filling two glasses with ice and Ketel One, I could sense him standing behind me. When I turned around, ready to hand the glass to him, I noticed he had a nervous expression on his face. He wanted to kiss me, but I could tell he was afraid.

I set the drinks down and made my way toward him, but he still didn't budge from his spot. Without hesitation, I went for it. Our lips collided, and he thrust his tongue inside my mouth, thrashing it around like a wild animal. It was wet and sloppy, and his breath had a stale garlic stench to it. His tongue reminded me of a cat slurping its milk. My body tensed up.

"John," I said. When I pulled away, I gagged a little when I noticed he still had the piece of seaweed stuck in his teeth. "I'm so sorry. You seem like a great guy, but I'm just not ready yet."

Sadly, I was ready, only not with John.

He gazed down at the tile floor and said, "It's okay," in a sweet and gentle voice that made me feel sorry for him.

"Thank you again for dinner," I said as I walked him to the front door.

As soon as he left, I ran upstairs and brushed my teeth hard and furiously before peeling off my clothes and jumping into bed. My wired eyes were mesmerized by the crescent-shaped waning moon that hung in the blackened sky outside my window. It gave off a subtle blue tinge that matched my mood. Sleep seemed far away. While I waited for my eyelids to get heavy, I rubbed the contours of the crystal tattoo that embellished my private region. It still had its perfect butterfly shape, but, *unfortunately*, I thought to myself, *nobody will ever get to see it.*

21

2013

NATURALLY, WHEN CHRISTOPHER DIED, my sex life died along with him. It had been over two years since my one-night stand with Richard. The longer I went without any kind of male penetration, the more I wanted it. But after my date with John, I was discouraged from searching for a male companion online. For the time being, the only kind of stimulation I could get was from a few lame sex toys and my imagination, which eventually led to a new obsession—erotica books. Since I wasn't going to get any real-life action, I could at least fantasize about the love lives of fictional characters.

After devouring *Fifty Shades of Grey* in one sitting, I was ravenous for another book, so I ran over to the local bookstore to see if they had any juicy stories for me to read. I walked past the clerk at the front of the store, whose head was buried in a magazine, and made my way to the erotica section, located along the back wall. Titles like *Love Me Hot, Into the Sex Zone*, and *Fondle Me Hard* grabbed my attention. I pulled them off the shelves and skimmed through the pages. The vivid sex scenes jumped out at me, and I couldn't wait to get home and get lost inside the stories.

"Hope?" a man said.

Startled, I looked up, and the books slipped out of my hand. Book covers with images of scantily dressed men and women in steamy embraces scattered on the floor between us. I didn't recognize the guy standing before me. Wearing his trucker hat backward, he had on distressed jeans and a ratty T-shirt that accentuated his sculpted arms. His model-like body resembled one of the characters from my romance novels.

"It's Jason," he said.

The name didn't ring a bell.

"We met a while ago at Kenichi. I'm the bartender."

"Oh, my God; yes, of course. I can't believe you remembered my name."

"It's kind of a thing I have. I'm really good at names."

Stuffy air was sucking all the oxygen from the store, and I could feel my body temperature rising.

"Here," he said, picking up the books from the floor. "Ooh, these look interesting," he said, glancing at the covers.

I was about to come up with some ridiculous lie and tell him they were for a friend, but instead, I came right out and said, "Well, it's about the only excitement in my life."

His full lips spread into a wide smile. "Hey, I'm not working tonight. I was thinking about grabbing some beers at the J-Bar. Why don't you join me?"

"Uh, I guess so. I just need to make sure I can get a sitter at the last minute."

"All right, good."

We exchanged phone numbers, and then I admired his luscious ass as he walked away. After purchasing my books, I sent Tracy a text inquiring about Jason.

She replied, "Hottest guy in town. Why, what's up?"

"Meeting him tonight for a drink."

"Do yourself a favor and let Jason wake up your sleeping pussy."

My body melted at the thought.

After getting the green light from Tracy, I started fantasizing about taking Jason home after our date. I was imagining him naked, when I suddenly remembered that I needed to find a babysitter for the kids.

I called Dani, who was always willing to help at the last minute if I couldn't get a sitter.

"Any chance my kids can spend the night at your house this evening?" I asked when she answered the phone.

"Of course," Dani said.

"You're a lifesaver. Thank you."

"I'm the one who should be thanking you. Having your kids around makes my life so much easier."

I was lucky to have Dani as a friend, and it was a bonus that our kids got along so well. Megan babysat for her younger son, Beckett. And since Dani treated Megan like the daughter she had always wanted, Megan loved going to their house. "What do you have going on tonight?" she asked.

I filled her in on my exchange with Jason, promising to share the details with her in the morning.

* * *

After tearing through my closet, looking for something to wear that had sex appeal, I finally settled on black leather pants, wedges, and a low-cut scoop-neck sweater that showed off my cleavage. I put on a heavy layer of black and gray eye shadow, giving my eyes a smoky look. Satisfied with my appearance, I hopped on the bus to town and then walked to the J-bar, located in the iconic Hotel Jerome.

My leather pants were making me perspire as I made my way through the eclectic lobby. Objects from the Wild West, Native Americans, Prohibition, and silver mining days decorated the stately room, along with European antiques. I discreetly slipped my fingers under my pits to make sure they weren't sweating through my shirt. I had put deodorant on, but it didn't feel like it was working too well. Once inside the J-bar, which resembled an Old West saloon, I spotted Jason, dressed in a red flannel shirt, sitting on one of the leather-back chairs at the corner of the bar. When he noticed me, he waved his hand.

"Hey, I'm so glad you made it," he said, giving me a peck on the cheek. His unshaven face scratched like sandpaper against my skin, but in a strange way, I liked his manly touch. "What can I get you to drink?"

I noticed he was drinking a beer. "I'll take an IPA."

He signaled to the young bartender, a voluptuous brunette with bleach-blonde streaks in her hair, and ordered a pitcher of beer. While we waited for our drinks, Jason looked at me with an impish expression. "So, how are your new books?"

"Quite entertaining."

"I bet. Maybe you can tell me about them later."

The bartender poured me a tall glass of beer. "Maybe," I said, blushing as I took a sip.

"Can I get you guys anything to eat?" the bartender asked.

Jason turned to me. "You hungry? The wings are awesome here."

The last time I had polished off a plate of wings was during my post-college days in Aspen, back when we lived off cheap beer and cheap food. "Sounds good," I said. "I'm starving."

He placed the order and then took a sip of his drink. The frothy beer landed on his upper lip. I watched as he licked it off with his tongue.

"So, what do you do in town?" he asked.

"Not much. I'm a stay-at-home mom. It's not that exciting. What about you? Do you do anything besides work at Kenichi?"

"I ski a lot in the winter and mountain bike in the summer, but that's about it. Just living the life."

Jason didn't exactly fit my criteria for a future mate, but I wasn't looking for that this evening.

The spicy smell of the buffalo wings cleared my nasal passages when the server placed them in front of us. I couldn't wait to slather the saucy fried chicken wings in the chunky blue cheese dressing.

"These are so good," I said after taking a bite of a messy wing. We both nibbled meat off the bones until there was nothing left.

"I like a woman who eats," Jason said.

I knew he meant it as a compliment, but it didn't make me feel ladylike.

"I think I could use a Wet-Nap," I said, noticing my saucy hands and the red-stained napkin draped on my lap.

"Here," he said, "I can help." Jason picked up my sticky hand. "Do you mind?"

"Go right ahead," I said.

Parting his lips, he placed my greasy index finger into his warm mouth, gently sucking off the sauce. The sensation sent me whirling.

"Tasty?" I asked, before taking a large sip of my beer to cool myself down.

"Very."

This was moving a lot faster than I would have imagined. "Should I ask how old you are?"

He placed his hand on my knee. "Does it matter?"

"To be honest, no—I don't really give a shit." Erotic thoughts about Jason were howling inside me. I had no interest in telling him about my life or beating myself up for being with a guy that was probably fifteen years younger than me. I wanted sex, and I wanted it now. "My kids are out for the night."

"Do you live near town?" he asked.

"About a mile away."

"I'd like to see where you live," he said.

"I'd like to show you."

Jason signaled to the waiter to bring our bill, and then he threw a wad of cash on the counter. Anxious to get home, we jumped into a cab outside the hotel entrance. For the entire ride, he rubbed his masculine hand on my inner thigh, making my legs sizzle inside my hot leather pants. As soon as we pulled into the driveway, Jason handed the cab driver money, and we rushed into the house.

"Want a drink?" I asked when we walked into the family room.

Grabbing my arm, he pulled me into him. "No, I'm good," he said tenderly.

Then he guided his lips toward mine, and his tongue probed the inside of my mouth in an urgent way. My burning fire escalated as our kissing grew harder, deeper, and more intense. I tugged his belt open and unfastened his jeans, while he reached behind my back to unhook my bra. Ripping the rest of each other's clothes off, we somehow made our way toward the couch. I rubbed my hands all over the contours of his pectorals, reveling in the warmth and curves of his body. He grabbed his crumbled jeans off the floor and pulled a condom from one of the pockets. I made a strange animal sound when he thrust inside me. We moved back and forth with rhythmic pleasure. It was pure sex, the kind my body was aching for.

When it was over, I quivered with exhaustion—a reminder of how good it felt to have a man inside of me.

I got up from underneath him and sat up. "Thank you," I said.

"Thank you, Hope. I had a great time tonight. We should definitely hang out again."

I picked my shirt up off the floor and put it on. I looked at his perfectly mussed hair and lightly tanned skin and said, "Definitely."

On his way to the door, Jason stopped in front of one of my old paintings that was hanging on the wall. It was an image of a bright red Aspen leaf suspended in midair and about to land on the ground. "Cool painting," he said.

"Thanks. I painted it years ago."

"No shit, really? You're an artist?"

"I was. I haven't picked up a brush in years."

"Why not? You're obviously talented."

"I don't know. I lost my inspiration a long time ago." I opened the front door to let him out. "Good night," I said as he stepped outside into the cool night air. Feeling satiated, I ran into my bedroom, got ready for bed, and fell into a deep sleep.

The following morning, Jason sent me a text asking when he could see me again.

I replied, *How about late tonight after the kids are asleep?*

Can't wait, he texted back.

For the rest of the day, all I thought about was having sex with Jason again. Just like the water boiling on the stove while I prepared dinner, my body was bubbling with images of Jason touching my naked flesh. Bouncing around the kitchen, I prepared the kids their favorite meal.

"Guys, dinner is ready," I yelled.

Bobby ran to the table first. "Yay! Baked ziti," he cheered. Once seated, he clutched his fork and started to inhale the food.

Unlike her brother, Megan took her time walking into the kitchen and taking a seat at the table. Tiny red pimples had sprouted all over her face. At thirteen, my little girl had crossed the threshold into the teenage years. Along with the acne came the attitude, the moodiness, and the changing body. It was the latest roller-coaster ride that I was trying to manage the best I could.

"Mom, we started a huge project on Ancient Egypt," Megan said. "We're going to be working on it for the next few months, and then there's going to be a huge presentation in the spring." She took a piece of garlic bread off the platter. "All the parents will be invited to it," she said between mouthfuls of food. "And we're supposed to dress up in costumes."

Hearing this, my creative light bulb turned on. "Why don't we make something? We can go to the craft store and buy the material. It's a pretty simple costume to make. We just need a white sheet, gold spray paint, and beads." I poured the kids glasses of water. "And we can get ribbon too."

"Seriously?" Megan said, rolling her eyes. "Why can't we just order a costume on Amazon? That's what everyone else in my class is doing."

Bobby had red sauce all over his face. I got up from the table and wet a paper towel. He didn't budge when I wiped his cheek, which I noticed had been slimming down. Although he was beginning to lose his baby fat, he was still another three years away from becoming a testy teenager like his sister.

"It'll be more fun to make a costume than buy one online," I told Megan before biting into a piece of garlic bread and moistening my lips with grease.

"It's kind of funny that you always complain about Grandma Audrey's crafts. And you're, like, the exact same!"

Megan got up from the table, brought her dish over to the sink, and stormed out of the kitchen. I fought the urge to call her a bitch. It must have been Megan's hormones acting up. I wasn't like my mother at all. The only thing my mother ever talked about was her deviled eggs, crocheted designs, and bizarre crafts. I had never made a deviled egg in my life, and I had no idea how to crotchet. Not to mention, unlike my mom, who never went to college, I had a bachelor's degree in fine arts.

* * *

Jason had become my human sex toy. A few nights a week, after the kids were asleep, I would text him to come over. He never refused unless he was working late, and even then, he would text me afterward to see if I was awake. Our relationship was purely physical. Once in a while, he would pass out in my bed, but I would always wake him up before sunrise and make him leave just in case the kids woke up.

A few months into my trysts with Jason, I started growing bored with him. Our late-night booty calls were waning, and as much as I enjoyed the sex, I still yearned for more—to connect with someone on a deeper level—the way I had with Christopher. My body was into it, but my heart wasn't.

"That was great," Jason said after sex one night.

Sitting up, I rested my head on my hand and looked at him. "Are you happy with your life, Jason?"

"Fuck yeah. What isn't there to be happy about? I live in this incredible town, ski over a hundred days a year, and get to have regular sex with a hot mamma."

"But where do you see yourself in ten, twenty years from now?"

"Why does it matter? I like to live in the here and now and not think about tomorrow. Why are you getting all deep on me, Hope? We have a good thing here."

Carpe diem, I thought to myself, wondering if he even knew what that meant. "Yeah, you're right," I said in a flat voice. I got off the bed and threw on a T-shirt and sweatpants. "You better get going. I think the next bus is coming soon."

I slept intermittently that night. Something was tugging at my heart. One of the things I loved about living in Aspen was that it embraced a community where one could nourish the mind, body, and spirit. When I moved back to Aspen, I had rediscovered two out of the three—nature and exercise—both of which had helped feed my spirit and body. But ever since I had stopped painting years earlier, I'd lost the mental stimulation.

After dropping the kids off at school the following morning, I rushed home and parked my car in the driveway. On the way into the house, I noticed the yellow glow of the sun moving over the mountaintops. Tiny buds reared their heads on the trees and flowers that surrounded the house, getting ready to blossom in the next couple of weeks. As I gazed at the wonders of the changing seasons, an image of a scene that I had painted a long time ago popped into my head.

Stepping into the garage, I made a beeline past the bucket of balls, sporting equipment, skis, poles, and bicycles. I made my way toward a pile of unopened boxes in the back corner. A wave of relief came over me when I found what I was searching for, as though I had been connected with a long-lost friend.

I frantically ripped the tape off the box labeled "ART SUPPLIES." Inside was my plein air easel. I pulled it out, ignoring the crumbled newspapers that fell alongside the box and the musty scent that tickled my nose. My parents had given me this small portable easel made of unfinished beechwood my senior year of college. When folded, it was about the same size as a briefcase. I adjusted the three legs to its fullest height. The drawer was filled with tubes of paint, hard and dried-out paintbrushes in various sizes, oil sticks, and turpentine. My fingers were aching to wet the brushes and squeeze the paint on the palette.

Years ago, I had started a painting that I had named *Springtime Thaw*. It was an image of a thawing lake blanketed with chunks of melting snow. After a quick search, I located the unfinished painting in a box in the back of the garage. When I pulled it out, I could almost hear it speaking to me, begging me to show it love again.

I placed *Springtime Thaw* securely on the easel. Right away, I could see what was wrong with this painting—there wasn't enough expression, feeling, or energy in it. It had been difficult to capture the effervescent water bubbling under the heavy snow that covered the rocks, and I hadn't painted the rocks substantially enough. But now, years later, in an entirely different state of mind, I could create what was lacking in the original piece. I could feel the emotional weight and translate the color and the cold depth of the scene. When I first started the painting, I had been a young newlywed living a peaceful and happy life. An artist's work was guided by her emotional state, reflecting her feelings through her craft. Back then, I couldn't accurately portray the melting water rising above, even on my darkest day—but today I could. Today, I finally understood.

I prepared a palette of blacks, whites, and shades of gray. Next, I wet my brushes and let my fingers guide me along the landscape of the dichotic image that I was attempting to recreate—representing a dismal landscape, as well as one that showed change and movement. The music had finally come back, and while I painted, I heard the melody playing in my mind, awakening my senses and guiding me into another world. The hours passed while I lost myself inside the scene, unaware of time and oblivious to standing on the cold concrete in the garage.

I almost had a heart attack when, out of nowhere, I was startled by the roaring sound and vibration of the garage door opening. Looking at the rising door, I spotted Bobby's Nike sneakers and Megan's chocolate brown boots, then their jeans, their jackets, and eventually their faces. *Shit. I forgot about the kids.*

When our eyes met, Bobby yelled, "Mom, why didn't you meet us at the bus stop?"

"What are you painting?" Megan asked as she walked over to look at my painting.

"I'm so sorry. I was so caught up in working on this that I must have lost track of time."

"I can't believe you made this. It's amazing," Megan said.

"You can totally sell it and make lots of money," Bobby chimed in.

Chuckling, I said, "Thank you, but I don't know about that. For now, I'm just happy to be painting again. It's been a long time." I placed the paints back inside the drawer in my easel. "Do you guys want an afterschool snack?"

"Yes, I'm starving," Bobby said. "But, Mom, you should wash yourself before coming inside. You have paint all over your clothes and in your eyebrows."

"Okay, you two, you head inside. I'll be in soon."

Megan turned around before opening the door, "Mom, remember when you suggested we make a costume for my Ancient Egypt presentation?"

"Oh yeah, I totally forgot. We need to order something. Isn't it due in a few weeks?"

"Yeah, it's due at the end of the month. My teacher said that some of the kids made their costumes last year and they were really good. So, if it's okay, could we drive down valley this weekend and buy the supplies?"

"You bet, sweetheart."

Smiling, she said, "Thank you, Mommy." Megan paused for a moment with her hand on the door handle. "I'm sorry I was mean about the costume when you first suggested it, and I'm glad you're like Grandma Audrey."

I couldn't believe she had said that to me again. I was nothing like my mother with her silly crafts and lowbrow homemade party food. Was I?

When Megan needed a costume, it hadn't even occurred to me to buy one. I had gotten excited about the prospect of doing a crafty project—just like my mother. Maybe Megan was right. Her apology spoke volumes about her level of maturity, and it made me think about how I had treated my mother over the years. Throughout my entire life, she had always put my needs before her own, without expecting anything in return. It was about time I grew up and followed Megan's lead.

I picked up the phone and called my mother.

"Hi, Mom."

"Oh, hi, honey. It's so good to hear your voice. I haven't spoken to you in quite some time."

"I know. I'm sorry. I've been kind of busy," I told her. "The kids are waiting for me, so I only have a minute."

"Is everything all right?"

"Yes, there's something I want to tell you."

"What is it, dear?" There was a slight inflection in her voice.

"I want to apologize."

"For what?"

"For all the times I haven't treated you well, and for all the times I've snapped at you when all you've ever done is try to help me." I swallowed the lump in my throat. "I also want to thank you for teaching me how to mother my children with the same unconditional love that you've always shown me."

"Oh, Hope. Thank you for saying that to me. Your words are choking me up."

"I love you, Mom."

After I hung up, I glanced back at my painting hanging on the easel and let the tears spill down my face. My kids were getting older, and before long they were going to fly away from their nest. If I didn't find a way to be inspired—to be passionate—I would be frozen forever.

These tears felt different than all the other tears I'd cried over the years. These tears were washing away the anger, the sadness, and the self-pity. *Springtime Thaw* meant that even under the heaviest layers of icy snow on a somber, gray day, when the sun was hidden beyond the bleak sky, nature never stopped its perfect cycle, moving through life from season to season.

I wiped away the last of my tears and thanked Christopher for showing me that painting could be my guiding light. Ultimately, the sun's rays would melt winter away, the rivers and streams would flow again, the animals would awaken from a long hibernation, and life would begin anew.

22

AFTER I FINISHED *SPRINGTIME THAW*, I began to work on a new collection of art. Somewhere in the back of my garage, I had found an old box filled with tree slices varying in size, from six inches to two feet in diameter and about two inches thick. I picked up one of the wood slices and brushed my hand along the rough edge and coarse surface. Following the black rings on the face of the slice with my eyes, I wondered what stories the wheels of wood told, what secrets they held, and if there was a way they could impart their wisdom.

Back in college, I had learned a method of art known as encaustic, painting on a surface with hot colored wax. My plan was to bring these pieces of wood back to life, uplifting them with beauty and deep meaning. One after the other, I painted each slice of wood in an array of bold colors that spoke to me, making each one shine. Then I added an inspirational word using a letterpress: *Love. Beauty. Faith. Change. Light. Believe. Dream. Ignite. Live. Gratitude.*

When I completed ten of them, I hung the series of circles in a random display along an empty wall in my living room, and then I took a deeply satisfying breath and admired them from my couch. I decided to name the collection *Wall of Intention*. The stamp of emotion that the slices of wood embodied told a new story, one that replaced a life of emptiness and tragedy with joy, abundance, and serenity.

Picking up my phone to check the time, I noticed two missed calls and a text message from Dani. *Where are you? The game is starting in fifteen minutes.*

Holy shit! I hadn't realized what time it was. "Bobby!" I screamed. "We have to hurry up. We're late for your lacrosse game."

Running around the house like lunatics, we gathered his equipment and got dressed. At the last minute, Megan decided to join us. Even though we jumped into the car in record time, I still blamed myself for not paying attention to the time as we sped across town toward the field, praying we'd make it there before the game started.

"Grab your stuff and move fast," I told Bobby when we pulled into the parking lot. I let out a deep exhale, relieved that we had arrived in the nick of time. Watching my boy run toward the field, dressed in his pads and oversized black and red lacrosse jersey, warmed my insides. He had asked the coach for number sixty-four, the same number his dad had worn in high school. "And good luck, sweetheart," I called out through the open window.

There was a brisk chill in the air, even though the cloudless sky was a clear, sapphire blue. The weather was unpredictable in May. One week it could be warm, melting the winter snow off the mountains, and the next week we could get another snowstorm. Dressing in layers was critical this time of year. I grabbed a blanket from the back of my car, and then Megan and I headed toward the bleachers to find Dani.

"Over here," she called, waving to us. Dani was wearing designer ripped jeans, combat boots, and a sweater underneath a black, down-filled Moncler vest. Rose-gold-rimmed sunglasses covered her eyes, and she wore a touch of pink gloss on her lips. Her understated chic style was making me feel self-conscious in my black leggings and North Face jacket. Her six-year-old son,

Becket, was sitting next to her. He had a fluffy head of blond curly hair, and his big blue eyes lit up when he saw Megan.

"I was worried about you guys," Dani said when we sat down. Becket climbed over his mother and crawled onto Megan's lap. Little kids always gravitated to her. I wondered if it was because she had a younger sibling or if she just had a natural affinity for children.

"If you hadn't texted me, I'm not sure we would have made it here," I told Dani.

"What were you doing?" she asked.

"I started working on a new collection of art and lost track of time."

While we waited for the game to begin, I twisted my simple white gold wedding band around my finger a few times, thankful that I had remembered to wear it today. Each time I turned it, I prayed that Christopher would bring our son good luck.

"Have you considered showing your work in any of the local galleries?"

"No, not yet. I mean, I would love to, but at this point I'm just happy to be painting again after all these years."

Ten minutes into the game, the crowd started screaming and clapping when a boy scooped the ball off the ground and charged toward the goal. I looked over to see who it was, and held my breath when I realized it was Bobby. I stood up and called out in excitement, "Go, Bobby!" He sped past two boys, who swung their sticks toward his helmet. He dodged them both and shot the ball directly into the net. It bounced over the goalie's head and landed in the back corner. "Way to go," I yelled again, still in shock that he had just scored a goal.

"What an amazing goal!" Dani said, congratulating me. A feeling of pride plunged through me. "Drew has been helping out during their practices. He told me that Bobby's been working hard."

Dani's husband, Drew, reminded me a lot of Christopher. Raised in an affluent home, he had attended prestigious private schools, yet he was down-to-earth and a loving family man with a big heart. Without a doubt, our husbands would have been great friends.

The Aspen team lost the game, but I didn't care. I was excited that Bobby had scored his first goal. Dani and I made our way down the bleachers to the field. Following behind us, Megan held Becket's hand.

"Do you and the kids want to join us for dinner tonight at The Meatball Shack?" Dani asked as we walked toward the team to congratulate the boys. A successful entrepreneur, Drew had sold his business in New York City and opened The Meatball Shack when they had moved to Aspen.

I couldn't think of a better way to spend Saturday night. The kids could play at the park across from the restaurant, while Dani and I enjoyed some wine and an adult conversation. "Sure, we'd love to. I'm actually craving the chicken parmesan."

I saw Bobby gulping from his water bottle. His hair looked greasy and matted down from his helmet, and his forehead was dripping with sweat. "Great game, honey!" I told him, smiling proudly.

"That was an impressive goal you scored," Dani said.

I watched with envy as Drew greeted his wife with a peck on the lips. He was wearing a white, Aspen Lacrosse practice T-shirt, and his black curly hair was sticking out of a Yankees baseball cap. He turned toward Bobby and said, "Good game, Whitmore," and gave him a fist bump. Then he looked at me and said, "You've got a great kid here, Hope."

"Thank you," I told him, as warmth spread through my veins. Despite everything we had been through, I knew I had two amazing kids who were all right—our family was all right.

"Are you guys ready to go to The Meatball Shack for dinner?" I asked Bobby and Megan.

"Yeah!" the kids yelled in unison.

On the drive to town, I thought about everything Dani had done for me since we had become friends. She and Drew had treated us to many dinners at the restaurant, and she was always available to help with Bobby and Megan. I wanted to show my gratitude for her friendship.

I texted Dani to let her know that I needed to make a quick stop at home and would be a few minutes late for dinner. Then I let the kids wait in the car while I ran inside. I grabbed the largest wheel off the wall and placed it in a shopping bag. The word *Grateful* floated in the center of the tree slice, surrounded by a subtle, swirly texture of seafoam green.

By the time we arrived at the restaurant, the sun had warmed the outside temperature, making it a pleasant evening to sit outside, assuming I kept my lightweight jacket on. Dani was sitting at a corner table on the patio, not a hair out of place. Jack and Becket were fidgeting in their chairs nearby.

As soon as they saw us, Jack leaped out of his chair. "Can we go to the playground now?"

I turned to Megan. "Do you want to take the boys over there?"

"Yeah, sure." She then picked up Becket and gave him a bear hug.

"Thank you, Megan. You're the best," Dani said.

We watched as Jack and Bobby raced each other across the cobblestone walkway, while Megan carried Becket behind them.

"Rosé?" Dani asked.

"Yes, please."

She poured me a large glass.

"Here," I said, handing her the shopping bag. "I brought you something."

Dani flashed me a curious look before opening the bag. She pulled out the piece of art and held it in her hands, examining it for a moment. "Hope, this is amazing. It's so inspirational. I love it."

"I'm glad you like it," I said, taking a sip of my wine.

"This is one of the most beautiful gifts anyone has ever given me."

"It's the least I can do. You and Drew are always treating me and the kids to dinner."

"Well, I'm truly grateful, no pun intended."

The waitress brought us a plate piled with meatballs, blanketed in a reddish orange sauce and embellished with swirly curls of carrots and celery. I started to salivate as soon as the spicy smell hit my nose.

"I hope it's okay," Dani said. "I ordered these before you got here. Buffalo chicken meatballs. They're one of my favorites on the menu."

"These look insane," I said, taking a meatball and putting it on my plate. "I can't believe I never ordered them before." After dipping it into the blue cheese, I took a bite. The spicy meatball melted in my mouth, and eating them with a fork was a lot neater than eating chicken wings with my hands. "The last time I ate wings was with Jason."

"How are things going with him?"

"I don't know. I'm kind of over him. I think I need to find someone my own age, someone with life goals and ambition."

Drew came outside dressed in jeans and a black sweater with his sleeves pulled up to his elbows, and he headed to our table. His black unshaven facial hair against his olive skin and curly chest hair sticking out from his V-neck made me wonder if he was part Greek or Italian, or maybe even Israeli.

"Hey, ladies," he said, leaning over to kiss his wife, making me ooze with envy.

"Hi, honey. Why don't you sit and eat with us?" Dani asked.

"I'd love to, but tonight is asshole night at the restaurant. For some reason, all the assholes have decided to eat here for dinner. A guy came in and ordered the rack of lamb special. The schmuck ate the entire meal, practically licked his plate clean, and then told the waitress he didn't like it and thought it was too expensive. Do you believe the nerve?"

"I can't believe someone would do that. What did you say to him?" I asked.

"I told him if he doesn't pay for his meal I would call my good friend Sheriff Thompson and have him arrested. And then I told him never to come back." He took a sip of Dani's wine. "Do you want me to order food for the kids?"

"They seem busy over at the playground. We should probably wait until they come back," Dani said.

"I better get back inside the restaurant for some more damage control."

When he walked away, I refilled both our glasses with wine. "Drew seems like a great husband."

"Like any married couple, we've had our ups and downs. We've been together since college, but overall, I do appreciate how lucky I am." She took a bite of a meatball. "I know you told me once before, but remind me again how you met Christopher."

I smiled at the memory. "We were both living in Aspen after we graduated from college. Believe it or not, I met him at the Red Onion. He was working as a bartender. I think I fell in love with him the moment I laid eyes on him." My voice cracked slightly. "He was my everything—tall, handsome, athletic, kind, and funny."

Dani placed her hand on mine and said, "It sounds like he was special."

"He was. I often fantasize about finding another Christopher to sweep me off my feet and help me take care of the kids, but no matter how hard I look, I'll never be able to replace him." My eyes wandered in the direction of the playground. Jack and Bobby were walking across the rope bridge toward Megan and Becket, who were sitting on top of the climbing rock.

"What do you say we have one more glass of wine before calling the kids over for dinner?" Dani asked.

The waitress placed two new glasses of wine on the table, and then she cleared our dirty dishes. When she walked away, Dani looked at me with wide eyes. "Hope, I was thinking..." She paused for a second. "Maybe you're still in love with Christopher, and maybe you can't replace him or fall in love with someone else because you haven't been able to let go and move on."

As much as I loved Marcy and Tracy and appreciated their close friendship and support, neither one of them had ever suffered any kind of tragic loss, which made it difficult for them to understand what I was going through. Dani's father had died of a heart attack when she was a little girl. Sadly, both of us had experienced a spontaneous incident that changed our lives forever, forcing us to cope with something that felt so painfully unjust. I wondered if certain people came in and out of our lives for a reason. Maybe we crossed paths at different points, showing up only when we were ready to listen, and then it was our job to learn and grow from those relationships.

My eyes welled up. I knew, deep down, even after all these years, I was still in love with my dead husband. Lowering my gaze, I said, "I know. It's true. I don't know how to let go." There was a part of me that had gotten used to the empty space, almost like it was an invisible security blanket.

"For starters, I think it might be a good idea to take off your wedding band. I noticed you were wearing it at the lacrosse game this morning."

I twisted the ring around while she spoke.

"How many years ago did Christopher pass away?"

"Next March will be seven years."

"I once read an article in a yoga magazine that the number seven is a spiritual number. It may sound kind of strange, but it makes sense if you consider the significance of the number. Our bodies are made up of seven chakras, there are seven days of the week, and the number seven indicates a new cycle of change in a person's life, a completeness. I think we should plan a special ceremony that will allow you to symbolically release Christopher and help you move forward? And who knows? Maybe afterward you'll be able to fall in love again."

The sun was beginning to set behind the mountaintop, yet I could see a thin ray of light shimmering on one side of Aspen Mountain.

"I understand what you're saying, but I'm just not quite there yet."

"Well, I guess you'll know when the time is right."

When I got home from dinner, I sat on my couch to take another look at my *Wall of Intention*, mesmerized by the powerful words on the tree slices. They were alive. I could feel their energy bouncing off the walls, melding into my inner core. Somehow, I had managed to take something that had been dormant and unloved for years—something that had been cut off from its root—and I had turned it into a transformative piece of art.

That night, while I was lying in bed, Jason texted me. *You around tonight? I haven't seen you in a while.*

I'm really tired, I wrote back.

I can give you some energy, he wrote.

I felt bad texting this, but I needed to tell him that it was time to move on. *You're a great guy, but I think we both need to try to find someone our own age.* I pushed send immediately.

A moment later, he texted back, *Can we still be friends?*

Absolutely! I replied.

Relieved, I put my phone on airplane mode and went to sleep.

23

2015

IT WAS ONE OF THOSE epic Aspen days—the kind we pined for throughout the winter season. All night long the sky dumped massive snowflakes, and we woke up to two feet of fresh powder on a bluebird day. School was canceled, which was fine with me—I was excited for a family ski day.

I ran into the kids' rooms to wake them up. Bobby jumped out of bed when I told him we were going skiing. Megan wasn't as thrilled as her brother. Lying in bed, relishing the unexpected day off, she begged me to stay home and have a lazy day.

"Not a chance. Hurry up and get your ski clothes on. It's going to be incredible on the mountain," I told her, confident that once she got on the slopes, she'd love it.

I rushed the kids out the door nearly an hour before the Silver Queen gondola opened. I was chomping at the bit to get on the mountain and ski the fresh, untracked runs. Before long, we were floating down the cloud-like terrain, skiing for hours until our weary legs finally gave out on us. Over the years, the kids had become incredible skiers. I was sure Christopher was watching us from above with a fat grin on his face. It seemed like a lifetime ago when their father had taught them to make pizza shapes with their skis on our first family vacation in Aspen. Now they carved turns seamlessly down every expert run.

Ever since Christopher put a ring on my finger, I had held onto my dream of moving back to Aspen. Each time I had nagged him about it, he promised it would happen one day. But *one day* seemed light years away back then. In reality, he had no intention of turning away from his career until he proved to himself and his father that he had what it took to be a successful businessman. Sooner than expected, the universe granted my wish, only it wasn't the way I had imagined. In a heartbeat, I would trade Aspen for my former life in Concord with my husband. But I wasn't given that choice, so all I could do was accept my destiny and appreciate that my greatest loss had given me the precious gift of living here.

* * *

A few days after our magical ski day, Dani and Drew invited me to a small cocktail party at their house. I was looking forward to mingling with people my own age. Now that the kids were older, I didn't have to hire a babysitter, which made it easier to go out. I yelled goodbye to them and got into my car. The temperature had been in the single digits all day, turning the powdery snow that covered the town into a slick sheet of ice. Cranking up the heat to full blast, I anxiously waited for it to warm me up. It wasn't until I was halfway across town when I finally felt the hot air blowing through the vent.

My cell phone rang from inside my purse. I reached over to the passenger seat and into my purse to pull out my phone. I was concerned it was one of the kids. *I can't find my purple pajama pants,* Megan had texted.

Relieved it wasn't anything serious, I started to type back, alternating between looking at the keyboard and the road. The car began to slide out of control, and when I impulsively put my foot on the brake, I lost control and veered off to the side. It all happened so fast. The spinning car. The large animal with horns that sprang onto the street. And my body lashing forward when I came to an abrupt halt.

I clenched the steering wheel with all my might as an explosive pounding penetrated my chest. Squinting my eyes, I tried to decipher what I was looking at. It was a buck, followed by a doe and two fawns. They had crossed the road directly in front of me. I had nearly killed the buck. He was one second away from being whacked by my SUV—and it would have been my fault. An accident. It would have been an accident.

When I thought back to the night Christopher was hit, for the first time it dawned on me that it was just an accident. I flashed back to the priest who had spoken to me while I was in the hospital, asking me to forgive the woman who had hit us, and I remembered the rage that had pierced me when he mentioned her name.

I no longer felt that seething resentment. As time moved forward, the anger had subsided.

I stared ahead, unblinking, watching the deer family cross safely to the other side of the highway. Then I got back on the road and drove at a snail's pace. In the solace of my car, the words "I forgive you" fell from my lips. A heavy curtain began to lift from my shoulders and the back of my neck. "I forgive you," I repeated, increasing in decibel each time, until I pulled into Dani's driveway. These three simple words made me feel as though pounds of weight had melted off me.

* * *

The exterior lighting surrounding Dani and Drew's home looked bright and inviting against the blackened sky. Recently finished, their custom-built house was stunning, and no matter how many times I'd been inside, the architecture never ceased to amaze me, with its wide-plank oak floors, gray limestone and steel finishes, and large retractable glass doors that opened to an expansive deck, offering sweeping mountain views.

With trembling hands, I rang the doorbell. The near accident felt as though a storm was passing through me, colliding with the rainbow coming from the other side. Waiting for someone to answer the door, I squeezed my fists in a feeble attempt to push it away for good. I wanted the beauty that shined in the aftermath to take over—but I still heard the echo of thunder.

"You're finally here," Dani said when she opened the door. She was wearing a black silk jumpsuit with a halter top that revealed half her back. Noticing my weak smile, she asked, "Are you okay?"

"No. I mean, yes," I said, shaking my head left to right in rapid succession. I didn't want to ruin her night. Playing the part of the pathetic widow was exhausting. I was done with it.

"Come with me." Grabbing my hand, she took me into the powder room and shut the door. "What's wrong?"

I glanced in the mirror. My complexion was pallid. I told her about the incident on the road. She hugged me and said, "But you're okay. Nothing happened. Nobody was hurt."

"I know, but the accident was a wake-up call."

"What do you mean?" she asked, scrunching her eyebrows. "A wake-up call for what?"

"For all these years, I've been harboring anger and blame over losing Christopher. It's like the love and the hurt are so mixed up inside me that it shut my heart down."

"Hope, stop. You have the most beautiful heart. You're a wonderful mother and a wonderful friend."

"Thanks, but that's not what this is about. I'll never be able to move forward, unless I relinquish these feelings and accept my fate."

"Stop beating yourself up. You will."

"No, I won't. It's been seven years already. I need to let go once and for all. I think you were right. I should have some kind of ceremony to release Christopher's ashes."

Dani's eyes lit up. "Yes! Let's do it. I have a great idea. How about we hike up Buttermilk in the evening under the stars on the anniversary of Christopher's death, and we'll do it there?"

I nodded, and a tear slipped from the corner of my eye.

Dani rubbed my arm affectionately and then grabbed a tissue. "Here," she said, handing it to me. "Wipe your mascara, and let's get out of the bathroom and get you a drink."

I gently blotted the black smudges from under my eyes and then took a deep breath. When the air blew out of my mouth, the storm went with it.

"Ready?" Dani asked.

"Ready," I replied.

"Before we get you a drink," she said, opening the door, "there's someone important I want you to meet."

I prayed she wasn't trying to set me up with some guy. I wasn't in the mood. I followed her into the living room, which flowed seamlessly into the dining room. Candles were scattered on the shelves around the lit fireplace. Platters of appetizers sat on the oval wooden coffee table. I noticed a man wearing thick red-rimmed glasses talking to Drew. His paisley button-down shirt was open to reveal far too much gray chest hair. They were standing near the dining table, which was surrounded by cream-colored leather chairs. The prayer wheel that I had given to Dani was hanging on the wall separating the dining room from the kitchen, adding an element of interest to the minimalist decor.

"Jean-Claude, I would like you to meet the talented artist, Hope Whitmore," Dani said.

"Enchanté," Jean-Claude said, as he leaned in to air-kiss both of my cheeks. "You're just the woman I've been wanting to meet. Darling, I've been told that you are the master behind this piece of art. It's the work of a deep-thinking, creative genius."

"Thank you." I blushed slightly, flattered by the compliment.

"Jean-Claude and his partner, Owen, own L'art in Aspen," Dani said.

L'art was one of the exclusive, high-end art galleries in town. I had wandered in and out of it many times, admiring the artists' work. A petite man wearing a white cashmere sweater walked out of the kitchen, swaying his hips back and forth as he moved toward us, holding a glass of wine in his hand.

"There you are, Owen," Jean-Claude said. "This is the artist, Hope."

"Hope, it's a pleasure to meet you." A shower of spit shot out of his mouth, landing in my eye. I blinked a few times, but he didn't notice. "We've anxiously been awaiting your arrival," Owen said, smiling and showing off his pearly teeth. "Did you tell her, lovey?"

"No, darling, I was waiting for you." Jean-Claude winked at Owen and then looked at me. "We're having an exhibition with local artists in mid-March. Do you have a studio? We would love to see more of your work and further discuss the possibility of showcasing your art."

My heart started to race and my knees weakened. I raised my eyebrows in disbelief. "That would be amazing," I said, pinching myself to make sure this wasn't a dream.

"Why don't you give me your contact information so we can set something up for next week?"

I gave him my phone number and then added self-consciously, "I work out of my garage."

"Wonderful. We'll chit-chat on Monday," Jean-Claude said.

"I need to get Hope a glass of wine," Dani interjected, grabbing my arm and pulling me toward the built-in bar on the other side of the living room.

When I was sure they couldn't hear us, I whispered in Dani's ear, "I don't know if I can do this."

"Yes, Hope, you can. This is the break you've been waiting for your entire life. You'll buckle down over the next few weeks and work your ass off. I'm happy to help with the kids. Now that we're finally settled in the house, I'll have a lot of free time on my hands." She handed me a glass of wine. "Come on. I want you to meet my other guests."

The rest of the night flew by. There were about ten other people at the party, all couples—husbands, wives, and partners. I was the only single woman there. For the first time since Christopher had passed away, I didn't care that I was at a party alone. It could have been because now I had something else to focus on—a potential art career. As I was heading toward the seventh anniversary of Christopher's death, I was finally shedding a layer of old skin.

Before I left, Dani said, "I can't wait to head up the mountain for our special ceremony. It's only two weeks from today."

Like clockwork, every year, I could sense the date approaching. Somehow, I managed to find a way to channel my sadness into my creative work, and with the possibility of an upcoming exhibition, I would be too busy for sorrow. It took me a long time to figure out how to reignite my inner pilot light. The flame had burned out many years ago. I now realized that my husband's death was part of some greater plan, altering the way I would go through life. It may not have been a curse after all, but a catalyst that had allowed me to become someone else—a woman who was strong, resilient, independent, and capable.

Unlike so many widows, I was one of the luckier ones. Christopher's life insurance policy allowed me to maintain my lifestyle, and for the time being, I could raise my kids without having to go back to work. I was surrounded by loving friends and family members who always had my back. Like a spider tangled in my own web of selfish suffering, I had failed to appreciate all the good in my life. I had failed to see that everything was a mind-set. But now I realized that you could change your mind-set—and change the way you see the world.

24

IT WAS A BLUSTERY WINTER day. An angry wind blew the snow across the landscape, and the sky had a stale, shallow gray tone that hid the sun beyond the clouds. The foreboding weather at midday pleaded with people to stay inside to keep warm. The last thing I wanted to do was hike up the mountain at sundown.

I texted Dani to try to get out of it. *The weather is pretty ugly out there. Should we postpone the pilgrimage?*

Absolutely not, she responded. *Today is the anniversary. Layer up and take hand warmers. I'll see you tonight.*

I knew she was right, but the thought of tackling the mountain when the weather was like this sent a chill through my bones. Throughout the afternoon, I was hoping she would change her mind and call it off, but I never heard from her again.

Before leaving, I went upstairs to my bedroom with a large plastic Ziploc bag and a teaspoon. The shiny bronze urn, with gold and ebony finishes, was sitting in the center of my night table. Despite its heavy appearance, it was actually lightweight. My hands were unsteady as I took off the top and opened the sealed bag inside, revealing the remains of my husband's body. I used the teaspoon to shovel spoonfuls into the Ziploc bag, trying not to spill it on the tan carpeting and counting silently in my head until I reached seven scoops. I sealed the bag and placed the urn back, noticing a faint stain outlining where it had been sitting in the same spot for so many years. With the bag held firmly in my hand, I rushed downstairs to get the rest of my stuff.

The kids were watching TV. Bobby was curled up on the couch underneath a soft fleece blanket in the corner. Megan was on her iPhone, clicking funny photos of herself on Snapchat. For a moment, I felt guilty about not including them tonight, but then I reminded myself that this was about my journey. I was the one still holding on to Christopher, not them. The anniversary of his death was just another day in their lives. Too young to remember, it didn't affect them the way it affected me. The pain of losing their father struck them at different times during the year, while mine was like a permanent scar on my body that was raised, red, and bumpy—and the only way for it to properly heal was to stop touching it.

I kissed them goodbye and told them how much I loved them before I left for Buttermilk.

Dani was already there when I pulled into the dark parking lot. She was sitting on the edge of her trunk, buckling her boots. "Did you remember to bring everything?" she asked when I stepped out of the car.

"Yeah, I've got it in my backpack."

"Tracy just sent me a text. She'll be here in a few minutes."

I considered Dani and Tracy my Aspen sisters, and couldn't imagine doing something like this without them by my side.

Just when I opened the back of my car to grab my stuff, Tracy sped into the lot. "Sorry, I was running late," she called through her window. The bright lights of her car were shining in my eyes when I looked up, so I turned in the other direction and continued to get on my gear. With my boots securely fastened, I threw my skis over my shoulder and walked toward Tracy's car to say hello. Another person stepped out of the passenger side, and when I recognized the face, I burst into an uncontrollable sob. Dropping my skis, I yelled "Marcy!" She ran toward me, and we hugged each other.

"I can't believe you're here," I said.

"I wouldn't miss this for the world."

"But I thought you were supposed to be in Paris for the fashion show."

"I was. I changed my plans after you told me about this, and then I decided it would be more fun if I surprised you."

"Best surprise ever!" I said, wiping away my tears with my gloved hand.

Dani walked over to us, smiling. "It's great to finally meet you," she said to Marcy.

Still in shock that Marcy was here, I had forgotten to make an introduction.

"Likewise," Marcy said.

Tracy had brought an extra set of equipment for Marcy, and she helped her get ready. Once we were all dressed and situated at the base of the mountain, I clipped my boots into the bindings of my skis, took a deep breath, and said, "All right, I'm ready. Let's do this."

We started our uphill trek together. Skinning, a popular sport in Aspen, was a way to mobilize up the mountain without using the lift. Many hardcore skiers skin in the backcountry in search of fresh, untracked powder. My friends and I preferred going up the inbound trails. It was a challenging workout, but the thrill of the exercise was arriving at the top, pulling off the adhesive material attached to our skis, and skiing down the hill.

My skis glided over the soft arctic-white snow as I made my way up the mountain. The early afternoon winds had abated, and the temperature was mild for a winter evening. I wondered if the change in weather from earlier in the day was a sign from above: hang in there; don't give up; as bad as it seems—it will get better. We wore headlamps for added light, but I hadn't felt a need to turn mine on yet. Radiant stars gave off a luminous glow that spilled over the jagged edges of the snow-covered peaks. The thinly sliced opalescent moon framed the darkened sky.

Dani led the way, while Tracy and I were right behind her. Marcy followed at her own pace. Having just arrived from sea level, I was impressed that she could do it at all. Progressing farther up the mountain, I felt a magical stillness envelop me—a quiet greeting from the evergreen trees that lined my path and an eerie emptiness from the daunting, unmoving chairlift overhead. The scene could have been straight out of a horror movie—four women hiking up the mountain at night, waiting for something or someone to jump out at them. But none of us were frightened. It was as if there was a protective presence surrounding us.

It took us a little over an hour to make it to the Cliff House, a restaurant on top of Buttermilk Mountain, which closed when the ski lift stopped running. We took our skis off, rested them against the metal rack, and walked over to the picnic bench behind the cabin. I took off my backpack and pulled out the plastic Ziploc bag. Tracy reached into her bag and raised her hand to reveal what she had brought.

"I think we should make a toast," she said, holding a bottle of Prosecco.

Marcy was sucking wind from the extreme exercise. With a heavy breath, she said, "Can we toast that I made it up the mountain? That was the hardest fucking thing I've ever done!"

We all laughed. Tracy passed around clear plastic cups and opened the bottle, which made a loud popping noise. After she poured the bubbly drink in everyone's cup, we walked to the edge of the mountain.

I turned to look at the beautiful women standing around me and spoke with tear-filled eyes. "I am overwhelmed with gratitude to be standing on this summit with my three best friends. Each of you represents an important chapter in my life, and yet tonight, we are all together."

Pausing for a moment, I made eye contact with Tracy. "You and I have known each other the longest. You knew me when I was young, single, and as you love to point out, a prude. You've stuck by me every step of the way, through my marriage, my children, becoming a widow, and helping me readjust to Aspen a second time. And through it all, you remind me every day that life should be treated like one big party."

Tracy hugged me. "I love you, Hope. And mark my words, when we're ninety years old and roomies in the old-age home, we're still going to party like it's 1999, or in our case 1996."

"I don't doubt it for a second," I said, smiling.

Next, I faced Marcy. "As you know, I never would have survived my move to Boston or those first few years of motherhood without you. Always my rock, my sounding board, you carried me through the most difficult time in my life. Without you by my side, I'm not sure I would be where I am today. And, of course, I am so touched and honored that you're here tonight."

"It goes both ways, Hope. You've always been there for me too." Marcy moved forward, pulling me into a tight embrace. We held on for a moment, and then she placed her hands on my shoulders, and our eyes met. "The day you told me you were moving back to Aspen was one of the hardest days for me, but you promised me that distance would never keep our friendship apart—and you were right."

I sealed my lips tight to keep the rising lump in my throat from bursting out, and I hugged her again.

When we let go, I looked at Dani. "You're a gift that came much later in my life. Even though I've only known you for a few short years, I feel like we've been friends forever. An incredible mother, wife, and friend, you lead by example—always putting everyone else's needs before your own. I've often wondered if Christopher sent you to me for a reason. You taught me that if we can learn to rise above the shit that life hands us and not let it swallow us, then we can take that shit and mold it into something meaningful and beautiful."

A single tear dripped down her cheek. "I'm equally as blessed to have you in my life." We moved in at the same time to embrace, and then she squeezed my hand when we stepped apart.

"When Dani came up with the idea to have this pilgrimage, she mentioned that seven is a spiritual number, indicating a cycle of change, a transitioning of sorts. Here we are—March nineteenth, the seven-year anniversary of the day that changed my life forever. I stand here before you to release the ashes of the one man who stole my heart and taught me to love deeply. Christopher, wherever you are..." I looked up at the starry sky. "I know you're with me—right in here." I patted my heart. "I had always imagined that one day you and I would end up back in Aspen together, but the universe had other plans for you. Your physical presence may not be with us, but your spirit will forever guide me."

I opened the Ziploc bag and threw his gray ashes into the air. They floated like fairy dust, a faint shimmer sprinkling around me as they evaporated into the night.

We raised our glasses and Dani called out, "To Christopher, and to Hope, who finally found her north star."

I took a sip of my sparkling wine. Then we gathered together in a group hug, and my boundless appreciation and love poured inside my friends. After we finished our drinks, we packed our belongings, threw our skins into our backpacks, and prepared for the descent. Inhaling the crisp air, I took one final look at the panoramic view, turned my headlamp on, and let go. Like a bird, I flew down the mountain on my skis, exhilarated. The wind blew in my hair, and the cathartic tears ran down my face—I was free at last.

* * *

Chattering voices filled the airy art gallery, which was divided into four sections, each featuring a different artist. Track lighting hung from the ceiling, shooting spotlights on the art. A bar was set up in the corner, along with cheese and dessert tables at the other end of the gallery.

Jean-Claude had sent over two of his employees to pick up my artwork from my garage a few days before the event and had them installed in the gallery. I was instructed to just show up the night of the opening. About twenty of my wooden circles, each with a different word, were scattered on the wall. In addition to the series, I had refurbished a stool and replaced the seat with a log slice. The word *passion* was written on the face. It stood proudly, taking center stage.

Standing in a gallery that was exhibiting my work, surrounded by my friends and my entire family, was like an out-of-body experience. Taking turns, every one of them congratulated me—my in-laws, my parents, Bethany and Edward, and Aunt Myrna, along with her fiancé, a robust little man who reminded me of Danny DeVito. Megan had invited her new boyfriend, and the two of them spent most of the night flirting with each other while they sipped Shirley Temples. Meanwhile, not wanting to ruin my buzz, I ignored Bobby and his sidekick, Jack, as they shoved mini-pies in their mouths at the dessert table.

"Honey, I am so proud of you," my mom said as she leaned in to hug me. "You know, I never told anyone this, but I always had a silly little fantasy that I would sell my crafts at the Ohio Arts and Crafts show."

"Mom, you should definitely do it. Don't be afraid to put yourself out there." It was hard to believe that I was the one uttering those words. It sure as hell took me a long time to get where I was.

"Darling, darling." Jean-Claude came sashaying over to me. He whistled when he saw me. "That dress looks fabulous on you."

I was wearing an off-the-shoulder black silk dress that was cut above my knees, hugging my body in all the right spots. After he air kissed me on both cheeks, he tried to whisper in my ear, but instead he squealed with excitement, "The most eligible bachelor in Aspen just bought your entire collection!"

"You're kidding," I said incredulously.

"Darling, would I joke about that? It gets better. The guy is worth a fortune. He owns the largest cannabis operation in Colorado, and he said he knows who you are."

"Who is it? I don't know anyone in the marijuana business."

Jean-Claude waved to a guy at the other end of the room, signaling for him to come over to us. As he made his way in our direction, I thought my heart was going to burst out of my chest. His skin was deeply tanned, and his five o'clock shadow appeared a little less unkempt than usual. I sure did know this guy. I wanted to bolt out the door, when I remembered sharting in front of him on the gondola.

"Jeff," Jean-Claude said. "This is Hope."

"We've seen each other around town," he said, winking at me.

An intense fire rose through my neck, burning all the way into my cheeks, as I forced myself to smile. He gave me a full-fledged grin, and when our eyes met, there was a depth in them that drew me right in. I reached out and shook Jeff's hand, and my body lit up as our clasped hands lingered longer than was customary. There was something between us, and we both felt it.

In the years since Christopher's death, dating had led to nothing but a string of disappointments. And yet, I was sure all those failed relationships had happened for a reason—they helped me figure out who I was. As much as I was tempted to run away from this guy, I knew I couldn't give up. Anything was possible. He and I might end up having a wild one-night stand. Or maybe we'd get involved, only to realize we weren't compatible. Or maybe something special and long-lasting would transpire. If life had taught me anything, it was that regardless of how the story played out, I had to keep trying—to keep fighting—for Hope.

ACKNOWLEDGMENTS

The idea for this book was inspired by a real-life event: My dear friend Nicole lost her husband, the love of her life, in an avalanche. On the evening of the seven-year anniversary of his passing, Nicole and I, along with five other friends, hiked up Buttermilk Mountain and released his ashes. Soon afterward, she and I came up with the story idea for *This is Hope*. Nicole's painful loss, along with her humor, wit, and journey as a widow were the driving forces behind the main character, Hope Whitmore.

Like Nicole, my mother lost her husband, who was her Prince Charming, in a tragic car accident. It wasn't until I wrote this book that I could understand what it was like to walk in my mother's shoes or how difficult it was to move on—for the sake of her children. I may have grown up without a father, but I have been blessed with a mother who always gives me her unconditional love and support—not just in writing this book—but in everything I do. I want to thank my mother for listening to me ramble on about Hope and meticulously reading and editing the manuscript.

I would like to thank Melissa Donovan for guiding, teaching, editing, and steering me through the entire writing process. Melissa is like my writing angel, setting me on my path and helping me find my passion. I also want to thank my amazing literary agent, Jennifer Cohen, for helping to make my dream a reality;

my publisher Anthony Ziccardi, for giving life to this book, along with the opportunity to continue pursuing a writing career, and, of course, Billie Brownell for her meticulous editing and always keeping me on-task.

I don't have any blood sisters, but I have a sister-in-law and many friends who have become my sisters. Scattered from the East Coast to the West Coast, they reside in New York, New Jersey, Connecticut, Ohio, South Carolina, California, and of course, Aspen, Colorado. My girlfriends mean so much to me. We laugh, we cry, we listen, we laugh some more, and we help each other. To all my dear friends, thank you for cheering for me while I wrote this book. And to Allison, who is watching over all of us from above and has taught me so much about giving, her spirit will be with me forever.

Last but not least, I want to thank my family: My two grandmothers, Bunty and Nan, both of whom became widows later in their lives. These two matriarchs reign supreme in my world. Sadly, my mother-in-law lost her husband too, right before the birth of our daughter, their first grandchild. My father-in-law passed on a legacy of love, and my mother-in-law carries the torch, always spreading her magnanimous heart. And of course, my brother and his wife, who always have my back.

I have been gifted with two of the most incredible children. They are my greatest joy. I will spend every waking hour on this Earth and after I leave rooting for them. Hopefully they will learn from their father, my husband, who is a shining example of someone with unyielding grit. Watching him has taught us how to live passionately, persevere, and do whatever it takes to get the job done. I love you all so much.